Playing with the Moon

ELIZA
GRAHAM

*Playing with
the Moon*

MACMILLAN NEW WRITING

First published 2007 by Macmillan New Writing
an imprint of Pan Macmillan Ltd
Pan Macmillan, 20 New Wharf Road, London N1 9RR
Basingstoke and Oxford
Associated companies throughout the world
www.panmacmillan.com

ISBN 978-0-230-52887-1

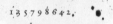

A CIP catalogue record for this book is available from
the British Library.

Typeset by Intype London Ltd
Printed and bound in Great Britain by
Mackays of Chatham plc, Chatham, Kent

This is a work of fiction and is the production of the author's imagination.
Any relationship with real events, places or people is entirely coincidental.

Visit **www.panmacmillan.com** to read more about all our books
and to buy them. You will also find features, author interviews and
news of any author events, and you can sign up for e-newsletters
so that you're always first to hear about our new releases.

for Johnnie

Acknowledgements

A big thanks to Cave and Trollop members,
especially Mark Vender and Kristina Riggle,
for all their encouragement and help.

I would also like to acknowledge the use I made of the following books in researching this novel: *When Jim Crow met John Bull*, Graham Smith (I.B. Tauris & Co Ltd, 1987); *London*, Peter Ackroyd (Chatto & Windus, 2000); *London at War*, Philip Ziegler (Pimlico, 2002); *The Myth of the Blitz*, Angus Calder (Pimlico, 2002).

Part One

One

Minna

Our second wedding anniversary. I'm about to tell Tom our marriage is over when he spots something in the sand.

His brow crinkles. 'What the hell's that?'

'What's what?' My heart gives a little jump: half irritation, half relief he's interrupted the conversation. He springs to his feet and walks towards the rocks through the seaweed and driftwood blown up by last week's storm. The sun comes out and something glints on the sand below us, now smooth as a linen tablecloth. I screw up my eyes to try and make out the object. Bottle top? Coin? I get up and follow him, feet scrunching over the shingle until I reach the sandy foreshore.

Tom holds out his hand. 'Stay there.' The firmness in his voice makes me blink.

'What's the matter?'

He crouches, his back to me, and digs with both hands like a dog. 'Oh God.' His hands cease their movement.

'What?'

'You might not want to see . . .' I push past his restraining arm and see what he's dug up: a long white object. A bone. The metallic thing lies about a foot away from it.

'Is it human?' I lean closer.

'Probably just a sheep, or cow.' But I can hear hesitation in his voice. My knowledge of anatomy is shaky but I know this isn't animal; it's a human leg bone. Tom digs a little more and exposes a row of ivory-coloured arches. A ribcage.

'Jesus!'

His arm curls round me, pulling me away. 'Don't look. Go and ring the police.'

I nod. As I stand I catch sight of the coin again. Only it isn't a coin, but two strips of rusty metal hanging from a metal chain. Dog-tags, like you see in old black-and-white war films. I pick them up and rub at the inscription on one of them with my handkerchief. LEWIS J CAMPBELL and a number.

'So they'll be able to identify him.' Something starts to prickle behind my eyelids. I blink and look away, passing the tags to Tom. So ridiculous to feel this emotion for someone so long dead. 'Poor, poor man, whoever he is.'

'Are you all right?' His tone expresses just the right amount of concern: not enough to show me he's worried but not so little he could be accused, or accuse himself, of callousness. He walks this fine line with me the whole time.

'I'll go and make that call.' I remember something. 'We probably shouldn't touch anything.'

'God, no, you're right.' We've watched enough crime drama to know about not disturbing bodies. He drops the tags and they clatter onto the vertebrae. I shudder. 'Sorry,' he says.

I stand and walk across the shingle to my rucksack and push the nines on the mobile. Lucky the signal's good down here, one reason why we chose Rosebank House for the summer. Tom would be in trouble if his clients couldn't get him round the clock.

The emergency services woman with the slow rolling burr permits herself little animation at the news and asks us to wait on the beach for the police.

'Quite exciting really,' I tell Tom in a bright voice.

He stares at me. 'If you say so.'

What a crass thing to say. He was probably thinking about the last time we waited for the emergency services. I fiddle with my wedding ring, now loose on my finger. I've had to stop wearing my engagement ring, it kept sliding off.

I haven't bought him a card for our anniversary. He laid a big bunch of delphiniums on the breakfast table for me this morning – safe flowers because we didn't have them at our wedding or the cremation.

He sits down on the sand beside me again and I see a tiny vein

4

pulsing in his neck. Only months ago I'd have longed to kiss it. Now I observe it and feel nothing. Below us waves hiss incessantly onto the sand. 'We need to talk,' I say. It's killing him, living with me. It can't go on.

Blue lights flash above us by the old pillbox on the cliff.

'Rough seas in these parts a month or so back,' the sergeant tells us. 'Bad spring storms. Probably eroded some of the sand so the body rose to the surface again.'

'Else he was stuck on those rocks till the waves pushed him off,' offers the constable, pointing towards the jagged stones that mark the end of the cove.

The sergeant sniffs to show what he thinks of that idea. 'No skull. Lucky for us that dog-tag's still with the bones. Should make it easier to work out who he is.'

'Do you think he's local?' I ask.

The sergeant turns his head. 'The ID looks American to me. Lots of Yanks were camped round here, especially early in 1944.'

'He probably drowned in some training fiasco,' Tom says.

The constable frowns at Tom. 'That an Ulster accent, Mr Byrne?'

I stiffen, a reflex action from back when I used to feel protective towards Tom. 'He's British.'

'I grew up in Belfast.' Tom's accent is slight now; the local bobby has sharp ears. Tom's probably trying to work out whether it's good or bad I stood up for him.

The sergeant picks up his radio. 'No point us all hanging round down here, this chap's been dead a good few years. Expect you'd like to get on with your holiday, Mr and Mrs Byrne.'

And the use of our married titles reminds me of the conversation I was starting when Tom spotted the bones. Tom sees me flinch and I blush. This sequence of reactions surprises me – it's been weeks since I felt anything at all.

Dead Fontwell Soldier was American

Holidaymakers have discovered the remains of an American GI, sixty years after he drowned. American military officials have confirmed his identity as Private Lew Campbell, believed to have died in 1944 during training exercises for the Normandy Landings.

The body was found on Tuesday in Fontwell Cove, five miles east of Lulworth. Police believe recent rough weather and cliff erosion dislodged it from a resting place further along the coast.

Fontwell lies on MOD land and was evacuated in November 1943 so it could be used as a training ground for the invasion of Europe. Its former inhabitants never returned to the village. The land is open to the public at set dates in the year.

MOD and Foreign Office officials are attempting to trace any surviving family of Private Campbell in his home state of Georgia. It is likely the body will be buried in the American War Cemetery at Madingley, Cambridgeshire.

Two

Felix

Something thuds beside Felicity.

She turns to see a boy dribbling a football the colour of a ripe damson towards his brother. For a second she thinks they're kicking Lew's swollen head across the grass. She clutches the wall while the world spins. Damn. She's been an idiot, coming back here.

When the spell passes she's relieved to see that nobody is looking in her direction – invisibility is one of the advantages of ageing.

And of course there's no black man lying there, head bloodied and bruised, one hand still raised in an attempt to protect himself. Just two small boys with their football, enjoying a perfect summer afternoon among the crumbling walls of the village.

Ever since she read that newspaper article she's started seeing Lew again. He appears on the end of her bed, calling her name until she wakes. She thought she'd put a stop to that years ago. 'Go away,' she told him last night. He said nothing, never does. Just looked at her with those coal-black eyes.

Nearly time to go. The village only opens for set hours on set days. If you outstay these times you run the risk of being shelled or shot. Felicity, known to her friends as Felix, is relieved, even though she's driven all the way down from the North to see this place, renting a cottage nearby so she can return to Fontwell as often as she wants. The village is open every day during the summer months.

Someone calls the football-playing boys. She sees a woman wearing a floating, bohemian-looking skirt and a top in pale colours, long gold hair dropping over milky shoulders. She reminds Felix of Isabel, but of course the woman is just a holidaymaker keen to see the local sights. Nothing more romantic than an abandoned village.

'Not sure you should be playing football here.' The floaty woman picks up their ball and throws her an apologetic glance. Felix smiles to show she doesn't mind: Sam and his brother always kicked balls around on this sward of green. She can't bear to have the village thought of as a museum.

She wanders back to the car park and sits for a minute in her Vauxhall, eyes closed, deciding whether or not she can go through with the next part of her pilgrimage. Perhaps it would be better to return to the holiday cottage. She's visited her mother's grave, now completely given over to grass, bindweed and sticky-willy, so there's really no need to linger in Fontwell. The pretty woman and her boys return to their Volvo and drive off. They'll sit outside some picturesque cottage, drinking tea and lemonade and planning the next day's trip.

What the hell. She's come all this way so she may as well see the old place. She starts the engine and drives through the village. Rosebank now lies outside the restricted area; the Ministry of Defence has decided it no longer needs the parish in its entirety. She waves to the soldier at the barrier and watches him lower it behind her – last one out. Just like 1943.

Felix takes her foot off the brake. The village is left to itself, with only its memories and the intermittent thumping of guns for company. She turns up the track to the house. They've restored it now. Apparently it wasn't as badly damaged by mortars and shelling as the other houses and the MOD kept the roof repaired over the years, possibly considering it suitable for officer accommodation. But now they've sold Rosebank House and the land around it to a local environmental charity, the Barrows Trust, which in turn has paid a holiday rental company to let it. The first visitors have already arrived.

When Felix rented her own holiday cottage she told the lady at the booking office she used to live in Rosebank. Mrs Ogle had insisted on shutting up her office for an afternoon to show her round.

'You must be aching to see your old home.'

Felix wasn't sure she was aching at all. Dreading it, more like. 'Won't the people renting it mind?'

'I'll ask. They're a nice young couple.'

And they didn't mind, even suggesting an afternoon when they'd be out.

Felix has to control her hands and feet to prevent them from braking and turning the car round. She remembers taking a ferry from Poole to Cherbourg once, years ago. She'd had to sit in her stuffy cabin until they were safely out to sea, fearing that she might look back at the receding cliffs and recognize Fontwell's cove. So silly.

The trust has resurfaced the drive. In Felix's day the potholes destroyed the suspensions of several cars. The large chestnut tree in the field has survived the mortars. So have the two elms. The drive bends to allow the first glimpse of the house. How small it looks in comparison with her home in Harrogate. She's remembered it as a large place, looming over her.

A silver Mercedes sits outside. Felix parks next to it, noting how shabby her ten-year-old Vauxhall looks in comparison. Renovations on the house have only just finished: a final skipload of old bricks and timbers awaits collection. The new windowpanes still bear their manufacturers' stickers, and paint pots and brushes sit in cardboard boxes by the door.

She walks to the front of the house, peering up at first-floor windows until she works out which was hers: the one underneath the left-hand gable. She used to climb down the wisteria – lucky she was a skinny girl – and jump down to the lawn. The wisteria has long since withered away and the exterior walls are a darker colour than the cream she remembers. But this is still unmistakably the house her doctor father bought in June 1933 to accommodate the family he imagined would keep on growing.

Felix realizes she's staring at something small and shiny in the skip and pulls it out. A miniature brandy bottle, label long since gone. She replaces it, feeling a band tighten across her brow. To distract herself she turns to examine the flowerbeds. Could any of the roses have survived the half century and more? A naive hope. Anyway, her father tore Tricolore de Flandre, Félicité Parmentier

9

and Madame Hardy out when they were Digging for Victory. These lupins and stocks are new, tender green leaves curling up from weedless compost. Perfect. Felix shivers.

'Here you are!' Mrs Ogle bustles in from the back garden, a slim woman in her early fifties in Armani or another of those Italian designers. Felix smoothes down her own aqua-coloured linen dress, which looked so good in the shop in Harrogate but creased badly in the car. 'Nice young couple have taken the house. He's in PR and she's an interior designer. Or was.' She lowers her voice. 'Something went wrong, I gather. They want seclusion, he told me.' Her eyes glitter, obviously conjecturing about what had happened to the unnamed couple. 'No dogs and no children. Ideal first tenants for Rosebank.'

No dogs, no children. Felix remembers the quiet Sunday afternoons of her childhood when she longed for pets and siblings to help pass the hours. If she hadn't had David to play with, she'd have been a lonely girl. And David was fifteen minutes' walk away, hardly on her doorstep.

Mrs Ogle unlocks the front door. 'Let me show you inside.'

'It's kind of you to take the time,' Felix murmurs, wishing she could think of some emergency requiring her immediate departure.

'Shame for you to come all this way without seeing your old home. And we're so pleased with how the refurbishment's gone.' Mrs Ogle gives the entrance hall wall a pat. 'This is a proud moment for local people. We had to fight off the developers, you know.'

Felix shudders at the thought of caravan parks or retirement villages.

'And they've still got their eyes on the next tranche of land.'

'There's more to be released?'

'That little hamlet just before you reach the crossroads.'

Felix remembers. 'That's Upper Farm. Or was.'

'The farmhouse has almost completely crumbled away now and the remaining farm buildings aren't much to look at, rusty corrugated-iron barns.'

'The old Squire always wanted to renovate them. But events overtook him.'

Mrs Ogle shakes her head and smoothes out an imaginary crease in her skirt. 'Property companies would love to build a little executive housing estate up there.'

'Heaven preserve us.'

Mrs Ogle gives her an approving nod. 'How old were you when you left Fontwell?'

'Thirteen.'

She sighs. 'It must have been a wrench? Will you move back down here now?'

Felix smiles to avoid answering. Mrs Ogle, more sensitive than her cheerful exterior suggests, takes her hesitation for emotion.

She nods towards the back garden. 'I'm going to check the gardener's tidied the shed. Call me when you're finished and I'll lock up.'

The entrance hall is camomile instead of the pea-green Felix remembers. The floor tiles have been restored – blacks and whites, like a chessboard. An image of Lew standing beside Isabel, so dark against her fairness, floats into her mind. She walks through the hall to the back of the house, catching glimpses of terracotta sofas, stripped floorboards and caramel walls in the drawing room, which used to be the dining room. A large flat-screen television occupies the space where the piano used to stand, a black vase or ornament on the shelf above it. Felix doesn't bother going in to have a closer look; even in its transformed state the old dining room reminds her of silent meals with her widowed father. She continues up the corridor.

The old parlour, used only for waiting patients and Sunday callers, is now a study, with beech desk and grey office-chair. Smart. Neat piles of papers cover the desk. Felix sits for second and imagines herself writing letters or phoning friends in here, gazing at the crumbling church tower through the waving branches, a view that's hardly changed at all in more than half a century. Her gaze drops back to the desk, to the photograph of the young man and woman. The woman has eyes the colour of ground coffee and a shock of wavy chestnut hair. The man's arm drapes her slender shoulders and his smile is proud.

Without really knowing where she wants to look, Felix wanders into the kitchen, all cream-painted cupboards and granite: light and airy, instead of the dark, womb-like space she spent so many evenings in.

What a relief to see the renovators haven't knocked into Mrs Derby's pantry – cooler and larger than any fridge. So many younger people don't understand about pantries. She opens one of the cupboard doors and admires the neat stacks of white china plates and bowls. Then she remembers the couple renting the house and blushes. What the hell would they think if they knew she was going through their cupboards? Very trusting of Mrs Ogle to let her wander around alone.

The builders have taken out the wall between the surgery and the conservatory, creating a single room big enough to act as a dining room, with small sofas and table at the garden end. If she lived here Felix would spend all summer in this room, with its newly exposed beams and creamy walls.

A chrome light-switch reminds her that electricity now reaches this house, in place of the gas that used to light the lamps in her day. How her father would have relished such bright light at the flick of a switch, the luxury of examining patients and writing up notes without eye-strain. But electric lights wouldn't give out the warm and hissing glow that kept her company through winter nights in the kitchen, while the wireless blared out Tommy Handley. And Felix knows the night-time dark outside will still be absolute: a darkness that could contain anything.

'Get a grip, woman,' she mutters to herself. 'Johnson's been dead for years now.'

She's moved into what was once the dispensary, now a utility room, spick and span and ready for use. The tiles she remembers still line the walls, white and clinical, and these must be the same old pine shelves her father put up to store his bottles and packets. The chemist in Swanham supplied his patients satisfactorily, but Dr Valance liked to keep some essential medicines in the house, especially when petrol became scarce and was reserved for emergency trips. These days the authorities would have a fit if they found a doctor was keeping so many drugs on his premises. She runs a hand along the bottom shelf, not certain what she's searching for. Not brandy bottles, not this time.

Her fingers touch paper jammed up against the wall in the far corner. She pulls out a small yellowed sheet. She blows on it and the dust disperses to expose a cormorant, poised to dive, head slightly tilted, eyes intent on its prey. Seeing the bird is like receiving an electric shock; she remembers Lew drawing it as though it was yesterday.

Felix slides the drawing back onto the shelf. It belongs in Rosebank House, with the girl she once was. Away from the valley, it would disintegrate. After all, she did.

Three

Minna

I sit for hours at a time in the conservatory, my eyes fixed on the spot at the end of the field where the sky sheers upwards and red cliffs drop thirty feet to the beach. I wrap my arms around my body to hold myself together. Sometimes, if I'm lucky, the vista distracts me from my thoughts. At other times I picture myself running out of the back door, through the meadow with its wild mallow, eyebright and poppies, and plunging over the cliff. Only I'm not sure I possess the necessary energy.

'Shame we can't see the beach.' Tom comes to stand beside me. 'We used to stay in a cottage right on the beach in Donegal as children. You could lie in bed and watch the waves breaking.' He looks away. Childhood holidays, another subject now taboo.

'We used to stay in a house like that in Wales when I was a kid,' I say, to prove I can talk about it. In fact, a five-minute walk and a row of cottages separated us from the Irish Channel. 'We'd be the first ones paddling in the sea in the mornings.'

There, my jutting chin tells him. He nods as though he's spotted my purpose.

'We could have people down here for weekends,' I say, imagining them sprawling on the lawn with newspapers and cups of coffee, me in an apron bringing out bacon sandwiches, busying myself with Sunday roasts and apple crumbles. Would it help me forget for a few hours? 'Michael, anyway.'

Tom's face brightens at his brother's name. 'And Gareth.'

'Of course.'

'Matthew and Jill,' offers Tom. 'Or Liz. And Kris, of course.'

Kris. One of my oldest friends. Unseen, unspoken to, since I fled London. She leaves emails and messages on my mobile and I read them, promising myself I'll answer at some point in the future, knowing I won't.

'And the Frobishers, with little Marina.' I want to knock down any ideas Tom might have about shielding me from other people's children. 'She'd love it here. And the garden's quite safe—'

He thumps a fist onto the windowsill. 'Why are you doing this, Minna?'

'Doing what?'

'You know damn well, pretending you're fine.'

I pick at the curtain fabric, a loosely woven Madras check in yellows and blues. 'I wasn't aware I was doing anything.' I hear frost in my answer. *Stop this now,* a little voice warns me. But I can't. 'And I'm fine. Doing better every day.'

'You were trying to say something on the beach yesterday. What was it?'

I shake my head, not because I feel any more hopeful about our relationship but because the moment has passed and I lack the energy for confrontation. Greyness presses down on my body most of the time, sometimes replaced by a jerky, acid-green energy that drives me for miles along the coastal path.

Last night Tom didn't draw the curtains properly. I lay in bed sleepless for hours, clutching the sleep-suit that's become my comforter and watching the full moon, so fat you could imagine it dripping silvery-yellow juice. My grandmother used to tell me full moons curdled people's dreams. I didn't bother getting out of bed to close the curtains: how could my dreams get any worse?

Tom's sigh seems to fill the conservatory, bringing me back to the present. 'I'm going for a drive. Need anything?' No internet supermarket deliveries here, and Swanham is five miles away. That's why we rented the place – complete seclusion.

'I did a big shop.' To avoid being here when the former occupant turned up, I walked down every aisle of the local supermarket, examining almost every item.

'There's a directory I need to look at in the library.'

'If there's fresh bread in that nice baker's, pick up a loaf. Or any

15

vegetables you like the look of.' I can't imagine ever getting enthusiastic about eating again but I cook for Tom with more devotion than I ever did before. The individual fish pies with their garnishes of dill and the perfectly timed pan-fried duck breasts make him uncomfortable, I can tell. But he eats them. Probably worried about precipitating another shouting match. Or one of the even more deadly silences. Why do I go to such trouble in the kitchen? Probably because I go to so little elsewhere.

'You're a long way from Putney, aren't you?' He makes a big effort, giving my nose a tweak, just like he always used to when he teased me.

'Haven't seen a nail bar for days.' My feeble effort raises a smile. 'Let alone Starbucks.' I haven't seen anything except sea and sky. The nothingness around me scares me, makes me feel exposed. But I chose this exile and I'm damned if I'll run away.

I stand at the window, twisting my ring round my finger, and watch him drive off in our Passat. Tom hates four-by-fours – something about the way he was brought up. His continuing lack of materialism is probably what I love most about him. Or used to. Sometimes I think I'll never be able to love anyone again. I used to imagine grief as a purifying process. How naive.

What the hell am I to do with myself? I've already completed my daily exercise routine – no need to let it slip. A lady from Swanham drives down to clean the house twice a week, and a gardener takes care of the outdoor tasks ('although you are invited to dead-head the flowers and positively urged to pick the sweetpeas!' the welcome pack says), so I'm hardly overwhelmed with domestic duties. I drift upstairs to our bedroom, east-facing and full of morning sunlight, and pull up my side of the goosefeather duvet to ensure everything's in place. I like to check once or twice a day. After I agreed to let that woman look at the house yesterday I started to panic. Then I calmed down, telling myself it was extremely unlikely she'd want to poke around in our bed. And Mrs Ogle from the lettings office would be there to keep an eye on her. All the same, it made me feel weird imagining her looking at our things – Tom's laptop, my unopened watercolour set, our books, CDs and DVDs – in her old home. And the urn on the shelf above the television.

I come downstairs, still restless, needing something to do with my hands. The magazines Tom bought for me fail to hold my attention with their bright covers showing beaming women in bikinis. Too early to start cooking. I could iron, in the utility room. The windows are small and high but this promises to be another perfect day. Sometimes I feel worse on bright days, as though the weather's mocking me, the sun scorning my loss. I don't feel like that about the moon, her silent stare feels restful, compassionate. The sun's just a ball of heedless energy.

I turn on the lavender-trimmed Roberts radio and linger over the smell of fresh linen and steam. After a few minutes the rhythms of the task start to soothe me. The hiss of the iron, the scent of hot cotton and the test-match commentary in the background – something I'd never normally listen to – all blend into a restful mix.

I fold a T-shirt and place it on the shelf. My hand touches paper. I draw out a small sheet with something drawn on it. A kid's doodle? I put it on top of the washing machine for adding to the recycling box. Then I look again at the long-legged bird, with its intent eyes and tense sinews. No child drew this. Tom might like to look at it, he's fond of drawing and has always enjoyed my silly sketches; or used to, before his business grew so demanding. Initials curl across the bottom corner of the paper: *LC*. I trace the outline of the bird with a finger.

The iron hisses again to remind me of my abandoned task, and I fold the scrap into my jeans pocket.

Four

Felix

At dawn Felix makes tea in a stained Silver Jubilee commemorative mug, trying to ignore the incessant dripping of a tap. Sleep had eluded her for most of the night and birdsong had roused her long before she'd wanted to wake. She'd risen, feeling oppressed by responsibilities.

The roof of the house she's abandoned in Yorkshire needs repairing, the last battle in a long war against subsidence, wiring gremlins and crumbling slates. Dear Lord, hasn't most of her life been a battle against something or other? Coming down here was an indulgence she couldn't really afford. If only she'd missed the short newspaper article about the discovery of a dead American soldier. If only he'd stayed hidden.

She tries to relax her tense shoulders and calm the hands that can't convey a teaspoon of sugar to a mug without shaking it all over the table. 'Damn you,' she mutters. 'You've had me on edge since the night I met you.'

1943

The too-sweet odour of death filled Felix's senses, making her stomach turn. She tried to ignore the dead badger's body, swollen and black under the holly bush.

'Bet that was Johnson.' David stopped, shining his feeble blackout torch at the badger, the creature's jaws open in a last grimace. 'He just does it because he likes killing, not because it's necessary.'

'Why doesn't he just join up and kill Germans?' The smell seemed to insinuate itself between the layers of her clothes. Her stomach lurched.

'Gassed at the end of the last war. Dodgy lungs. And he's forty.'

'Bet he's just using that as an excuse. Come on.' She didn't want to look at the badger. A bramble caught her calf and drew a red scratch. From the branch of an oak came the cireek of a tawny owl. Finding herself clutching David's arm, Felix let go, red-faced. He'd think her a sissy.

Somewhere out here in the gloom Johnson, the gamekeeper, was searching for poachers and predators. If he found David and Felix he'd haul them off to David's uncle, giving David a quick cuff, and Felix a curse for good measure. A month back he'd discovered them releasing magpies from a cage. The expression on his face still haunted Felix's dreams.

Something screamed. Felix's nails bit into her palms.

David's hand touched hers. 'Just a fox.'

Her heartbeat slowed. She hoped he hadn't noticed her shiver. Tiredness replaced fear and she yawned – getting out of bed on cold nights made her feel her head was filled with sand. Only the prospect of fox cubs had persuaded her this outing was worthwhile. A twig cracked and she turned – nothing.

'Probably just a deer.' David must have seen her startled face.

'A deer in jackboots.'

'Sounds seem louder at night.'

'Hope not. Or Johnson will hear us.'

David motioned her down behind the brambles. 'This is where I saw them yesterday. Keep very still.' The full moon washed the glade with light; Felix could make out every dead leaf, every branch. The breeze had dropped. She heard a second twig crack. This time David turned, eyes narrowing. 'Stay here.'

'Where are you going?' Her heart raced.

'There's someone there.' His voice squeaked at the end of the sentence. She'd noticed this happening increasingly often.

She tugged at his sleeve. 'It's probably Johnson, he'll tell your uncle.'

He shook himself free. 'It's not him – too tall.' She watched him stride away, wishing she'd stayed in bed. She'd managed to keep her fear of the dark from David but now she wondered whether pride was such a good thing. Even with the moon shining overhead she felt her heart race.

Something rustled in the glade and she looked round. Three fox cubs tumbled in front of her, clawing one another, taking play bites, yelping. Under a beech tree the vixen watched her family, immobile but with eyes that didn't lose their wariness for a second.

The fox raised her head and caught sight of Felix. Felix willed herself to absolute stillness, not breathing, not blinking, wishing her heart would beat more quietly. She felt two searing marks on her face where yellow eyes bored into her.

Seeming to find her acceptable the animal dropped her gaze back to the cubs rolling and growling. Felix forgot her heavy eyelids and the warm bed she'd abandoned, forgot they were only a month away from moving out. For a few minutes the world shrank to the foxes and this small patch of woodland. David had to call her twice before she heard him.

'Felix.' His tone warned her something was up. When she saw who was with him she jumped to her feet, not sure that her eyes weren't playing tricks.

She'd never seen a negro so close. His skin reminded her of the Squire's favourite saddle, glossy and expensive. Her fingers almost itched to stroke his face to see if it felt as smooth. And he was tall, taller even than her father. His shoulders were those of a super-being. Even his uniform was superior to English soldiers', the material well pressed, his boots supple and shiny. She stared, knowing it was rude but unable to help herself.

'Felix.' David's voice had an urgent note. 'Have you got anything to eat?' They always took food on these midnight excursions. Tonight she'd helped herself to a piece of precious Dundee cake she'd found in the pantry. Mrs Derby, her father's housekeeper, would assume the doctor had eaten it on his return from some nocturnal medical emergency.

'Here.' Felix held out the greaseproof-paper-wrapped morsel and David passed it to the black man. Felix stared at his shining white teeth as they bit through sultanas and glacé cherries.

'I've got a flask of tea.' David took it out of the satchel slung over his shoulder. 'When did you last eat?'

The soldier took a swig, closing his eyes as he did. He sighed and wiped a hand over his mouth. 'Yesterday. But it was thirst drove me crazy. Tried drinking from the stream but it tasted salty.' His voice was deep, cadenced in a way that made Felix think of long, slow summer days. 'Kept longing for cool sodas or a glass of milk.'

'You should have gone upstream.'

'You're right, boy.' Felix's eyes must still have been wide as marbles because the black man smiled at her. 'Pardon me, missy.' He extended a hand. 'Private Lew Campbell at your service.'

She shook the hand, with its long fingers and smooth nails, the palms calloused. 'I'm Felix.'

'Felix?' He raised an eyebrow. 'That a girl's name?'

'It's really Felicity but David calls me Felix because he says I climb like a cat. You've got a Scottish surname?'

'My ancestors worked a plantation owned by a Scottish family.'

'But you come from America?' David asked.

'From Georgia. Been training at a camp down the coast.' He looked from one to the other. 'You brother and sister?'

'Friends. What brings you to Fontwell?' she asked.

'Wanted to walk east from our camp towards Swanham. Guess I must have taken a wrong turning.'

'You did rather,' David said. 'Swanham's a good five miles away.'

Lew Campbell's face fell. 'I couldn't see any signposts.'

'They took them down to confuse the Germans. Not that it would have stopped the Wehrmacht for long.' David sounded very grown-up. In the last months Felix had observed a new confidence in him, dented only when his voice shot up or down. Her father said this often happened to boys his age.

'Then I caught my ankle and couldn't walk till the swelling went down.' Lew turned his head and frowned. 'That someone coming?' He gave off a note of panic disconcerting in one who could have snapped mere mortals in two.

'Johnson. Quick – this way.' David led them through the woods, Lew hobbling and biting his lip.

They reached a bank. 'We have to jump down. Can you make it on that ankle?'

He nodded.

'We'll go first and break your fall.'

He shook his head. 'I land on you and you're in trouble, boy. I'll go first.' He rolled to the ground and swung himself down the bank, suspending himself by his hands for a second before letting himself fall. David and Felix dropped into the leaf-filled ditch after him.

Lew stood, sweat beading his forehead. 'Let's go.'

David led them down the lane towards the back gate of his uncle's estate, stopping occasionally to listen for the gamekeeper. 'You can hide in one of the outhouses tonight. Nobody'll go there till morning.'

'I'll be off by then.' Lew took a deep breath. 'Don't want to get nobody into trouble.'

'You won't.'

They stood in the lane, moon high above, bathing the Manor in pale light so every stone and window pane was distinct, a film set of a view. Lew whistled. 'That where you live?'

'Yes,' David said. 'It's my uncle's house.' In his tone Felix heard a mixture of pride and wistfulness.

Lew shook his head. 'You must be rich folk.'

'Come on.' David led the way to the back gates, but Lew limped after them for only a few yards. The grimace on his face told them he was struggling.

'It'll take all night at this rate.' Felix detected a note of panic in David's whisper.

She turned back to Lew, who was gripping the gatepost. 'I'll run back and get a bandage from Father's dispensary,' she said. 'You'll move faster if the ankle's supported.'

'We need to get him under cover.' David peered over his shoulder.

'I'll be very quick.' Before he could object she ran off down the lane. It would have been quicker for her to cut through the woods but she couldn't bear the prospect of the dark boughs waving like outstretched arms. And Johnson was still prowling around. The lane skirted the graveyard – the one part of the route Felix feared. She ran with her hands over her ears, eyes fixed ahead of her until she'd passed it, then shot into the drive to Rosebank House, slowing because it was potholed and treacherous and what on earth would they do if she twisted her ankle, too?

The doctor always left the French windows open. She crept through the conservatory, given over to earwigs and dying ferns instead of jasmine and oleander since her mother's death. He locked the surgery but kept the key in a pot on the hall table. She unlocked the door without a sound.

In the dispensary she stood on tiptoe to pull down a roll of bandage. There were more bottles here than she remembered. She pulled one down – brandy, the label told her. Empty. She reached for another and found it was the same. Strange. Perhaps he was saving them for recycling – glass was valuable. But usually Mrs Derby stored empties in a cardboard box in the pantry.

She rearranged bottles of iodine and Dettol and jars of senna pods to disguise the gap in the display. On her way back out of the French windows she paused and took a deep breath before plunging back into the shadows.

Her legs were slower, heavier this time. A stitch nagged under her ribs. When she reached the other two they were sheltering behind a bank of browning pampas grass edging the Manor's lawn. 'You were ages,' David whispered, eyes darting towards the woods.

'I had to find the stuff, didn't I?' She leant over to relieve the stitch. 'Let's see that ankle.'

Lew sat and rolled up his trouser leg. His calf was nearly as wide as her thigh. The ankle was puffy. She remembered sitting in her father's surgery when a farm worker came in with a sprain; it had looked swollen like this. 'What did you do to it?'

'Caught it in a rabbit hole, like a darn fool.' He watched her efforts. 'You think it's broken?'

'If it was, you wouldn't be able to walk on it. Or jump down that bank. It's just a sprain. You need to rest it for a day or two.'

He watched her as she rolled the bandage round his ankle. 'You sure know your stuff. You'd make a fine nurse.'

She blushed. 'I've sat in on morning surgery often enough.'

'Let's get moving,' David helped Lew to his feet. To reach the outhouses they needed to cross the drive sweeping up to the main entrance. 'Make for the red door,' he whispered to Lew. 'Left of the stalls.'

Above them the large pale shape of Fontwell Manor loomed like a ghostly ship. Felix prayed Isabel wasn't suffering from the insomnia David said plagued her. They reached the outhouses and David pushed open the red door of the shed. 'There are sacks you can sleep on. Lucky it's a mild night.' From his pocket he pulled his torch, papered over in accordance with blackout regulations. 'Shut the door.' The feeble glow revealed a pile of hessian sacks in the corner.

'We've got to go now but we'll be back first thing.' David tugged Felix's shoulder.

'I'm truly grateful.' Lew's eyes shone in the light of the torch.

'Is there someone we should ring for you?' She knew as she spoke that there wouldn't be. Why else would they be hiding him in the outhouse?

'Ring?' He looked puzzled. 'Excuse me?'

'Telephone.'

He shook his head.

David ushered her out. 'Good night, Lew.'

'Night. And thanks.'

David closed the door without a sound.

'What's going on?' she asked.

'I'll tell you tomorrow.' He yawned.

'Suppose he's an enemy?'

'He's hardly the right colour for a German spy, is he? Remember how Hitler hated that negro runner, Jesse Owens?'

'But shouldn't we tell the police?'

'He's American, Felix, he's on our side.'

Felix heard something. 'What was that?'

'I can't hear anything.'

She listened again, couldn't make out the noise. 'Sounded like a door closing.'

'Probably just the wind. We should go to bed now, the moon's set. Want me to walk back with you?'

She looked at the shadowy expanse of the woods and willed herself to be brave. 'I'll be fine. I'll come and find you after breakfast.'

'Start thinking of safe places for Lew.'

Felix waited until he'd gone and ran over the lawn to the lane. She didn't want him to know she was going to avoid the woods. For the second time in an hour she sprinted past the churchyard, hardly daring to breathe in case she alerted anything to her presence. Her mother was in a grave there, she reminded herself. But she couldn't imagine gentle Martha Valance holding back the forces of darkness. She didn't slow down until she'd reached Rosebank's French windows.

When she reached her bedroom she threw herself fully clothed into bed, too weary to light the lamp. Even *Climbing on the Himalaya and other Mountain Ranges*, a favourite treasure from the Manor library, couldn't tempt her with descriptions of climbs she longed to make when she was grown up. Again she heard the tawny owl in the forest and she pulled the eiderdown over her head to block out its screech.

Five

Minna

Swanham Herald
Cruel Sea Kills Romance
Following the discovery of GI Lew Campbell's body at
Fontwell last week, a Bournemouth woman has told how
a tragic military accident destroyed her parents' mixed-
race romance.

Louise Miller, 63, is Lew Campbell's daughter, the
result of his relationship with her mother, Phoebe
Lambert. Mrs Lambert met the Georgia-born GI in
Swanham in 1942, following his arrival in England. Lew,
then 19, was the talk of the town, according to Mrs Miller.
'The girls hadn't seen many black men before and they
were intrigued by Lew. But he only had eyes for my
mother. They fell in love.'

But the budding romance was disrupted when Lew
was posted to a training camp in west Dorset. 'Lew was
kept really busy as D-Day approached. Mum kept writing
to him but heard nothing back. After the Normandy
Landings she assumed he'd fallen on the beaches like so
many American soldiers. Now I discover he probably
drowned in a training accident.'

Phoebe died in 1993. Her daughter hopes to attend
Pte. Campbell's funeral when the body is released.

'It's such a relief to find out what really happened to
him after all these years.'

I read the article with more interest than I've been able to summon
for any other news in the last few months. 'Did you see this?'

Tom raises an eyebrow at the headline and scans the article.

'Our skeleton had a history. And he was black, which is interesting.'

Tom lifts his head. 'Jim Crow meets John Bull, eh?'

'What?'

'Jim Crow's what Yanks called black GIs. Apparently they created quite a stir when they came over here.' Tom reads widely and watches all those documentaries on the History Channel. 'Poor fellow, all those miles from home.' He's interested, but not drawn to the story like me.

I take back the *Herald*. 'And he never even made it to the Front.'

'There's a place in Devon, Slapton Sands, where hundreds of Americans drowned while they were training,' he says. 'The authorities hushed it up.'

'Perhaps they thought it would be bad for morale.'

He shrugs. 'Tea?' A mug of Tom's tea is like a meal, reviving and strengthening. When I was pregnant I worried that too much of it would be bad for the foetus so I cut back to two cups a day, just to be safe. Just as I stopped applying paint stripper to my clients' door frames and windowsills in case the fumes damaged the baby. As if you can make deals with fate.

He brings the mugs out to me in the garden. He's chosen the bone china. I've always hated drinking tea from pottery: it simply tastes better out of china. When we were first together he used to call me Princess, with a twinkle in his eye that told me such finicky behaviour would be unknown in Belfast.

We sit at the teak table. A lark sings high above and the air is already heavy with the scent of honeysuckle and roses. I haven't done my exercises, twenty minutes of stretching and isometrics every day – part of my routine. If my body keeps busy my mind can't dwell on things. Some days I can't bring myself to do it, can't bring myself to do anything. I long for night so I can slip back into sleep.

Tom's texting someone on his mobile, brow furrowed.

'Do you think we should go to the funeral?' I ask.

He puts down the mobile. 'Why would we do that?'

'We found him.'

He stares out towards the sea for such a long time I think he's decided to ignore the suggestion. 'We can go if you want, but don't you . . .?'

'Don't I what?' Every time he says something I jump down his throat.

'Think it might be unsettling for you?'

Black clothes, hushed voices, the stuffy air in the crematorium chapel, someone weeping far away: my mother, Tom's?

'It wouldn't be like that for a sixty-years-dead soldier.' I stand and clear the mugs. 'It would just be the padre and Louise Miller, the daughter. And she didn't even know her father.'

'I found it a bit harrowing when we found his body.' He blinks and looks away.

I stare at him. 'Did you?' I've been so wrapped up in my own reactions I haven't even thought to make sure Tom is OK. I used to look out for him, used to tease him if I thought he was growing too heated about the Middle East or the state of the London Underground or the demands of his clients. And he watched me, too, telling me off when I tired myself out with a project or got myself too worked up about an incorrectly mixed paint or imperfectly matched cushion cover. We'd formed an emotional seesaw, not always perfectly balanced, but calibrated to prevent one another dashing to the ground or shooting too high. Only now the equilibrium's gone. I don't look out for Tom any more; I stopped at about midnight on a Saturday three months ago, while rain lashed the windscreen.

Now I just concentrate on myself, on getting through each day. I make bargains with myself. If I keep myself under constant supervision, I might just make it.

So why am I threatening my fragile compromise with life with this interest in a long-dead soldier? 'You're right, it would be a mistake to go.' I glance back at him over my shoulder as I take the mugs into the kitchen to refill them. He's still staring towards the sea.

The mobile trills and he gives a start and grabs it, eyes narrowing as he answers.

'Hello, Jeremy. No, I haven't tracked down all the councillors yet but I'm going into Swanham this afternoon.' He listens to Jeremy's reply, the tip of his tongue just visible through his lips. As I come back out, Jeremy's telling him something long and complicated. Tom nods and bites his lip.

I switch my attention back to the newspaper and reread a report about the Red Arrows display on Bournemouth beach. It sounds familiar. I realize I've read the paragraph twice already this morning.

Six

Felix 1943

Dr Valance concentrated on his *Times*, which was a relief as Felix was certain last night's adventure must be painted all over her face. He finished the crossword and sighed, before pulling out the brown envelope from his inside jacket pocket. He unfolded the letter from the ministry and studied it for the twentieth time, though they both knew it by heart.

'It is regretted that, in the National Interest, it is necessary to move you from your homes. Everything possible will be done to help you, both by payment of compensation and by finding other accommodation for you if you are unable to do so yourself.'

An automaton must have written the letter, some contraption buried deep below a Whitehall ministry. Her father said the most devastating letters were always written in the same passive and impersonal style. His sky-blue eyes met hers and he frowned, as though remembering something.

'I rang St Agatha's again.'

'Oh.' Her heart lurched.

'They can take you in November. Don't look so gloomy, child, it's a very good school.'

'Yes.'

'If it hadn't been so convenient sending you up to the Manor for lessons every morning, I'd have done this years ago. It'll be good for you to have more female company. You've become a hoyden, tearing round the countryside, climbing trees. Your mother would have liked you to learn some of the accomplishments: piano, French conversation, that kind of thing.' As always when he mentioned his dead wife his face stiffened.

'Mummy liked me having lots of fresh air. And she liked David.'

His hand reached across the breakfast table to touch hers. She noticed how it shook. 'David's a splendid chap. Shame you don't get along as well with his cousin.'

'Isabel hates me.'

The hand withdrew. 'Hate is a word you shouldn't use. Hate causes wars. Isabel could teach you things.'

'How to paint my lips and keep my hands soft?'

His eyes narrowed. 'She's the perfect model of a young lady. And she's had a difficult time of late. She needs your sympathy.'

Isabel, who stayed in bed until ten in the morning and still ordered Elizabeth Arden from a shop in Bond Street, having a difficult time? 'You mean her swollen glands? But that was months ago. What's wrong with her now?' But she knew, of course, that he'd never tell her. Patient confidentiality – inviolable, he called it, whatever that meant. Her father was forcing a smile. 'St Agatha's will give you a good start in life. Think of the friends you'll make.'

She sighed. Perhaps something would happen before December – the Germans would invade England, or the Allies France – and the war would be over. David's tutor, Mr Stewart, had already joined the navy, David was bound for Harrow, and Felix for this institution where girls wore serge gym tunics and velour hats, played lacrosse and had passions for sixth-formers. She'd read all about boarding schools and didn't like the sound of them. Felix already knew she wasn't a team player and suspected this would cost her dearly at St Agatha's.

If only she could stay here. If only Fontwell could go on for ever, or at least until she was old enough to head to the Alps or Himalayas for some serious climbing. Thinking about the future tightened a band across Felix's chest. To distract herself she studied the food on the table. Four years into the war and rations were growing scarce. Lucky that patients often sent Father home with eggs and bacon, or they'd be struggling, Mrs Derby said.

Dr Valance picked up *The Times* again. Felix cut another slice of bread and spread it with a thin layer of margarine, topped with honey made by the Squire's bees. 'Margarine *or* honey, Felicity.' He lowered his paper. 'Not both.'

'Sorry.' She waited until he was immersed again and scooped the slice, together with her untouched boiled egg, into the napkin on her lap. 'Please may I leave the table?'

'Goodness child, you'll give yourself indigestion if you eat at that rate.' He looked up briefly.

'Yes, Daddy.'

'You won't make old bones if you don't chew properly.' He frowned at the paper. 'There's a chap here claims the Germans will attack us with pilotless planes and rockets, would you believe. Off you go.'

She scuttled out with the stolen food stuffed up her jumper.

In the lane Sam Fuller rolled marbles through the dust and beamed at her from a grimy face. 'Can I come to the beach with you?'

'Miss James will tell you off if you miss school again.' Like most of the local children, Sam attended the village school. Felix's father hadn't wanted her to be a pupil there.

'It's not for the likes of you,' Mrs Derby had told her. 'Not for young ladies.' So Felix had joined David for lessons with Mr Stewart at the Manor instead.

'Miss James's mother is poorly.' Sam scooped up his marbles. 'She's gone to Swanham to visit her. Can I come with you?'

'Later.' His small frame slumped. Most of the time you'd hardly know Sam was around. He wasn't bad, for a kid of seven – quiet enough and happy to carry out errands. Felix and David didn't take him out at nights: that would be irresponsible. People Sam's age needed nine or ten hours' good sleep. And besides, she and David sometimes talked about things that weren't suitable for young ears. Like Isabel, all those letters she got with the addresses written in firm, masculine writing, and flowers too, sometimes, even in wartime. And the raised voices when she sat in the library with the Squire at night.

Felix was still thinking about the older girl when she met David, hiding behind the pampas grass and clutching a roll of blankets secured with a belt. 'There you are.' He looked flustered.

'What's up?'

'Nothing. Just Isabel.'

'Surely she's not up so early?'

'Still in her bedroom all day and insisting on a fire even though fuel's in such short supply, and refusing to do anything to help the Squire around the place.' He let out a long breath. 'Not that I do much.'

'You help in the garden. I've seen you hoeing the potato patch.'

'I like that kind of thing. Isabel hates it.'

'Well she can't just lounge around for ever reading her *Tatler*s. Perhaps they'll make her join the Wrens.'

David rolled his eyes. 'Can you see Isabel in uniform? Obeying orders?'

'Getting up early in the morning.'

'Learning drill.'

Felix laughed. 'She'll just have to get married quickly and start having brats. She's nineteen now, old enough.'

'Not much older than me, really.'

He'd just turned fifteen, a year and a half older than her.

David was frowning.

'What is it?'

'Probably nothing. But I think Johnson likes her.'

'Johnson? What do you mean, he likes her?'

'I've seen them talking a few times. He stares at her as though she's some kind of oracle.' David grinned. 'Can't imagine they'd have much in common.'

They'd reached the outhouses. Lew jumped to his feet as they opened the door to the shed, shoulders set, knuckles clenched.

'Only us,' David said.

In daylight Felix noticed blue lines under the fugitive's eyes and a greyish tinge to his skin. She wondered how far he'd dragged himself on his swollen ankle yesterday. 'I got you more food.' She placed the egg, bread and honey on the sacking in front of him.

'Thanks, missy.' He fell upon it, eating the egg in swift bites. Even ravenous he couldn't be graceless, he moved as though his body was a finely calibrated machine. She couldn't help staring at him. At Sunday School before the war they'd collected money for the missionaries who worked among the piccaninnies, as Mrs Baker called them. Felix hadn't pictured the recipients of the charity being so well developed.

'We need to get you out of here.' David folded up the sacks Lew had used as his bed. 'The Squire's going to prune his fruit trees this morning and he'll come in here for the shears.'

'The Squire?' Lew frowned. 'Who's that? Sounds like someone in a movie.'

David blushed. 'My uncle.'

'I thought a squire was like a lord.'

'Not so grand,' David said. 'And he doesn't have a title. Just Mr.'

'But why don't you call him Uncle?'

David shrugged. 'Isabel and I – Isabel's my cousin – have always known him as the Squire.'

Lew grinned. 'My aunt always calls my uncle Pastor, 'stead of Joseph. 'Cept for when he's late for mealtimes, then she calls him Joseph Campbell in a voice that could freeze hell.' He licked a speck of honey off his finger. 'So you live with this Squire?'

'Always have done, apart from when I was away at school.'

'You don't go to school now?' Lew grinned. 'Hey, bet you don't mind.'

'It was evacuated to Cornwall. And I got measles rather badly at the same time. So it seemed easier for me to come home. But now the Squire thinks I should go to public school.'

'You in a public school?' Lew shook his head. 'Not somewhere smart? Thought you'd go to one of those schools where boys wear the hats.' He raised his hands above his head and drew a top hat in the air.

David smiled. 'We call them public schools but they're not at all public really, you have to pay to go.'

'Talkin' of going places,' Lew ate the last mouthful of bread, 'what happens now?' He spoke casually but Felix noticed a guarded expression in his eyes.

David looked at Felix for inspiration. 'The woods would be safe enough by day.'

'But cold. And Johnson's always hanging around there.' She shivered at the thought of going back among the trees in the dark.

'The woodshed?'

'Full of spiders.'

'Lew's a soldier, spiders won't bother him.'

His words reminded her they still knew very little of Lew and what he was doing here. She glanced at the big man in the American uniform eating her breakfast leftovers. He lifted his head.

'Seems to me,' he said, 'that folks who take a risk for someone they hardly know deserve answers.' David started to say something but Lew waved him to silence. 'You don't know me at all. Or the punishment for going absent without leave. Or for hiding someone like me.'

'You're absent without leave?' Felix shrank a little.

'That's what they call it. I was due back at the camp yesterday and I didn't show.' His dark eyes met hers and held her gaze. She'd always pictured deserters as weedy youths, too scared of fighting to cope with army life. Lew looked as though he could take on the entire German army without blinking.

'Why didn't you show?'

'Shh!' David pointed to the door. Footsteps were coming towards them.

Seven

Felix 1943

'. . . Think I'll pick the last of the Bramleys and move on to the Worcesters if I have time.' A silence, then a sigh.

'What's the point? We won't be able to take them all with us.' The female speaker was Isabel. She'd dragged herself out of bed at last.

'I know I'm a sentimental old fool but I just keep hoping something will happen before next month.'

'A miracle?'

'Well, no point letting the place go to rack and ruin in the meantime. Just wish I could have done something about Upper Farm.'

'The corrugated horrors?' Isabel sounded bored.

'I'd have liked to have renovated the barns. Shame to leave them in that state.'

'There's a war on.'

A sigh like wind through trees. 'I know. What are you going to do this morning, my dear?'

'Promised I'd dig the potato patch, didn't I?' Her tone held little enthusiasm.

'You don't look up to it. Still very pale.' A pause. 'I told you not to do it.'

'I know.'

'Don't take it to heart, it's just the way she is.'

Who? Felix wondered. Beside her David sighed. Perhaps he felt ashamed about eavesdropping.

'Damn,' the Squire said.

'What is it?' Isabel didn't sound very concerned.

'Meant to tell Johnson I saw a roe nibbling at the saplings this morning.'

'What's it matter, now we're going?'

'Good estate management is good estate management, my dear.' A sharper note in the Squire's voice.

'I'll tell him if you want.'

'Would you? He'll be in the woods with his traps.'

She said something they couldn't make out and their footsteps moved on.

'Blast.' David's face was pale. 'Let's go.'

'But where to?'

'The beach. Lew can hide out in the cave until his leg is better. He can light a fire down there and keep warm and dry.'

'Should be jigging round soon. Feels better since missy bandaged it.' Lew rose, gritting his teeth. 'How far's this beach?'

'Ten minutes. Think you're up to it?' David picked up the roll of blankets.

'Yup.' But Lew shuffled out of the shed like an old man. She glanced at David. He gave a slight shake of his head, letting her know now wasn't the right time to voice fears. She wanted to ask him about Isabel, too, what she'd been talking about. It would have to wait. Nine o'clock, the village would be humming with activity. And because today was fine and there were no lessons children would mill around, trying to avoid parents who might want them to collect eggs or clean out pigsties.

At the end of the drive David waved them behind the stone gateposts. 'I'm going to go ahead and make sure the road's clear. If you hear me whistle "The British Grenadiers" stay where you are. If it's "Rule Britannia", the coast's clear.'

'Hope you know these tunes, missy,' Lew whispered to Felix. 'Because I never heard them in my life.' As she huddled close to him by the wall she caught his scent, exotic, deeper than that of sweaty farm labourers, muskier than her father's smell of Palmolive soap and pressed cotton.

The opening notes of 'Rule Britannia' shrilled through the morning air. 'Let's go,' Felix whispered, moving across the road. Lew hobbled after her. David waited for them by the telephone box. 'So far, so good.' Then a shadow crossed his face. 'Damn.' She spotted Sam ambling across the green. 'He hasn't seen us yet. In here, quick.' She pointed over the stone wall to Miss Foss's garden. Miss Foss was a birdwatcher and believed in shrubs. Her garden provided good cover. The wall was low enough for Lew to step over with just the faintest intake of breath. They crouched behind a laurel and heard Sam's footsteps pounding their way along the lane.

'Felix? You there?'

Felix stiffened. David turned and put a finger over his lips. As if she'd betray them. All the same, it felt rotten hiding from Sam. 'Felix?' Sam called again.

She held her breath and heard him shuffle away.

'Let's go.' They climbed back over the wall to the lane. David paused near where it split: left to the post office; right towards the cliff-top path, which continued down to the beach. Ahead of them, Sam stood with his back to them, hands stuck in pockets. Felix muttered a prayer that he wasn't heading for the cove. He spent a few moments digging his toes into the dirt and drawing patterns with his shoes and turned left. Probably going to press his nose against the post office window, hoping against hope that the shop-keeper had been able to get hold of gobstoppers or toffees.

The lane narrowed into a path clinging to the sides of the steep hill, covered in its lowest section with yellowing leaves from chestnuts and oaks. They could only manage it in single file, Felix first, with Lew in the middle, and David bringing up the rear. Conversation dried up as they climbed. When she turned to see how Lew was managing, she saw that his brow was covered in perspiration.

'I'm doing fine, missy.' He smiled at her but she could see the concentration on his face.

As they ascended they left behind the trees and their fallen leaves. Sheep grazed the turf. A breeze, fanning their glowing faces, her-alded the cliff top. At last they could see the Channel, shimmering slate and azure a hundred feet below, the surf hissing on shingle. Felix's heart gave its customary lift.

Lew whistled. 'See why you kids like it here. Where's the cave?'

David pointed at the rocks marking the far end of the beach. 'The entrance is down there.'

Lew squinted at it. 'Can't see nothing at all.' They descended to the cove, Lew's breath coming in starts as he limped down. Once or twice he gave a low groan. Felix was relieved to reach the level beach.

'If we sit behind the rocks we can still be in the sun but nobody can see us,' she suggested as they neared the cave. David helped Lew across the rocks until they reached the little circle of sand in their middle. Felix noted its dryness. When was the next high tide? They unrolled the blankets and sank down, facing the cliff path so nobody could approach unnoticed.

'So tell us where you're going.' Felix fixed Lew with her sternest gaze. 'And why you were running off to Swanham at a time of international peril.' She liked the last part of her question; it reminded her of the language in the Pathé news films.

'Felicity!' David glared.

'No, she's right.' Lew bowed his head, swallowed. 'What I done is wrong. But I didn't mean for it to happen.'

'So why did you do it?'

He drew a line in the sand with his finger. 'A friend's in trouble.'

'A friend?'

'You don't mean a woman, do you?' David sounded like a grown-up.

Lew started drawing a second line. 'Phoebe's her name.'

'What kind of trouble?' David asked.

Lew's gaze stayed on the ground. 'I have to give her some money. I had two days' leave but I didn't think it would take so long to reach Swanham. Should have reported back for duty last night.'

'Couldn't you have used the post?'

Lew blinked. 'The post?'

'The mail.'

'To send money? No, not a big amount like this. If it got lost, Phoebe'd be stuck.'

'How were you planning on getting to Swanham?'

'Walking.'

'And you say you'll give yourself up once you've seen Phoebe?'

'Sure will.' His dark glance moved to David. 'I want to see those Germans beat same as you folks.'

'It must be great knowing you'll get to fight them.' David, normally the gentlest of boys, sounded wistful.

'Trouble is, they don't let many coloured men into the combat troops. We mainly do support stuff, drive jeeps, work in supply depots, that kind of thing.'

'That's so unfair.' A man as strong as Lew seemed wasted in those roles, Felix thought.

'You're telling me, missy. But that's southern whites.'

'Southern whites?'

'Yankees aren't so particular.'

Yankees? Weren't they all Yanks – Americans? Felix's confusion must have shown because he smiled at her.

'Yankees are folk from the north.'

'The Confederates were the ones in the plantations, with the slaves,' said David, who had recently seen *Gone with the Wind*. 'The Yankees were the ones they were fighting.'

'But you said the Yankees were the baddies.'

Lew guffawed. 'Some of the whites at home are good people. But some don't think we're worthy to clean their boots.'

'How do English people react to you?' asked David.

'They're kind. Mostly. There was this minister's wife near the camp—'

'Minister?' Felix frowned.

'I think Lew means the vicar,' David said.

'Vicar.' Lew spoke the word carefully. 'This vicar's wife wrote letters to all the white women who lived near the camp, telling them how they should treat us. "Be kind, but don't let them into your homes," she said. "Don't chat to them. They're not like us, they're more animal."'

Felix and David were silent. Felix felt the kind of gloom she felt when her father talked about the war, telling her about people in Europe being arrested in the middle of the night or put in camps if

40

they disagreed with the authorities. She hunted around for a more cheerful subject and her mind switched to Phoebe.

'Why can't we just telephone Phoebe and tell her to come here for the money?' The idea struck Felix as inspired, but David pulled a face.

'How would she get here?'

'Bus.'

'They're not exactly regular at the moment. You should hear Isabel complaining about them.'

So Isabel'd been travelling. Interesting.

David flushed, probably realizing he'd revealed more than he'd intended. 'I don't know.'

Felix still didn't understand the urgency. 'Why exactly does Phoebe need the money?'

Lew looked at her and then away again, biting his lip. 'She's in a difficult situation.' His eyes met David's.

'That explains it.' David nodded.

Felix started to say something but David's frown told her to drop the subject.

'You've got her address?'

'Yes.'

'Is she on the telephone?' said David. 'Could we ring and tell her to meet us somewhere between here and Swanham? She could walk or borrow a bike.'

'There's no phone.' Lew spoke quietly. 'Phoebe moves round.'

'So how'd you know where to meet her?'

'There's a pub she goes to most evenings.' Lew pulled at a whelk stuck to a rock.

Felix felt better about him now. He was a deserter, no doubt, but for a noble reason. It was kind of him to want to help this girl. 'We can ring the camp for you, tell them there was an accident.'

'Maybe that'd be best.' But his face looked troubled.

'And perhaps we can help get the money to Phoebe for you,' Felix added.

'Missy, you done enough for me.'

'The Squire goes into Swanham sometimes to see his accountant,' David said. 'Perhaps I could drive in with him and find her for you.'

'Don't put yourself out.' But Lew's eyes were warm on David.

Felix looked at his ankle in its boot. 'We should undo the bandage so you can stick your foot in the sea. The cold water will help the swelling.'

'Good plan, missy. In fact, I was thinking of taking a dip when it's a little more private round here.'

David gave Felix a pointed look. She rose, cheeks turning pink. 'I'll walk up the beach while you have a swim.'

'Oh, I won't be swimming, I can't.' Lew grinned at her. 'Just want to freshen up.' It struck Felix again how confident he seemed that they'd sort things out for him.

She started to walk away, hearing David's intake of breath as he ran into the water and Lew's gasp seconds later. Lucky for them this was such a fine autumn day, almost warm enough to deceive you into thinking it was still summer. High on the cliff to the west, sunlight gleamed on metal – probably another man from the ministry surveying Fontwell and its beach and salivating over its possibilities. He wouldn't be able to see Lew and David from there.

The military could hardly wait for the villagers to leave. In another month or so they would cover the beach with grey metal tanks and landing craft, or whatever they used to practise invasions. Felix remembered the invasion fever earlier in the war, when she and David had only been able to gaze at the cove from the headland until it was decided Hitler was so busy elsewhere he wouldn't be coming to Fontwell. The loss of the beach had felt like bereavement. But this time it would be worse and the beach wouldn't even be left in peaceful loneliness. Nor would the village. Soldiers would toss cigarette ends into Miss Foss's flowerbeds and trample down shrubs and bushes. Jeeps would carve up the Manor lawns. And Felix and David would be conjugating irregular French verbs and wrestling with quadratic equations and playing team games with silly children who'd never crawled over rocks to watch grey seals at play. She kicked out at the shingle.

A shadow fell on her. 'You'll scuff your shoes.'

Felix froze.

Eight

Minna

'The mystery grows.' Tom raises an eyebrow. 'There you go, Miss
Marple, you can start interviewing suspects.'

'That's the trouble with living in an abandoned village,' I say. 'No
suspicious locals with motives.' I go into the kitchen and lob my
half-eaten piece of toast into the bin. Tom's followed me out. I keep
explaining that I don't like breakfast. Please, please don't let him
start nagging me again. To distract him I keep on talking. 'Strange,
though. What was a GI doing here if he wasn't training?'

44

Tom shrugs. 'Visiting friends? Taking the sea air? But you'd think he'd go somewhere more lively for his leave.'

'Whatever he was doing he ended up drowning.'

'It happens.'

I open my mouth to object to this comment but close it again. He closes the dishwasher. 'So what'll you do today?'

'I don't know. Potter round. Go for a walk, perhaps.'

'You could paint . . .' Tom makes the suggestion with hesitation.

'Yes.' It's what I'd advise a friend in similar circumstances to do. Once or twice I've even gone as far as taking out the wooden box containing my watercolours. I felt nothing. No excitement at the colours, no urge to reproduce what's around me, or, God forbid, inside me. 'Actually, I thought I might cut the sweet peas.'

'Very country-lady-ish.' His look is ironic, almost as though we're back to normal and he's about to tease me.

I grew up in a large Edwardian house with a well-stocked garden and a mother who doted on plants. From an early age I snipped and mulched and weeded. As a child in Belfast, Tom didn't have much of a garden, although his father used to grow a few flowers for the house. I still catch him looking at this house or our flat in Putney as though he's wandered into the wrong place and someone will tell him off for trespassing.

'I've got work to finish for Waymark, but first I thought I'd go through our bank statements. It's been a while since we took stock.' Is he making a dig at me – the one who used to manage all our financial affairs?

He settles down in the dining room with the folder of bank statements and cashpoint receipts, a frown creasing his brow. Tom really, really hates money matters and it's one more chore he's had to shoulder lately. I wish I could summon up the energy to offer to do it for him. Instead I drift into the garden. Cutting the sweet peas takes no more than five minutes, and even when I've removed every weed in the flowerbeds the blank expanse of the morning stretches ahead. I've already done my exercises and made our bed. I've even cleaned the kitchen, polishing the draining board and hob and sweeping the floor, although the cleaning lady's due in this afternoon.

When Tom told me he'd booked Rosebank I made all kinds of plans: long hikes along cliffs, visits to National Trust gardens, sketching and painting. And indeed I've walked miles, but I couldn't tell you a single thing I've observed on these expeditions. Except for the village. Somehow, Fontwell draws me out of my indifference. Probably because it's sad and sad is the only station I'm tuned to these days.

Checking the flags to make sure the range isn't in use I walk over the field leading to the footpath. My mother would love the wildflowers scattered through the grass. We should ask my parents down here, really. Put their minds at rest about me. But I know I won't pick up the telephone and make the call. Tom sometimes rings them on his mobile. Several times I've picked up snatches of conversation, broken off when he notices me.

'Not much change,' he said to them a few days ago. Well, what do they expect?

This land forms part of the South Coast path. From the conservatory I often observe walkers, stepping out, purposeful and determined. They smile and wish me a good morning. I feel a pang at the engaged expressions on their faces. I was purposeful once.

Below me the sea still whispers its accusations. *Should have taken more care, should have stopped to think, should have, should, should, should* . . . Trying to block out the indictment, I don't even notice my feet dragging me past the pillbox towards the village until I turn off the path and take the steep track down through the trees. Only when shadows brush my face do I realize where I'm going and look up with a start.

The village pulls me into its crumbling embrace and despite myself I look around as I emerge from the trees. Something about this place mirrors my own sense of existing outside time. I walked round the houses when we arrived a few days ago, but that was with Tom. Coming here alone feels different. No small children scamper

46

here today. I can see only a couple of teenage girls sunbathing on a verge, trying to get signals on their mobiles.

I find myself standing at the fence circling the old Manor, now too dilapidated for the public to be allowed near it. A notice tells me that the panelling in the dining room went to a museum in the United States, where it was reconstructed to house a permanent exhibition of eighteenth-century furniture, and the beams to another country house in Wiltshire. The Manor is slowly letting itself die, releasing itself, stone by stone, into the ground. I wander on down the lane past the telephone box. A sign tells me it had only just been installed when the village was evacuated.

'I wonder how the telephone engineer felt about that,' a middle-aged man beside me says.

'Surely they must have known the village was going to be evacuated,' adds the woman with him.

'Perhaps they didn't know until the last minute,' says the man.

The woman turns to me. 'Breaks your heart, doesn't it?' The accent's not local, but it's not London, either.

I nod. 'It's sad.' I make a movement with my lips which I hope approximates to a smile, and shuffle off.

I'm standing in front of the church. Ivy has wound itself round the remaining yew and seems intent on choking it to death. I feel a pang for the tree. If my mother were here she'd be climbing over the wall to rip it off. The information board says the font and stained glass were bequeathed to the church in the next village. The roof's almost gone; if you stood inside you'd see great squares of blue sky above you. Grass and weed cover the gravestones. At least they've lost that raw look new graves possess. But graves aren't a good place for me to linger. I notice a woman in her seventies hanging around, pulling sticky-willy and bindweed off one of the headstones. On the other side of the churchyard a young man squats to examine a tablet set into the ground. His clothes look too smart and he writes notes on a Blackberry. When he stands he pulls his courier bag over his shoulder and extracts folded papers. Plans. He studies them, making pencil notes. I know his type, he's a property man. He looks faintly familiar but I can't place him and can't be bothered to rack my brain to work out where I've seen him before.

I make for the village school and peep at the displays on the children's desks, essays about nature walks, decorated with wildflowers and drawings of mushrooms and berries. I picture the pupils exiled to strange villages and towns. Did they ask, over and over again, when they'd be going home?

But if they had come back here, they'd have found the place changed. They'd have changed, too. You can never turn back the hands. As I leave the schoolhouse I touch the stone wall as though it'll impart some message of hope or wisdom, but it just feels cool against my palm.

Perhaps I should tell Tom this extended holiday is a mistake? But I said I'd stay here for six weeks, until I was sure about myself, and begging for early release would be giving up. Not that Tom seems happy here, either. He spends hours in the office. I don't blame him, banished with me for company.

I pass a bench and realize my legs ache. Sometimes my body feels so separate from my mind I have to remind myself to feed it, rest it, care for it. I let myself flop down. Something crackles in my pocket. The cormorant drawing. I remove it carefully.

This must have been the bus-stop once, for villagers going into market a couple of times a week. I can picture the women getting off the bus with baskets full of shopping, fresh gossip in their minds, going home to cook supper for husbands who'd worked long days in the fields. How could they have guessed their world was coming to an end?

How can anyone know their life's about to shatter? Me, talking to friends, catching up on news. Tom, laughing and telling jokes, drinking wine and shouting for more music, more dancing. Yvonne, our hostess, telling him he'd wake Benjamin, who was asleep in a carry cot in their spare bedroom.

'And you were going to drive,' I reminded him. 'My first night back drinking, remember?' I'd started weaning Benjamin from the breast because he was six months old and I thought I might start working again for half the week.

He closed his eyes, contrite. 'Darling, sorry. You should have stopped me.'

I let out a sigh. 'When I frowned at you half an hour ago, what did you think that meant?'

'I thought you were angry because hordes of women were swarming round me.' He grabbed my waist. 'It probably looks worse than it is. I've had, what, three glasses?'

'Two too many.'

'Dance with me.' His arms round my waist. 'Moondance' was playing. Tom's always loved his fellow countryman Van Morrison.

'You won't be able to drive.'

'So? If push comes to shove we'll sleep over.'

'What about Benjamin?'

'Well I don't think he'll be driving himself home, do you?'

'I haven't got bottles and nappies.'

'We'll ring for a cab and collect the car in the morning.'

'Have you got cash? I've only got a fiver.'

'Dance, woman!' he muttered in my ear. 'You worry too much.' And perhaps I did. I'd always been the worrier in our relationship, the one who insisted on organic carrots for Benjamin's puree, who hadn't let a sip of formula touch his lips until now. Meanwhile Tom won client after client, companies and charities wooed by the Ulsterman with the warm eyes and the blunt tongue. MPs from all parties like him, too. My husband has charm, much as he'd despise the attribution.

That night was the first time I'd danced with him for, what, a year? And it reminded me how I'd felt about him when I was his girlfriend, rather than his wife and the mother of his child. We were just Minna and Tom again, back with the old crowd, having a good time. And I wasn't going to fret too much.

'Where did you get that?' The voice startles me back to the present. Its owner sounds astounded. I didn't even notice her taking a seat on the bench beside me.

49

I jump. 'I'm sorry?'

'That drawing, where did you find it?'

I look down at my lap and see I've unfolded the cormorant. 'In the house I'm renting.'

'Rosebank?'

'That's right.'

The woman is silent. 'You shouldn't have taken it,' she says.

All my life I've been allergic to the word 'shouldn't'. 'Why's that?' The words sound like two daggers.

'It belongs in the house.'

'I'm renting the house. And I'll put it back.' But why the hell am I defending myself to this old bag? 'What's it to you, anyway?' I realize what I've just said and blush.

She stands. 'You wouldn't understand.'

I watch her stomp away. Great. I've only been in my retreat a week or so and already I've managed to alienate a local. The village has lost its appeal. Time for home. I fold the drawing, replace it in my pocket, and rise from the bench.

Reaching the top of the path, I take a deep breath to steady myself. Below me holidaymakers enjoy the beach, children running into the sea and squealing when cold waves catch them: a scene of total happiness. Or so I think, until I notice a small boy crouching at the shore. He tries to catch the waves and hold the water in his hands, weeping as it leaks out onto the shingle. His mother runs to him with a yellow bucket and tries to persuade him to use it instead, but he pushes her away.

I turn away from the scene and lie back on the springy turf. Something's nagging at me. I frown, trying to work out what it is. Then I've got it: that old woman must have been the one who visited Rosebank while we were out. She once lived in our house. How else would she know about the cormorant? And I've just been rude to her. I try to decide whether or not I care.

I take the cormorant out of my pocket again, scrutinizing it once more in case I've missed something.

Nine

Felix walks away from the girl on the bench, longing to find somewhere cool where she can force her emotions back into submission. No need to jump on the girl like that over a scrap of paper, even if her voice was acid, even if the cormorant is special. The shock of seeing it again after all this time makes Felix's head spin. She hadn't even thought about the drawing for decades. How extraordinary that it should reappear in her life like this.

Perhaps she's mistaken and it isn't the drawing she remembers, just one very similar. There are enough cormorants on this part of the coast, and people who like drawing them.

But she saw his initials on the corner of the sheet.

She needs air and heads up the path to the cliff top, noting how her heart pounds. As a child she could run straight to the top almost without drawing breath. A young man coming down stands to the side for her to pass. As she pants a thank you she notices he wears a smart silver bag slung diagonally over his shoulder. Strange for the seaside.

The trees fall away and the breeze from the sea strokes her face. Her heartbeat slows and she feels the familiar joy at the sight of the beach. How smooth the shingle looks, as though the sea's ironed it. How small the holidaymakers are down there, like tiny animated dolls. She hears footsteps behind her and glimpses a shock of chestnut hair. The girl with the cormorant sketch is coming up here. Felix hurries along the cliff top until she's out of sight, feeling foolish and resentful both at once.

Sixty years ago Isabel had walked down to the beach unobserved while Lew and David were bathing in the shallows. She was daydreaming, gazing at the horizon, when Isabel came up behind her and made her jump.

As always she found it impossible not to stare at the older girl. Isabel's pale skin still retained a few tiny freckles from the summer – as though the sun had melted and dripped onto her, Felix thought. She wore white, as always – vastly impractical for a wartime autumn, Mrs Derby said, with such a shortage of soapflakes. Her skirt skimmed the tops of her knees and under her cream jacket Felix glimpsed a jumper made of the kind of wool royal babies probably wore. Her stockings were almost immaculate but Felix couldn't help feeling pleased when she noticed small darns on one of the knees. The only colour in today's ensemble came from a late rose Isabel had pinned to her lapel, and from the gold hair dropping to her shoulders.

Isabel's smoky-grey eyes narrowed. 'Where's David?'

'Don't know.' Felix tried to look uninterested, keeping her back to the rocks. 'Probably looking for seals by the rocks.'

'You look tired.'

'Find it hard to sleep.'

'I thought I heard you two in the garden late last night.'

Felix tried to retain a nonchalant expression. 'Father doesn't like me out after dark.'

'All the same, I thought I heard voices.'

Felix shrugged and racked her brain for a distraction. 'Have you heard from your mother?'

Isabel frowned at her. 'Why?'

She seemed jumpy. Isabel didn't often see her mother, David said. Felix wondered again what would happen to the older girl when they all left Fontwell. She didn't seem to have any plans. Felix had heard of girls finding jobs in all kinds of exotic places, but perhaps work didn't appeal to Isabel, even at a time like this.

'Let's go and see what that cousin of mine's up to.' Isabel was already walking away.

'No.' The older girl blinked. Miss Isabel Parham, squire's niece, wasn't used to being defied by Felicity Valance, doctor's daughter. 'Sorry. But I'm really keen to look for orchids.'

'A little late in the year, isn't it?' Her lips gave a slight curl.

'Sometimes you find them up on the cliff late in the season.'

'I've never seen them up there in October.' Isabel gave a half-smile at Felix's surprise. 'St Agatha's was hot on botany. It was about the only subject I liked.'

Wretched St Agatha's again.

'What's it like?' Felix's stomach turned cold at the thought of the place.

'Strict.' Isabel glanced at Felix's unpolished sandals with their undone buckles. 'The food used to be ghastly, too, all prunes and fatty cuts of meat. I used to tell the Squire he couldn't expect me to eat that kind of stuff. Probably even worse now, with the war.'

Felix felt she might as well go home and shut herself in her bedroom. The sun had gone in and the waves no longer sparkled.

Isabel's face softened. 'It's not so bad. The other girls are fun, we got up to all kinds of things. When the teachers found out I liked plants they let me help in the greenhouses.' Her nose wrinkled. 'Bit messy, mucking around with soil and grubby old pots, but better than lessons. The headmistress said I should concentrate on non-academic learning.'

'What did she mean?'

'That I was thick, darling. Thick, but presentable.' Isabel flicked back her hair. 'I have this problem with reading: the letters seem to bleed into one another.'

Felix had seen Isabel with the newspaper, tracing a line with her index finger, lips moving slightly. She'd thought it was one of Isabel's little affectations, like wearing white all the time. Imagine finding reading difficult.

'So they taught me how to advertise for servants, fold napkins and write seating plans. More useful for the kind of life I'll lead.'

'You'll have to do war work, won't you?'

Isabel sniffed. 'Have you seen some of those uniformed females? Ankles like milk bottles, voices like foghorns.'

'Girls work in factories, too.'

'Is that supposed to be funny?'

'Or you could become a land-girl.'

'Buried in some damp Welsh valley? I don't think so.' Isabel's eyes narrowed. 'Got your stuff ready for school?'

'I don't want to go.' Words tumbled out of Felix. 'I want to stay here.'

Isabel's glance took in the waves and the red cliffs and her face softened again. Then she laughed. 'You're such a country mouse. I can't wait to get to London. Soon as my glands are better I'll be going to dances and meeting all kinds of people.' *Prospective husbands,* she probably meant. 'When you've grown up a bit, you'll feel the same. You can't be a little tomboy for ever, you know.'

'Daddy says glandular fever can recur.' Isabel deserved a put-down, but guilt washed over Felix as the older girl's face fell. 'I've changed my mind about the orchids, I'm going to walk along the beach.'

Isabel yawned. 'Suit yourself. I'm going to go home and have a rest.'

'Another rest?'

She glared at Felix. 'I have to look after myself. I was very ill, you know. Your father said he'd never seen such a bad case. Too much exercise is bad for me.' Her full lips fell into a pout.

Felix opened her mouth to tell her she was wrong, her father had often said invalids could cut weeks off their convalescence with gentle walking. But what was the point of arguing with Isabel? With a last suspicious glance at the sea the older girl walked away.

Felix waited until Isabel had reached the top of the cliff before turning round. Now David had vanished, too, presumably hiding with Lew in the cave. She ran across the beach to look.

David sat on the rocks, hidden from the beach, hair in wet spikes. 'That was close.' His face was pale beneath its tan. 'Well done you for keeping her talking like that.'

'It took some doing.'

54

David frowned. 'This could get difficult. At least Lew's ankle looks better after the dip.'

'I'll bandage it up again.'

'He can't swim a stroke, you know.'

'Like Sam.' But Felix was thinking about something else. 'We'll have to find him something for lunch.' She sounded like Mrs Derby, fussing about meals. 'And he'll need supper as well.' Where were they to get the food? It wasn't as if they could simply pop into the village shop to buy Lew bread and milk, not these days, not without a ration card.

'I can probably scrounge something from our kitchen,' David said.

'We should telephone the camp and tell them Lew's here,' Felix whispered. 'Did he give you the number?'

David shook his head and frowned. 'He's still worried about going back, says they'll throw him into a cell. They're hard on the blacks, apparently.'

'But he'll have to go back sooner or later, won't he?' She puckered up her brow.

'Hope so.' David sighed. 'I like Lew but . . .'

'But what?'

'It doesn't matter.' He picked at a whelk.

'Tell me.'

'I'm worried about being muddled up in all this.' He shrugged. 'If we get caught helping him it could look bad for the Squire's campaign.'

'Is he still trying to stop the evacuation?'

'He's been up to London to talk to people he knows in the War Office. Suggested they use the land round Upper Farm and let us stay here. But they say they need access to the beach. And you can only get to the beach through Fontwell.'

They fell silent.

'So it's hopeless,' Felix burst out. 'We'll have to leave.'

'It doesn't look good.' He swallowed. 'Let's try and forget about it. What shall we do now?'

'Go and steal some food, I should think.' She started to understand why women like Sam's mother wore that look of perpetual weariness. 'It's going to take hours to get enough to feed him over the next day or so.' Thinking about Lew made her frown. 'I don't understand what this girl Phoebe's problem is.'

David shrugged. 'Who knows? Women of a certain type can be very clinging.'

Ten

Minna

'I don't feel welcome here.'

Tom lifts his head from the laptop and frowns. I tell him about the woman in Fontwell.

'Don't let it get to you. You know old people, they can be very blunt.'

True enough, even my adored grandmother didn't hesitate to speak her mind (she was American and felt no compunction about expressing things the British would leave unsaid). But the woman's outburst yesterday felt more visceral, more personal.

'Oh well.' I pick up my bag, a turquoise raffia nonsense, bought before it all happened. 'I haven't got time to worry about it. Need anything in town?' I don't actually need anything myself.

'Don't think so.' His expression as I leave the room is a mixture of rebuke and plea. 'Minna.'

'Yes?'

'Why did you wait till today to tell me what happened in the village?'

'I don't know.' And, really, I don't. An invisible tape covers my mouth these days.

Tourists swarm all over the small town, enjoying the sun and hunting for cold beer and charcoal for their barbecues. I wait in the supermarket car park while cars shunt in and out of spaces. Finally I spot a space and edge forward just as an old Vauxhall reverses into the rectangle. My predatory London instincts explode. I jump out of the car, slamming the door, and march over to the Vauxhall. 'I've been waiting five minutes for that space!'

The driver winds down her window. The woman from yesterday. Oh.

'So sorry.' She looks dazed and refastens her seatbelt. 'I'll move.'

'No.' For the second time in twenty-four hours I regret my hasty tongue. I put a hand on her window. 'Stay there. I'll find another space. I didn't mean to be rude.' Her blue eyes blink as she recognizes me. 'We got off to a bad start yesterday.'

'I'm sorry I snapped at you.' She grins. 'I felt bad, especially when I worked out you'd kindly let me look round Rosebank.' She catches sight of something in the wing mirror. 'If we're quick, one of us could grab that space by the trolley park.'

'I'll go.' I'm back in my car and easing into the parking place before the next wave of hopeful car-parkers has even noticed it's free.

'Bravo!' She comes over as I get out. She's clutching a leather-and-brocade summer handbag that must once have been very expensive and still looks elegant. 'That was nippy.'

'London training.'

'I never could drive in London, it always leaves me feeling pulverized.'

I swallow. 'I put the cormorant drawing back on the shelf. I'm sorry I took it, but it was interesting.'

Her eyes are sharp. 'Are you an artist?'

'A designer, interiors mainly. Why do you ask?'

'Something about the way you looked at it. And what does an interior designer make of the cormorant?' Her tone's amused now.

'I like the energy in it. And the simplicity. Did you do it? It reminds me of a Japanese drawing.'

'No, it's not mine.' But she looks pleased.

'Whoever did has a sharp eye.' The old woman smiles. 'So who was the artist?'

Felix seems to find something on the ground demanding her attention. 'Someone who came to the village years ago.' She looks as though she wants to tell me more. Four months ago curiosity would have swamped me, now I feel only mild interest. A woman pushes a drowsy baby past in a pram, shopping bags dangling from the handle. I swallow, force myself to say something, anything at all, that'll take my attention off the pair.

'Fontwell's been abandoned for more than half a century.'

'Yes.'

'So you must have known the artist before or during the war?' What on earth am I doing, pressing this poor woman while laden supermarket trolleys trundle past us? It's not as if I'm even that interested.

'They evacuated us.'

'But not until November 1943.' I paid more attention to the dates on the information boards in the village than I realized. I catch a glimpse of her face. 'Sorry. I don't usually stick my nose into people's business. Must be getting bored.'

'Why are you bored?'

The question should rattle me, but it doesn't. 'I can't seem to settle. I keep myself busy but the days still seem long.'

'Keep yourself busy doing what?'

'Plan meals, shop, exercise, keep on top of things.' I thought for a second. 'Well, for a while I did. I've been wondering if I can be bothered any more.' Why the hell am I telling a stranger all this?

'Perhaps you're depressed. When I'm depressed even the simplest tasks are beyond me. I can hardly be bothered to tie my shoelaces or brush my hair.'

My hand goes to my messy ponytail, pulled up in one of the elastic bands the postman wound round the morning's pile of letters for Tom.

'He was the kind who probably never knew what depression meant,' she continues.

'The artist?'

She nods.

'Fortunate man.' My tone is dry.

'Not so fortunate.'

'What do you mean?'

She looks as though she's said more than she meant to. Then her features relax into a smile for a second. 'Do you like Rosebank?'

'It's beautiful,' I say, without reservation.

She nods. 'We should be doing our shopping. Goodbye. I enjoyed our chat.'

I watch her make her way across the car park. She walks like a cat, holding herself very upright, like a much younger woman. In her youth she must have been stunning, with those dazzling blue eyes and slender legs.

She's probably going home and telling her husband how she met this poor young woman this morning. Me, a poor young thing. I still can't get used to this new role: Minna, who had an experience so dreadful it can only be discussed in hushed voices and with shaken heads.

Eleven

Nightmares drive Felix out of bed in the early hours. Lew doesn't feature in them, but Johnson moves through the darkness to murmur threats she can't hear. Then she's back in Harrogate and the roof's crumbling in, burying her in slates and plaster-dust. And her long-dead mother stands at the bedroom door holding a baby in her arms, which is all wrong – it was a tumour seeding in her womb, not the longed-for second child. Cancer killed Martha Valance before the shrubs she planted in Rosebank's garden reached maturity.

'Sorry, darling,' she whispered before they gave her the last dose of morphine. 'I'm letting you and Daddy down, aren't I?'

'Leave me in peace,' Felix mutters, before giving up and getting out of bed. It's July 2006, she tells herself. Not October 1943. Sometimes these dreams take a while to dissolve. She fumbles in the kitchen for mug and teabag and wishes she were back in Harrogate. If ever she were going to go back on the bottle it'd be at a time like this. God, the nights – and early mornings – she's drunk to forget them all: Lew, Johnson. David. Especially David. She huddles in the kitchen over the tea until the images recede, telling herself the hand moving back and forth behind the chintz curtain is just a rose that needs tying back. And the dripping tap is just a dripping tap, not a message beating itself out on the steel sink. Damn silly to be scared of the dark in your seventies. Coming back to the South has reduced her to this. And seeing that drawing again in that young woman's hand. She should have stayed in the cool of Yorkshire, in the company of rational North Country women, who'd tell her not to be so foolish.

Did nightmares still haunt David? Hard to imagine that someone so successful could be haunted by anything. He must have retired by now, of course, but he still holds various honorary positions on professional bodies and gives evidence in court cases involving child health. Felix has seen his name in the newspaper.

She could ring him, or write to him. He mightn't have seen the news about Lew. The local papers down here went to town on the story but elsewhere there was only that one short piece in *The Times*, easily missed. But what exactly would she say? 'Hello, David. Do you think we ought to tell the truth about Lew?' And he'd say, 'Felix, it's been on my conscience all these years. Let's pop straight down to the police station and make a statement'?

If they were going to own up, they'd have done it sixty-odd years ago, wouldn't they?

Get a grip, Felix, you daft old woman.

The girl with that mop of hair and the sad eyes, she'd be a distraction. When the clock shows her a respectable time Felix picks up the phone and asks directory inquiries for Rosebank's number. It's listed. She dials quickly, before she can change her mind.

'My name's Felicity Curtis, we met in the car park yesterday,' she says without a preamble when the girl answers. 'I wondered if you'd like to meet me in the village.'

A pause.

Felix continues, 'You sounded interested in local history. Perhaps I can tell you about the houses and who lived in them.'

'All right.' Hard to read the girl's tone. 'My name's Minna, by the way, Minna Byrne.'

'That's unusual.'

'I assume you mean the Minna part. Short for Wilhelmina, which I can't stand, even though it was my grandmother's name and I adored her.'

'Wilhelmina. Was your grandmother German?'

'American, but the family came from Holland originally.'

'I'm Felix, short for Felicity, which I can't stand either. And before you say anything, I'm aware Felix is a boy's name.'

'Sounds like we've both suffered for our names,' Minna says.

Felix likes the dryness in her voice. 'I could be at Fontwell about four.'

'Same bench we met at last time?'

'See you there.'

Holidaymakers wear T-shirts and shorts but Minna huddles in a cotton cardigan. 'Shall we walk round the village?' Felix asks.

Her nod is polite but Felix senses a note of curiosity, or hopes she does. Too awful to think the girl might be humouring her, merely feeling sorry for a lonely elderly woman. She leads her up Laundry Lane, towards the big house. Tourists cluster, cameras snapping.

'Tell me about these.' Minna points at a crumbling cottage. Felix senses she's making a supreme effort. What can have happened to close her up like this? 'Who lived here?'

'As it happens, my friend Sam. His mother got TB and died shortly after we moved out. My father always felt bad about that.'

Minna peeps at her. 'Why?'

'He was the village doctor.' Felix peers at the grey stones. 'He despaired of the dampness in these cottages.'

'So it wasn't all paradise lost.'

Felix snorts. 'Far from it. On dank February afternoons I'd have given my eye teeth to live somewhere with a cinema. Most of the time I loved it, though. I spent hours playing on the beach, except for when they closed it off for a year or so.'

'Why did they do that?' Minna gives a small, thin smile. 'Of course, in case the Germans landed.'

'Fortunately they decided Fontwell Cove wasn't a security risk and they let us move the barbed wire. Then the war seemed even further away.'

'No air raids nearby?'

'No. There were quite a few to the east, over Swanage and Poole. I remember seeing a German bomber come down.' She describes the Heinkel screaming overhead, its port engine on fire, how the wounded plane burned a scar across the sky. Minna seems interested.

Felix glances around. 'It's strange seeing the place so decrepit, but at least they haven't built over the whole valley with caravan parks or executive homes. Not yet, at least.'

'It's gorgeous.' Minna sounds forlorn.

'But?'

'I miss London.'

'Too quiet for you.' Felix gives her a sharp look. 'Did you come here for sea air?'

'I needed a break.' A shutter has fallen over her eyes. 'This is supposed to refresh me.'

'The coast's good for that. But even David got restless here sometimes and he loved the countryside and the coast.'

'David?'

'Sorry – my mind was wandering. David was my best friend. A real nature-lover.'

'Did he draw the cormorant?'

Felix kicks a piece of loose stone that's fallen from a wall. 'David couldn't draw to save his life. But he did love birds and animals, he used to look after anything that was wounded or sick. And if he couldn't heal it and it died, he cut it up to find out what had killed it.'

The girl seems to grow even paler. 'He sounds . . . interesting.'

'He was.' Felix shakes her head, remembering David as a boy. 'Even despite the birds' skeletons and sheeps' skulls he insisted on carrying round in his pockets.'

'Do you know we found a human skeleton on the beach? A soldier from the war, apparently.' Minna speaks very casually but her clenched hands give her away.

Felix clutches the railing outside Sam's cottage.

'Are you all right?' Minna frowns at her.

'I'm fine. It's warm, isn't it?' This girl and her husband touched Lew's bones, pulled him out of the sand. If she'd known this, she'd

64

never have made contact with Minna, never. Felix hears the blood roar in her ears. 'I think I might have overdone it.'

'Shall I walk you back to your car?'

'No, I'll be fine.' Breathe from the stomach, relax the shoulders. 'See those leaded windowpanes? They're Elizabethan. The oldest in this part of the world. All broken now, of course.'

Twelve

'Six foot tall negro.'

These American MPs, military police, were nothing like Lew. Even without taking the colour of their skin into account. And the guns in their holsters. One tall and gangly, one stout, they reminded Felix of Laurel and Hardy.

Mrs Derby fixed Laurel with her cold grey eyes. 'There's no one of that type in this village.'

'We had a confirmed sighting five miles up the valley a few days back, ma'am.'

Her lips tightened as though the village had been accused of harbouring escaped lunatics.

'It's quite wooded round the village,' Hardy observed. 'Might be worth a look.'

'Mr Johnson's very particular about the woods.' Mrs Derby folded her arms. 'He's up there most nights with his gun. And he won't thank you for disturbing his birds.'

'Mr Johnson, eh? And who's he?'

'The gamekeeper.'

Laurel frowned. 'Pardon me?'

'He looks after the pheasants and partridges the Squire shoots,' Felix explained.

'And where might we find this Mr Johnson?' He took a notebook from his pocket. Felix's heart thumped, the last thing they wanted was Johnson on the lookout for a runaway.

She crept towards the back door. She'd run ahead of the MPs to warn David. Perhaps they could find some distraction for Johnson, tell him they'd seen a stray dog in the woods, or something.

She sprinted down the drive and along Laundry Lane, rushing through the estate gates and reaching the back door of the Manor breathless and with a stitch stabbing her side. David sat in the scullery attending to one of the injured birds he kept there. 'The MPs are here.' She bent over to catch her breath.

He dabbed iodine onto the torn wing, replaced the blackbird in its cardboard box and put the box on the shelf next to a cage containing a hedgehog. 'Who?'

'Military police.' She took a breath. 'On their way over to talk to Johnson.'

He spun round. 'Bloody hell. Just a second.' He filled a jam-jar lid with water and shoved it into a cage housing a motionless rabbit. 'Let's go.'

Felix ran behind him over the grass and into the woods, hardly able to draw breath after the dash from her own home. The woods smelled of decaying leaves. No birds sang. They found Johnson in the clearing, attending to his magpie cages. A dead bird lay beside him and a crow flapped a broken wing on the grass. David drew in a breath as he saw it. 'Can I take that one home? When it's healed I'll release it in the fields so it doesn't come back here.'

Johnson's answer was to pick it up and wring its neck. He threw the body onto the ground beside its companion.

Felix swallowed. 'Why did you do that?' Usually she was too scared of him to dare to challenge him but today her indignation was stronger than fear.

He met her stare, his eyes mocking her. 'Why the hell shouldn't I? What do you kids want, anyway?'

'My uncle was looking for you.' David was still looking at the dead birds, his hands shaking.

'Where is he?'

'In the boathouse.'

'What?' Johnson scowled.

Felix couldn't think of a single reason why David's uncle would be at the boathouse, a place unvisited by anyone except Isabel in summer when she was in one of her dreamy moods and liked floating across the lake in the punt.

'Uncle wants to know if we should try and sell the fishing tackle before we leave.' David was doing some fast thinking, Felix noted with admiration. 'He wants you to have a look.'

Fishing wasn't really part of Johnson's territory – there were no longer any trout streams worthy of fishing in this valley, but it hadn't been so in previous generations and fifty years' worth of equipment had accumulated in the boathouse. Felix remembered overhearing conversations about rods and nets and where they should go when moving-out day came.

Johnson's stare switched from the cages to David. 'Well that's a bit inconvenient, young Master David, isn't it? I've my hands full out here.'

He'd guessed they were up to something. He wasn't going to leave the woods. The police would step through the trees any moment now and Johnson would track down Lew for them.

'It won't take long.' David was doing well at sounding authoritative and calm, every inch a squire's nephew. She prayed his voice wouldn't give one of its sudden warbles or croaks. 'The Squire said it was important.'

Johnson shut the cage and pulled on his cap. 'It better be.'

David led them on a circuitous route to the boathouse. Felix was opening her mouth to challenge him when she realized he was keeping them out of sight of the front door in case the MPs had already arrived.

'Why are we going this way?' Johnson snapped.

'I thought I saw fox prints here earlier. Now I'm not sure.'

Johnson glared at him. 'You wasting my time?'

'No.' David met his gaze, unblinking.

What on earth would they tell Johnson when they reached the empty boathouse and the man realized he'd been tricked?

David pushed open the door to reveal Isabel standing beside the punt. She blinked as the sun flooded in, as though she were a creature of shadows, uneasy in light. Behind her cobwebs shone.

'Johnson?' Her expression combined surprise and irritation. And something else Felix couldn't describe.

'Miss Parham.' There was a breathlessness in Johnson's tone.

'How did you know I was here?' Her lips curled into a faint smile. 'Have you been following me?'

'No, miss. I was expecting to see your uncle.' He spoke as though he had something stuck in his throat.

'He's taking the lawnmower to bits. Won't I do?' She tossed her hair off her shoulders. Johnson made a little sound like a gasp.

David was mouthing something at Felix. He nodded at the door and they slipped out.

'That was a piece of luck,' he said, when they were out of earshot.

'What do you mean?'

'He'll think we did it on purpose so he could see her. He'll be nice to us now. We've killed two birds with one stone.'

Felix couldn't help thinking of the dead crows, and shivered in the sun. 'Why does he like her?'

'She's supposed to be very beautiful. Uncle says she'll make a society marriage if the war doesn't turn everything upside down.'

'So why on earth does she encourage Johnson?'

'She likes pulling his strings, I suppose. He'd hardly even look at her when she first left boarding school, just doffed his cap and nodded. Then she started smiling at him and asking him to do things for her.'

'What kind of things?'

'Carry in logs so she could get a fire going in the drawing room. Or mend the tennis net so she could practise her serve. And she asked him questions about the pheasants.'

She stopped. 'Isabel asked about the pheasants?'

'She had him explaining about the pens he makes for the chicks.'

Felix shook her head in disbelief. 'I don't understand her.'

'None of us do. She's not like anyone else. The Squire says Isabel's . . .'

'Says what?'

'She needs gentle handling.' He glanced at her. 'I'm not really supposed to talk about her outside the family.'

'Not even to me?'

'C'mon, we need to go and warn Lew to keep well hidden. At least the police will be kept busy hunting for Johnson in the woods.'

'Does Isabel like Johnson?' She didn't want to drop the subject.

'Hard to tell. Sometimes I think she hates everyone.'

'She despises me.' Felix remembered something. 'She told me she'd heard us outside last night. I thought it was strange – her window was closed. But perhaps she was outdoors too?'

They reached the gates. Sam stood in the lane. David stopped. 'Hello.'

Sam grinned at them. 'Going to the beach?' Felix noticed a wistful note in his voice.

'Yes.'

He looked at her longingly.

'Can't you play with Philip?' Philip was Sam's older brother.

'He's helping Dad.'

If they kept Sam up the nearside of the beach away from the cave he need never know about Lew.

David gave a slight frown but shrugged at her imploring glance. 'Why not?' He seemed to have sunk into listlessness. Felix squinted at him as they followed Sam up the cliff path. He gave her a half-smile. 'Can't help thinking how little time we've got left.'

Of course. 'A month.' Every day she noted something happening for the last time, or for the last time she'd see it. And there were absences, too. Nobody had drilled the big field skirting the road out of the valley. Her father hadn't planted new spring bulbs in the garden. At least summer had passed without this pall falling over it. They hadn't known about the evacuation. They hadn't had to remind themselves that this was the very last time the horses would pull in the wagons laden with corn and hay, or the last time they'd ride on top, gazing up at the cotton-wool clouds, smelling the leather and sweat of the horses. The last time, the last time. It was getting harder and harder to push knowledge of the departure to the recesses of her mind. Mrs Derby was packing trunks, talking of the new job she'd take when she left Fontwell. Felix's father was looking for a new practice in the North of England. Name tapes had been ordered for her uniform. She was silent as the three of them descended to the cove.

'Keep Sam occupied.' David nodded towards the cave. 'I'll go and check on things.' His worries apparently cast aside, he ambled across the sand, hands in pockets, whistling to himself. Felix would never have dreamed he could be such a good actor. She was learning things about her best friend.

'Skim this.' Sam handed her a flat pebble. She threw it, flicking her wrist, so it jumped once, twice, three times, four times over the water before it sank. Sam's face fell. 'You can never do five.'

'No.' David could. All last summer Felix had practised the throw, but her pebbles only ever bounced four times.

They paddled, water shocking their legs until it numbed nerve-endings. Sam gasped. She wished again she had brothers and sisters of her own. Sam and David were wonderful but they weren't family.

'Remember you and David promised to teach me how to swim.' He reminded them of this every time they saw him.

'It's too cold now, look how blue your legs are.'

Sam considered this. 'Next summer?'

'We won't be here next summer.' Felix waded to the shore and rubbed her feet one at a time on her jumper before pulling on her shoes and socks.

'My dad says the war will end by then and we'll come home. He says the Americans and Russians will squash the Germans between them.'

'I hope he's right.' She drew a face in the fine shingle with the tip of her shoe and gave it a down-turned mouth.

'My mum says she doesn't want to come back. She wants to live in a town.'

'Because of her chest, probably.'

Sam nodded. 'She coughs a lot.' He frowned. 'But you promise you'll teach me to swim? I'm seven and I still can't.'

'Lots of people can't swim at seven.'

'But they should, if you can't swim and you fall in, you drown.'

He pointed out to sea. 'My dad says loads of ships sank out there hundreds of years ago. He says ghosts climb onto the rocks.'

David waved at them. 'Why don't you run home for your lunch now, Sam?'

'Don't you believe me about the ghosts?'

'No. I mean yes.'

'So why you sending me home?'

'We'll probably come out again this afternoon,' Felix said, to cheer him up.

He sighed and stomped over the beach towards the cliff path. She watched him climb and wondered what would become of him when the family left the village. Her father thought Mr Fuller would probably take a job in a munitions factory. 'He'll earn twice as much and they'll be able to rent a decent house that isn't damp half the year. With electricity,' he'd said, casting a frown at the oil lamp on his desk. 'Yes, but . . .' She'd thought of the bank opposite the Fullers' cottage, white with snowdrops each February.

And who would teach Sam to swim in the town?

She walked towards the cave. Autumn was losing its early golden warmth and taking on a crispness that made her move more quickly. She wondered whether Lew'd been able to keep the fire burning in his cave overnight. She closed her eyes and listened to the wish-wash of the sea and her feet on the shingle, imagining herself a tropical explorer wading across a lagoon, palm trees waving, parrots flying overhead. Then she remembered they had adventure enough here. She opened her eyes.

He sat on a rock on the far side of the cave entrance, hidden from the cliff path, back straight, shoulders relaxed, head dropping back in laughter at something David was telling him. She couldn't believe they were responsible for looking after him.

'Hey, missy, how you doing?' He winked at her. He was the protected, they the protectors, and yet he was so easy, so unbothered.

'The police are looking for you.' Her voice sounded prim, like Mrs Derby's when she was talking to the doctor's less reputable patients.

'So David said. But I'm safe down here, aren't I?' His expression grew watchful.

'I hope so.' She was starting to realize the seriousness of what they'd done when they'd hidden Lew.

David gave her a tight little smile. 'It would still be better to ring the camp, tell them what happened.'

'You're right. I just can't tear myself away from here. It's paradise, just paradise.' Lew looked out to sea. 'I never even seen the sea before I joined up and they shipped us over. When I leave the army I'm going to buy a fishing boat and earn my living on the ocean.'

'It looks calm enough now. But most Octobers there are bad storms.'

'Hard to believe, missy.' His mouth fell into a relaxed smile.

David squinted at the horizon. 'See that bank of clouds right out to sea?'

Lew screwed up his eyes.

'The weather's changing.'

'Don't look like nothing.'

'Uncle's barometer dropped this morning. Perhaps it would be better for you if we contacted the camp.'

Lew stretched his injured foot. 'Sure. Last thing I want is for folk to get into trouble. If I make my own way back perhaps they'll believe my story.'

'You really wouldn't consider handing yourself over to the military police?'

His eyes widened. 'You don't know what they do to us.'

'What do you mean?'

'You wouldn't believe how harsh they treat us. And the snow-drops, the white MPs, they're the worst.' He shook his head. 'I thought we were all supposed to be fighting Hitler together. But so far as they're concerned, it's business as usual. Worse than usual.'

'I promise we won't tell them,' Felix said.

'Should I go now?' Lew looked at David. 'I could, if you wanted.'

'You can't walk on that ankle, it's not properly healed,' Felix said. 'We'll take care of you, don't worry. Nobody will find you down here.

73

And when you're ready to leave, David will talk to them, make them see it wasn't your fault.' She felt an urge to touch wood, but there wasn't any nearby.

David was frowning. 'What about Phoebe, won't she be worrying about you?'

Lew sighed. 'Phoebe's no worrier, perhaps she should be, though.'

'Why's that?'

He shrugged. 'She'll have her hands full soon enough.' His eyes lost their glint. He caught Felix looking at him and mustered a grin. 'Just wish I could have got the darn money to her.' His gaze slipped past her.

'Is she very pretty?' Felix asked.

He nodded. 'Hair like silk. Lips like cherries. Never seen anyone like her. And kind, too. Everyone loves Phoebe.'

'How did you meet her?'

'I was in a pub, listening to the swing band. Phoebe was there, too. She asked me to dance.' Reminiscence softened his features. 'Then she found out I could sing. Next thing I know, she's talking to the band leader and he's callin' me up to the stage. After that, I saw Phoebe every night till they moved us west.'

'Did you have much to do with white girls back home?' David asked.

Lew let out a guffaw. 'Separate shops, separate restaurants, separate everything. If I even looked at a white girl there was trouble. It's so different in England. First time I went on a bus here I gave up my seat when a white boy came on. The conductress told me to stay where I was. I'd be lyin' if I said everyone loved us, but it's easier than home. We're chocolate soldiers here, not niggers.'

David was watching something. Lew turned his head to see what it was. A cormorant, poised to dive, eyes bright.

'Anyone have a piece of paper and pencil?' Lew'd cast off his worries so quickly Felix could hardly keep up.

David turned out his inside pocket, revealing a bird's skull, a pencil stub and a notepad. 'I keep it with me for noting down unusual birds or plants.'

'You don't mind me taking a sheet?'

'Of course not. Have it.' David passed him the pad and pencil stub.

'Thank you.' Lew's hand flew over the paper. He seemed to be making a series of sharp dashes with the pencil. The cormorant dived into the sea. 'Darn. But I think I got most of him.'

'Let's see?' He passed Felix the pad and there was the bird standing on the rock, eyes on a fish, waiting for the moment to dive.

'This is terrific.' The bird was alive. She could blink and imagine it had moved.

'Keep it.' He waved it away. 'A thank you for all you're doing.'

'Really?'

'Sure.'

She tore the sheet out and folded it very carefully so it would fit in her skirt pocket. 'Who taught you to draw?'

'My father liked to sketch in the evenings, if he had pencil and paper. He taught me. My uncle, that's the pastor, was always shaking his head and telling him he'd be better teaching me my bible. Where I come from folks aren't known for their accomplishments. 'Cept quilts, all the women sew quilts. And singing.'

'What kind of singing?' Felix asked.

'Gospel. Jazz, too. Ever hear of Paul Robeson?'

David and Felix looked blank.

'He's a coloured man who came to London to sing and act. No place's barred to him.' Lew's voice swelled with pride. 'Wouldn't happen back home. He's my hero. My father's got a fine voice, bit like his.'

'What does your father do?' David asked.

'Works in the fields, like all the men. But he can read and write and he taught me. He wants somethin' better for us kids. But the war come.' Lew pursed his lips. 'Seems like nobody gets to do what they want no more. Still, least Uncle Sam pays regular money. And driving the trucks ain't too bad. But really I want to fight those Nazis.'

His long limbs stretched gracefully over the rocks. What a waste, letting a natural warrior lug food and ammunition around, Felix thought. Lew looked twice the size of most English soldiers.

'Will you marry Phoebe when it's over?' David asked.

Something flashed over his face which might have been surprise. 'I'd marry her tomorrow if she'd have me.'

'You're tramping miles to give her the money,' David pointed out. 'Surely she'd marry you?'

Lew smiled. 'Liking a coloured man's one thing, marrying him's another. Even here.'

'I'd marry you.' Felix's words took her by surprise. 'If you ever asked me, I mean. Not that you would.'

He smiled at her. 'Reckon that's the biggest compliment I've ever had, missy.'

'We should go now.' David sounded reluctant. 'I want to see where those police have got to.'

Lew gave a relaxed wave. 'See you later.'

Thirteen

Minna

I curl up very still in the armchair. Please don't let Tom notice I'm back and feel obliged to talk to me. Please don't let me see that expression on his face, so guarded, worried. If only I could do something, anything, to make him relax in my presence. It's as though we are locked in these roles: me, the protected and resentful; he the protector and worrier. Life, or nature, or whatever you want to call it, didn't intend us for these parts.

I try to summon the energy to get up and cook him his supper – bass I bought in Swanham, which the fishmonger assured me was locally caught yesterday. I also found Jersey potatoes, and spinach which I planned to serve creamed but is really too fresh and tender to muck around with. Perhaps the spinach will tempt my appetite.

Tom will eat this meal, shower me with compliments, his tense smile revealing how difficult he finds my company. I'll nibble on the smallest possible portion. These days I find eating almost impossible. My clothes are starting to hang off me. Once I'd have been pleased about this; now I feel indifferent. I remember the meals I ate in the past: long leisurely lunches in France, lingering over plates of cheese; Chinese takeaways consumed in front of the television with greed after a long day decorating. A different life.

Weeks have passed since I bothered with make-up, except the merest touch of mascara. Sometimes I have to remind myself my hair needs washing. Lucky it's long enough to tie back and ignore for days at a time. I used to have it trimmed every four or five weeks to contain its wildness. Benjy's hair was fairer than mine but promised to be just as unruly. His eyes were the same blue as his father's.

The early evening light has shifted to the west now, shining through the French windows. They chose well when they decorated

Rosebank, though I'd have picked a slightly deeper yellow for this room, the same camomile they used in the hall, perhaps. But I like the drawing room's caramel walls, with red curtains and sofa complementing the rich colour. Only months ago, I'd have already mentally redecorated the entire house, even though it doesn't need it. The changing colours of the sea would have gripped me. I'd have sat on the shingle with a sketch pad, trying to capture how the slate grey reflects the overcast sky, or mirrors the sparkling azure when the sun breaks through, how inky pools appear on the surface when the weather's about to change. Hours would have passed while I struggled with the paints, happy hours. Now I can admire the colours of the sea, but I no longer feel them like an emotion. Blue is just blue.

It occurs to me that I mourn not only my son but my former self, the woman who spent happy solitary days in other people's houses singing along to the radio and painting walls. I was never one of those designers who won't pick up a paintbrush. I used to revel in the opening of a new tin of paint, feel my heartbeat quicken as I brushed the first dashes of colour onto a virgin wall. I'd stay inside all day painting before tidying myself up and catching the tube to Tom's office, where I'd sit in reception flirting with the couriers while I waited for him.

'Well, she's dead and gone,' I say aloud.

Talking to myself. Great.

I'm rinsing Jerseys for supper when Tom comes into the kitchen for a beer. He gives a small start when he sees me at the sink. 'When did you get back?'

'Half an hour ago. I thought you were busy so I didn't disturb you.'

'I wouldn't have minded.' His look is solemn. 'Minna—'

'Supper's about half an hour away, why don't you have a bath? I'll bring you up a glass of wine. Or why don't you go for a stroll? It's lovely on the headland this time of night.' If I keep on talking he won't be able to say what he wants to say, the words I can't bear to hear.

He drinks almost all the beer in a single swallow. 'All right, I'll go for a short walk.' He pauses at the kitchen door. 'Why don't you come too?'

'Oh, I couldn't possibly. There's this.' My hand sweeps across the ingredients on the worktop.

'I don't mind waiting for supper. I could help you when we get back.'

My hesitation lasts too long. His shoulders slump. 'OK. I won't be long.'

His little smile could have broken my heart once. But I don't brood about him for long. As I chop and fry and boil, my mind runs along familiar tracks. *Stop it.* I force myself to think about the cormorant and the old woman in the village. Why's she come back? To enjoy a nostalgic return to her childhood home? No. Something else has drawn her here, something she almost seems to fear.

I fry the bass in butter and sprinkle it with lemon zest and chopped dill. Flipped onto the plate it looks good, almost restaurant-quality. I watch Tom walk back through the garden, pausing to examine the lupins and delphiniums.

'That looks fantastic,' he says when he sees the food. A pause. 'Are you eating with me?' He's using the casual tone he employs when he doesn't want to sound worried.

'I had a sandwich with my tea.' He knows perfectly well I'm lying. I feel his gaze on my face and lift my head to force a smile, but he's already looking away. We carry the plates through to the dining room.

'This is outstanding.' Tom rolls his eyes in exaggerated approval. 'Sure you don't want to try a bit?'

'I'm going to have some pudding.' And I do: three or four of the early raspberries I found in the market. I hadn't planned to eat them and for a moment I feel quite panicky. At least I didn't have cream on them.

'I bought the local rag when I was in town this afternoon,' he says at last. 'Thought you might want to see if there's any more about our friend on the beach. It's on the hall table.'

'Thanks. By the way, I went down to the village this afternoon, with that old lady I told you about. We're buddies now.'

His eyes widen. 'You're getting caught up in the history of this place, aren't you?'

'Not really.' I stand up to get the paper. 'It's a distraction, I suppose. And she seems lonely, poor thing. I think all the people she knew round here as a child have gone or died.'

I fetch the *Herald*. An article in an inside page mentions that the drowned GI was black and describes the excitement caused by the arrival of coloured troops in 1944. Apparently locals often protested against the segregation imposed by white American officers. An old lady recalls the pressure on a Swanham publican to ban black GIs. He responded by banning white American soldiers. A cinema decided to hold black-only showings, but received a barrage of complaints from local girls who didn't want to lose their dark-skinned dates when they went to the pictures. I wish I'd talked to my grandmother about what she remembered of the war and attitudes to soldiers in America. But she was just a New York schoolgirl in the forties and probably had nothing to do with Jim Crows, as Tom calls the coloured GIs.

I blink and see I've drawn a lozenge around the word 'body' in the headline. It looks like a coffin.

'Glad to see you're reasserting your artistic talents,' Tom says. I pray he doesn't look too closely at my doodle.

'A way to go yet.'

He picks up his mobile. 'I'm going to make a few calls. I may need to go up to London this week.'

'Everything all right?'

'Just some stuff that needs a face-to-face.' He gives me his most reassuring smile, the smile that brings in the clients.

'Mind if I go back onto your laptop? I need the Internet.'

'Feel free.' He looks curious.

'I want to find out more about the American bases round here.'

'Oh.' His best neutral expression. 'Thought you weren't that interested?'

'I'd quite like to know what happened to the GI.' I try to sound nonchalant.

'Never thought you'd be one for local history.'

'It feels safe.'

'Safe?'

'It doesn't remind me of anything else.'

As I try to remember our password I realize this is the first time I've been online for a month. Tom's been nagging me for weeks to read the messages friends have sent. I wade through his business messages – dozens from Waymark, his biggest client – to find my emails. And I'm touched, almost overwhelmed, by the few I can bring myself to read.

'Don't go all frumpy and country-girlish as a result of this sojourn,' Mikey writes. 'Make sure you wear high heels at least three times a week. And make that brother of mine do some walking, he needs to chill. Gareth sends a hug.'

I feel homesick for Mikey and Gareth, Mikey's boyfriend. I've loved them from the moment I met them. I'm an only child and relished acquiring proxy brothers. Especially ones who liked thirties films and visiting art galleries in obscure parts of London.

Kris has also sent a message. 'Desperate to hear from you, Min.'

For a few seconds I relax into teenage memories of me and Kris and the things we used to do together, the bottles of cider smuggled into our bedrooms, the shopping trips, the endless telephone conversations.

'My job at the IWM finishes soon,' Kris goes on. 'I'm moving north – a new job in Leeds setting up a new archive. Can't stand the thought of living in the city, so I'll have to find somewhere outside. Haven't sold my flat yet so I'll have to rent for a while.'

Of course, Kris works at the one place almost guaranteed to provide answers about Private Campbell's background: the Imperial War Museum. I compose a quick reply, telling her I think the sea air is doing me good and about the discovery of the body. I ask if she can tell me anything about American military bases in the area, or recommend books about black GIs in Britain.

I click Send and decide I've had enough for one sitting. But then I spot Sara Frobisher's name and click on her message. After the accident Sara sat at my hospital bedside when Tom had to go home to rest. Later on, when I was home again, she brought over beef casseroles and apple crumbles to tempt me, and helped Tom around the house. She and Kris couldn't have given me more support – not that I acknowledged, or even noticed, it.

'Tom, here's the house. Love S.' And a URL.

I open the link and find myself looking at the details of a Victorian semi in Wandsworth – in need of renovation and redecoration, but with great potential, according to the estate agent. I feel a frown stretch over my brow. How out of touch I am. Are the Frobishers moving again? Surely they only bought their house in Clerkenwell a year ago? I make a mental note to ask Tom.

I do a web-search for American military bases in the south of England during the last war. Dozens of links come up. I pull a pad and pen out of the drawer to make notes, but feel almost overwhelmed. It's so long since I've used my brain. I decide to wait to hear from Kris. I am just closing down the laptop when the email inbox comes back into view, with a new message showing. From somewhere called *Computersonline*. An invoice for a laptop. A very expensive laptop. It could be for Tom's London office but I know he's only just updated their computers. And he bought his own laptop a month ago. Then I see the delivery details: 'Sara Frobisher, 142 Rainshall Road, Clerkenwell'.

My head feels too woolly to work out what this means. Switching off, I go upstairs to check my comforter is still hidden under the duvet.

I wake early and know I won't be able to get back to sleep. Beside me, Tom lies almost motionless. I creep downstairs and switch on the laptop. 'Black GIs UK WW2', I type in the search bar. A list of sites appears. The first includes photographs of black soldiers. But none of them are big or clear enough for me to get a feel for what kind of uniform Lew would have worn. I click on site after site, reading accounts of girls won, locals charmed, preparations for the D-Day landings, until my eyes ache.

'You're going to become the world expert on GIs.' Tom's standing behind me with two mugs of tea.

'Sorry.' I close the site.

'Carry on.'

'No.' I turn off the laptop, feeling like a teenager caught logging on to porn sites. 'Let's get breakfast going.'

He follows me into the kitchen and watches as I pull bacon and eggs out of the fridge. 'You don't need to do all this for me, you know.'

'I don't mind.'

'I'm going to have to take up running.' He pats his still-flat stomach. Tom never regained the weight he lost after the accident. 'Perhaps we should go for a long walk together this afternoon.'

'Good idea.' I chew on my toast, wishing he wasn't watching me so carefully and I could drop it into the kitchen bin. I wonder when I can see Felix again. I'd like her to see some of these websites, if Tom can spare the laptop.

By the time we finish breakfast it's midmorning and Kris has emailed me a reply.

> Still can't find any evidence that American troops trained on your part of the coast until 1944. I'll try and check a few more documents and talk to some contacts in the States. In the meantime, here's a list of books for you. Luv K

Same old Kris, hating to leave any leaf unturned. I go back into the kitchen.

'We need more milk.' Tom folds up the dishcloth and hangs it neatly over the taps. 'I'd go in myself but I need to get to the bottom of these.' He nods at the piles of bank statements and receipts on the table. 'And a client needs a report by lunchtime.'

'Waymark?'

He groans. 'Yes. Jeremy never seems to sleep.'

Jeremy Wilson, Waymark's MD. Young, ambitious, energetic. Driven. I've only met him once but I remember the man with the Blackberry in the churchyard. 'I thought I saw him in the village.'

'He pops down occasionally, knows the area well. Recommended this house, actually.'

'Did he?' Of course, I can't remember any of the details of how we booked Rosebank. 'What's his connection with this part of the world?' I ask, trying to show an interest.

'A possible project, just an idea, really . . .'

He doesn't seem inclined to talk about it and my head's still too full of GIs to pursue it.

'I'll sort out the finances, you get on with your report. Then I'll go and get the shopping.'

'Would you?' Relief floods his face. 'I don't want to keep you away from your research. Why don't you ask Felix up here?'

I shake my head. 'I'm not that bothered.'

He gives me a sharp look. I feel as though I'm being accused of something.

I sit at the kitchen table with the bank statements, chequebooks and receipts, ticking off items and growing gloomier by the minute as I see how bad our position is. How has all this passed me by? Our money has almost run out.

I stand up and the chair squeaks on the tiles. I need to be outdoors. 'Just getting some fresh air,' I tell Tom as I pass the study.

'How far have you got?'

'Nearly done.'

'When we know the damage I'll ring the bank and negotiate a proper loan facility. We're being stung for overdraft interest.'

I could easily go back into the kitchen and finish the job. And call the bank. Or hunt down cheap online loans. But I don't. Pulling my cardigan off the peg, I make for the beach via the cliff-top path that starts above Fontwell village.

I sit on the shingle where we found the skeleton, puffing from the brisk fifteen-minute walk, staring at the spot as if a message might be written there. The wind pulls my hair out of its carelessly tied ribbon. I lean back, propping myself up on my elbows, and fall into a reverie.

'Minna.'

I jump. Tom's standing behind me, red-cheeked and out of breath. He must have run after me.

'Sorry. I was daydreaming.'

'So I see.' He kneels beside me.

'I just wanted a bit of sea air.'

'But you chose to come all the way to this particular spot?' He glances at the disturbance where they dug up the remains. I shrug. 'You were going to get milk, remember?' He doesn't mention the abandoned finances.

'I'll go in now. And I'll ring the bank as soon as I'm back,' I promise.

In Sainsbury's I recognize a ramrod-straight back and shock of greying hair. 'Hello.' Felix stops loading plums into a plastic bag. 'Do you have time to talk?'

'What else can I tell you?'

'I'm still fascinated by the whole set-up, the abandoned village, the drawing. Could I ask you some more questions? Is there somewhere we can go?' I listen to myself gabbling.

She places her plums in the trolley and turns to the melons, hands pressing the tops of honeydews until she finds one she likes. 'There's not much in Swanham. Sometimes I think it's even more boring than when I was a girl. But there's a halfway decent pub across the road, the Cygnet. Give me ten minutes to finish here.' I detect wariness in her tone. Have I offended her again?

I take my basket to the checkout. There's a baby sitting in the trolley in front of me. I try not to make eye contact with her or her mother. I can't be too careful. The mother looks friendly. She probably wonders why I won't smile at her little girl, who's placing a socked foot into her mouth.

Behind me two girls of about fourteen giggle. Can they tell what's going on in my mind? Do they know what kind of woman I am? The basket shakes in my hand and a lemon drops onto the ground. One of the girls stoops and picks it up for me. 'Here you are.'

I take it, speechless, and uncertainty puckers her smooth creamy brow. 'Thank you,' I mutter, belatedly. They've already forgotten about me and giggle over a photograph in the magazine one of them's buying.

When the checkout assistant tries to use my debit card it refuses to cooperate. 'I'll call the bank if you want, see what the problem is?' she offers.

'Don't worry.' I rifle in my purse. Lucky I went to the cashpoint at the weekend.

We sit in the wood-beamed saloon of the Cygnet, facing each other over tomato juice (Felix) and Sauvignon Blanc (me). 'Are you sure I can't get you something to go with that?' I ask.

She raises an eyebrow. 'I'm a bit of a bore to take to pubs. But I'm partial to cheese and onion crisps, if it makes you feel better.'

'Why don't I get you a sandwich?' I stand up.

'You're very generous. Ham and pickle. Thank you.'

'You're not having anything yourself?' she asks when I return with it.

'I don't really eat lunch.'

She looks thoughtful but says nothing, biting into her sandwich. 'What did you want to ask me?' she says after a while.

'Do you know anything about the GI we found on the beach? Nobody seems to know what he was doing down there.'

She folds her paper napkin into a rectangle and sticks it neatly under the ashtray. I can tell she's thinking hard all the time, making up her mind whether or not she trusts me.

Finally she lifts her head. 'I need a coffee. Can I get one for you?'

'Please.'

She goes to the bar and returns with the cups.

'David and I used to get up in the night to look at wildlife. He was very keen.' She describes a midnight trip to see fox cubs. She talks about the woods, the same woods I walk through when I visit the village. And as she talks, Fontwell comes to life. Her eyes flash as she describes how she and her friend David hated the gamekeeper, Johnson. 'He moved so quietly, you never knew when he'd come up behind you. I think he liked scaring us.' She shakes her head. 'Then David came across the GI.'

'Our GI?'

'Yes.' A pause.

I feel the significance of this confession, as though my relationship with Felix has become more intense.

'It was as though something completely magical had happened, a black soldier, in our woods. Lew Campbell, his name was. I loved him almost on sight.' She smiles. 'I've heard terrible stories about how the West Indians were treated when they came over in the fifties and sixties, but back in the war a lot of us were smitten with the black Americans. They had such warmth, such a sense of fun.'

'Not all the Brits were smitten, I imagine.'

She half closes her eyes. 'Not all.' She stirs her coffee, adding milk from the jug. I watch as the dark liquid grows paler and paler.

'Did Lew say how he was treated over here?'

'He said the English were friendly. On the whole. There was an incident with a vicar's wife near the camp.' She tells me about a round-robin letter to local women, warning them to keep their distance from the black GIs.

'And you wanted to look out for him?'

'We worried about him. He seemed . . . vulnerable.' She puts down the teaspoon. 'Funny, really, given how big and strong he was.'

She tells me how they smuggled him down to the cave while the gamekeeper was distracted. 'Lew loved the beach. He drew your cormorant down there.'

I sit up. 'Lew was the artist?' I can hardly believe it. My blood tingles in my veins. Perhaps this is the reason I'm so drawn to the sketch; this long-dead soldier is reaching out to me through the quick dashes he made on a scrap of paper.

She smiles. 'He'd have laughed to hear himself described as an artist. He was very modest.'

'And you hid him away from the grown-ups, from the authorities?'

'We were terribly worried they'd find out what we'd done, and then we'd get into big trouble.' She sits back in her chair, frowning as she tries to remember. 'He was scared, too, told us how badly the military treated blacks. And then food became a problem.' She rolls her eyes. 'We had no idea Americans ate so much.'

Fourteen

Felix 1943

David and Felix spent the rest of the morning scavenging food for Lew. The pickings at Rosebank were meagre, but Felix managed to persuade Mrs Derby to give her two slices of bread and butter for elevenses instead of the usual one.

The housekeeper frowned. 'You must be going through a growth spurt. I'd better tell your father, he might want to give you extra cod liver oil.'

Felix cursed Lew under her breath and grabbed an apple from the fruit bowl.

'What a day,' Mrs Derby continued. 'I've been running backwards and forwards to answer that door.'

'Why are they all coming to the house?'

'The telephone's not working, lines down or something. Must have been the wind last night.'

'All the telephones?'

'Every one. Even that ivory receiver they say Miss Isabel has in her bedroom.' Mrs Derby's lips curled. 'So she won't be ringing her fine friends in London.'

'Is that what she does?'

Mrs Derby smoothed the front of her apron. 'So I've heard. She even went up to town to visit them last week. At a time like this, can you imagine?'

David and Felix met at the Manor gates. He carried a paper bag, which he opened to reveal slices of ham and two almost-fresh scones. He patted his pocket. 'I filched a bottle of ginger beer from the Manor pantry.'

'This must be enough for his lunch and some of his supper,' Felix said.

'Hope so. Isabel was giving me funny looks as I came out. Think she saw the bag under my jumper.'

She remembered what Mrs Derby had said. 'Is it true she went up to London last week?'

'Who told you that?' His voice was angry.

'I can't divulge my source.' She liked the phrase, it reminded her of spy films.

'Village gossip.' He pursed his lips. 'Why can't people mind their own damn business?'

'Sorry.' Her cheeks burned.

'You might as well know. Just keep your mouth shut. Isabel tried to see her mother.'

'*Tried* to see her?'

'She wasn't at home. So the maid said. Only, Isabel saw her at the window.'

'Her mother wouldn't see her own daughter?'

'So it seems.'

Poor Isabel.

'Are you having a picnic?' Sam had appeared from nowhere. He must have been lurking behind the telephone box. Felix hoped he hadn't overheard their conversation about Isabel.

'Not today.' Felix tried to soften the rejection with a smile.

'You hear the wires are down?' Sam nodded at the box. 'Wind blew them down, didn't he?'

The church clock struck noon. 'Your mother'll be expecting you home for lunch.'

Sam wrinkled up his nose. 'A bit of grey fish that smells like whale, call that lunch?'

'We need to hurry.' David pulled her elbow.

'See you later Sam,' Felix said.

'You're always going off without me.' His words followed them.

'I'll come and find you later, promise,' she called back over her shoulder.

They shot up the track at a speed that made her forehead run with sweat. As they came down the other side to the beach she eyed the sea and noticed how it swelled, throwing white spray over the rocks. The breeze that hit her cheek was moisture-laden and cold.

Lew rose like a giant from the rocks and greeted them with a grin. 'Sure am glad to see you two.'

'Sorry – took us some time to find this.' David handed over the two brown paper bags.

'Hey, nice lunch, much obliged.'

David's cheeks pinkened. 'You may want to keep some of it for supper.'

Lew's eyes seemed to lose their brightness.

'We'll try and find you a bit more,' Felix said.

Lew smiled and started to eat. Again. She wondered at the speed with which the food vanished. He finished all but one of the scones and wrapped it up in the bag as though worried he wouldn't be able to resist it while it was in sight.

'Say, you know we spoke about calling the camp and telling them I'm stuck here?'

'Calling?' David looked puzzled.

'Telephoning.'

'The lines are down.'

Lew shrugged. 'That wind sure was something last night. Oh well.' His eyes travelled the length of the bay. 'My ankle feels better. I'll be able to walk on it by evening. I'll sneak past them policemen.'

'There are footpaths out of the valley they won't know about. Best to hang on till dark.'

'Sure.' He grinned again and turned to look at something out at sea. How quickly his attention seemed to shift from one subject to another. Felix envied him. How wonderful it would be to excise her own worries – St Agatha's, the evacuation – from her mind so easily.

'What are you looking at?' she asked.

'This sea's awork with fish. You ever catch any off these rocks?'

'I've only caught trout in the stream. And that was years ago, they're all gone now.' David narrowed his eyes. 'Have you fished much?'

'Sure, I was always going after catfish in the creek with a bit of bait on a line. Easy. Then Mamma'd fry 'em up for me.'

'I could bring some rods up from the boathouse.' The idea seemed to grab David.

'They'd be the wrong kind, wouldn't they?' Felix didn't know much about fishing but couldn't imagine using the Squire's rods in the sea.

David shrugged. 'Probably. Different reels and lines and bait. Still might be worth a try. We could fiddle around with them.'

Felix tried to picture herself adapting rods and hoped her doubts didn't show on her face.

'We could use peeler crabs for bait. Or worms. No harm in trying. Then we could make a fire and roast what we catch.'

'Like pirates.' Felix liked the idea. 'We'd need to be careful about smoke.'

'They'd just think it was us pretending to be explorers like we did last summer.'

How long ago that seemed. That had just been kids' stuff, make believe.

'There are old cooking pots and forks in the garden shed, waiting for someone to come and take them away to be melted down for the war effort.' David was thinking aloud. 'I'll rescue them.'

Felix's face must have shown her disapproval.

'I'll take them back when we've finished with them,' he added.

Lew rubbed his hands together. 'All we need is some cornbread and iced tea and we got us a feast.' He glanced at the clouds racing in from the west. ''Cept maybe not the iced tea.'

'Iced tea?' David looked puzzled. 'Do you put milk in it?'

Lew made a face. 'Milk in iced tea? You mad, boy?'

After lunch David dragged her into the boathouse to look at rods. 'I don't know anything about fishing,' she protested.

'This one looks in reasonable condition.' He extracted it from a canvas bag.

'Suppose it snaps in the sea?'

'Carry the net down to the beach, won't you?' He shoved it into her arms. 'Now I need some weights. This'll do.' He picked up a bit of old wire. 'I can twist it into a ring.'

'What are we hoping to catch, anyway?' She wrinkled her nose. 'This net stinks.'

'Bass. They love crab bait, apparently. Or we might try for mackerel. Or plaice.'

'What do you know about plaice? You've never been sea fishing before.'

David's gaze slipped away from hers. 'Sam told me.'

'Sam! Are you mad? What are you doing telling him about our plans?'

'I didn't tell him, I met him in the lane, just before you turned up, and asked, very casually, if he'd ever done anything like this and he told me his brother uses crabs. Apparently there should be loads under the rocks by the cave.' He still couldn't meet her eyes.

'I just hope Sam doesn't come down to see what we're up to. Or bring Philip down to advise you.'

'You're the one who let Sam come with us yesterday.'

'I made sure he didn't see Lew, though.' Felix remembered something. 'Blast! I never went back to find him like I promised.'

David grinned. 'Don't I know it. He was complaining bitterly about your shabby treatment.'

'If I see him now he'll go on and on about the fishing. He'll want to join in.'

'Avoid him them.'

'Then I'll feel mean.'

'Please yourself.' David handed her a rod. 'Look, if we get enough fish we won't have to run around looking for food for Lew this evening. That should make you happy.'

'I thought he was leaving tonight?'

'He'll need something before he goes.'

'True.'

David's back stiffened. Framed in the doorway stood the two MPs.

'Afternoon,' Hardy said.

'Good afternoon.'

'We thought we heard something in here. Fishing?' Laurel nodded at the net.

Felix longed to congratulate him on his perceptiveness.

'Used to be fond of it myself.'

'We thought we'd try, help with the rationing.'

'Good idea, sonny,' Hardy said. 'Where'll you go?'

'On the rocks.'

'With that rod?' Laurel sucked his breath through his teeth.

'We know it's not perfect for sea fishing.'

'You'll find it a struggle.' Hardy shook his head.

'I know.' David gave a grin that was like a grimace and nodded to Felix to follow him out of the boathouse.

'Might wander down to the beach later and see how you're getting on.' Hardy stood back to let them pass. 'We haven't been down there yet to look for our runaway.' The men seemed more relaxed than she remembered them, as though the sea had put them in a holiday mood. 'You kids haven't seen our lost soldier down there?'

'No.' They looked straight at the men. Above David's lip a film of perspiration glistened.

'Well don't let us keep you from the fish.'

'I wish they'd push off,' Felix muttered, once they were out of earshot.

'So do I.'

'We've got to get him away from here. All this,' she shook her head at the tackle, 'is just wasting time. Suppose they really do come down to watch you fishing?'

'Lew's got to eat.'

'It would be quicker just to steal more food.'

'I don't think so.' His jaw was set in a way she hadn't seen before. They trudged towards the cliff path.

'We've managed fine so far,' she said as they started to climb.

'This is safer.'

'It's not.'

He stopped, spun round, eyes flashing. 'If you're so unhappy about this why don't you just go home, Felicity?'

Felicity. She dropped the net on the muddy ground. 'All right, I will! Lug your own stuff down to the beach and find your own crabs.' She turned on her heel. 'We should have left him in the woods!' she called as she walked away.

'You don't mean that, Felix. Come back.' His words bounced off her back as she strode away. He didn't follow her.

She slowed as she reached the telephone box, realizing how tired she was. Since Lew had arrived they'd barely stood still for five minutes. She looked around for Sam but he was nowhere to be seen. Feeling a mixture of guilt and relief she headed for Rosebank, creeping through the back garden and in the kitchen door. Mrs Derby was moving tins around in the larder; she could hear her sighing over gaps in the shelves. 'Are we supposed to live on air?' the housekeeper said to herself.

Felix tiptoed across the linoleum, her father's low tones reaching her through his closed surgery door. She paused for a moment.

'A drier house . . . your chest . . .'

'Reckon you're right, doctor. If I could just get out of this blessed valley my lungs would settle.' Sam's mother and her persistent cough.

In her room Felix kicked off her shoes and flung herself on to the bed. Her eyelids felt heavy. She closed them for a second.

Cooking smells roused her and she jumped up. Dark. She pulled down the blackout and lit the oil lamp beside her bed. Half past six. How had she managed to sleep away the afternoon? The lamp gave off a reassuring hiss, its glow pulsing gently through the glass as though it were a living creature. She wished she could stay here, safe in its amber radiance.

She picked it up and went downstairs. 'I feel a bit under the weather,' she told Mrs Derby, who was opening the range door to stir a dish of rice pudding. 'I don't want anything to eat.' Her stomach gave a contradictory growl.

Mrs Derby closed the door and stood straight, putting her hand to the small of her back and drawing a breath. She examined Felix. 'Getting on for fourteen. Perhaps . . .?'

'Perhaps what?'

'Nothing.' She walked to the breadbin and pulled out the loaf. 'Take some bread and margarine back up to bed with you. I'll do you a hot-water bottle.'

'No thanks.' But she remembered Lew. Suppose they hadn't caught any fish with the flimsy rod? He only had a single scone for his supper. 'On second thoughts, bread and margarine would be nice.'

'Have an aspirin too.' Mrs Derby went to the drawer where she stored stray bits of string and brown paper and removed a small brown bottle.

'Thank you.' It seemed easier to swallow the pill than argue. Mrs Derby poured Felix a glass of water from the jug.

'Your father's having an early supper, there's a meeting at the vicar's.' She shook her head. 'Plenty to be done before we're evacuated. Just a shame that wretched telephone's not working.'

'You don't think they'll change their minds about us leaving the village?'

Mrs Derby sighed and took away the glass to rinse it. 'Doesn't seem likely.' She dried the glass and eyed Felix. 'Doctor's in a state about leaving your mother's grave.'

Felix knew he still visited once a day. 'I'll go up now.' She took plate and lamp and stomped upstairs. In her room she blew out the flame and stuffed the bread and margarine into her pocket, before tiptoeing back downstairs in her socked feet and creeping out of the front door. Mrs Derby would be absorbed in Tommy Handley, no need to climb down the wisteria tonight.

Sleep had revived Felix. She ran head-down against the wind, trying not to let her eyes linger on shadows. She tore down the lane to the cliff path, racing to the top before stopping for a few seconds to draw breath and peer down at the beach. The waves' white crests were visible in the moonlight. And she could see something else:

smoke rising from the rocks, curling round the hidden entrance to the cave. Her heart sank. She ran down, disregarding rabbit holes and roots that wanted to send her head-over-heels.

Her feet crashed over the shingle until she stood on the rocks looking down at them. 'I could see your smoke from the top of the cliff.'

'Make room for the lady.' Lew brandished a rusty fork with a small roasted silver fish on the end of it.

David looked up. 'So what? We've done it before, back in the summer when we had those sausages.' His tight face told her he hadn't forgotten their earlier exchange.

'But that was in the day. You know what the punishment is for showing a light in the blackout. And those police are still crawling around.'

David shrugged.

There seemed no point pushing for a fight. She climbed down to join them. 'So you had luck with the fish?' The rod lay in sections on the cave floor, two bamboo canes and a length of string beside it.

'Luck weren't no part of it.' Lew pulled the fish off the fork, drawing a breath as hot flesh touched his thumbs. 'This is for you, missy.' His brown eyes seemed to release the tension in her.

'Mackerel, lovely.' She realized how hungry she was.

David passed her the brown paper bag they'd used to transport Lew's lunch. 'We don't have any plates.' His expression was softer; perhaps he'd realized she didn't want to argue.

The fish tasted sweet. She pulled away the fine, milky-white bones and crammed slivers of meat into her mouth, letting her anxiety blow away with the smoke. 'How did you catch it?'

'The rod was too light, we couldn't even cast it on the waves at first. Lew was worried it would snap. He sent me to the garden shed to get those bamboo sticks, so we could make a splint to strengthen it.' David looked pleased with himself. 'Then the line broke twice. But we just kept trying.' David swallowed. 'The only bad bit was the crabs.' She could imagine how he'd hate pulling them out and sticking hooks through their bellies. 'Lew baited the lines. But we still didn't catch much. So we dug for worms.'

'Ugh.'

'And finally we managed to cast the line. Then we just sat up there on the rocks, waiting and talking.'

'Boy did we talk.' Lew impaled another mackerel on the toasting fork. 'And caught a bass.'

'We ate that before you came, Felix.' David licked his fingers. 'Sorry.'

She felt a pang of exclusion. Still, it was her own fault. 'What did you talk about?'

Lew and David looked at one another. 'I talked 'bout summer back home, how the heat becomes part of you.' Lew's relaxed voice was even slower than normal. 'I told him how the women sing in the fields and the flowers smell strong in the yards at night. He told me how it is here. How you tie flowers and greenery to the church pews at harvest, how you make lanterns at Christmas and sing carols in the frost. And for all it sounded a world apart from Georgia, it seemed we wasn't so different, after all.' He leaned back against the rocks. 'David said you two sneak out at nights to free animals in the traps. My brother and me, we used to climb out the window to steal peaches from a white lady's garden. Mamma would have given me a licking if she'd knowed.'

'My father would be furious if he found out I went out at night.' Felix met his dark gaze. 'You're right, we're not so different.' Her eyes felt full. 'But we're losing all this.'

'Hell no, you're not losing it. It's in you, girl, in your blood, in your bones. You take it with you wherever you go. I haven't been home for a year now but Georgia's still part of me and I'm still part of it.' His smile seemed to reach deep inside her.

'I'm glad we met you.' She turned pink, it wasn't like her to say things like that.

He winked at her. 'Pass me my drink, boy.' David tossed over a bottle of beer. So he'd raided the pantry again. This was like a party. She felt herself relax. David handed her a bottle of ginger beer.

'Here's to you, missy.' Lew raised his bottle. 'May your exile be short and happy.'

'You certainly seem happy, and you're far away from home,' said Felix.

He grinned. 'I take my fun where I find it. Folks back home have hard times. If we can enjoy ourselves, we do.'

'It's a shame we can't store happiness for the future.' She was thinking of boarding school.

He shook his head. 'Tonight I enjoy my friends. Tomorrow I'll take my punishment.' Lew patted his pocket. 'I'll give you this money for Phoebe, like you so kindly offer. And I'll show them my ankle at the camp; perhaps they won't treat me so bad. If I take my punishment and work hard there's still a chance they'll let me drive trucks. Or even do some fighting. Some blacks get to the front line.' He sat back and stared out to sea.

'I'm sure everything will be fine,' David said.

'Just look at that moon.' Lew pointed up through the cave entrance at the big yellow circle. 'You could just reach out and squeeze it like a lemon.' He began to sing in a low voice. '*Do you want the moon to play with, the stars to run away with?*'

Felix gazed up at the skies.

'See, missy, when you leave your village you'll always be able to look up at the sky, at the moon. That's what I do. And I imagine Mamma and Pop and my brothers and sisters – I'm the eldest – sitting out on the veranda, looking up at it, too. Mamma's got her sewing and Pop's cut hisself a chew of tobacco and the kids are actin' up, squabblin'.'

'Tell us about your family.' As always, the mention of brothers and sisters stirred longing in Felix.

'There's Tom, he's a year younger'n me and he wants to go into the air force. Mamma says he's lazy but she don't know Tom like I do, and I tell you, get that boy into something he loves and he'll show everyone. There's coloured boys flying now, you know.' Lew took a slug of beer. 'Then there's Leenie, she's fifteen. Pretty. Clever, too. Could make a schoolmistress, Mamma says. And Marcus, he's the baby.' Lew's lips twitched. 'Mamma named Marcus after some Roman guy in a movie she saw about chariots.'

'What does your father do?'

'He's a share-cropper; that means he rents land and gives the farmer some of the crop in return. It's mostly cotton or oats round us. Mamma takes in washing and helps out at white folks' houses. But they had plans for me. Wanted me to get a job in a store, 'n' learn book-keeping in the evenings. Maybe wind up with my own store someday.' Lew yawned.

'Would you like that?'

'I'd rather be a singer in a band. But perhaps I'll learn book-keeping to keep myself till I make my name.' He yawned again. 'Sure hope I get to do all these things sometime.'

Above them the big bright moon smiled on.

Fifteen

Minna

'It must have been a wrench when Lew left Fontwell,' I say. The way she's described the picnic on the beach and Lew's accounts of his home makes it clear that Felix had become very fond of him.

She blinks. 'Yes.' She pushes back her coffee cup and stands, reaching for her bag. 'I need to get back and make more calls. You wouldn't believe how much time I spend chasing builders for my roof.'

'But he drowned sometime after that picnic on the beach?'

She looks down at the car keys in her hand. 'That's what they said in the papers, isn't it?'

'But you didn't know that's what had happened until you read the story in the *Herald*?' She must have suspected something had gone wrong, surely?

'I told you, we left the village shortly afterwards.' A note of something in her voice; I've pushed her too far.

The barmaid removes our coffee cups with a reproachful rattle. I notice for the first time how empty the saloon has become. The mobile in my pocket trills and we both jump. 'Damn. Sorry.' I take the mobile from my pocket to switch it off and see Tom's number on the screen. 'I'd better take this.'

'Minna?' Tom sounds worried. 'What happened?'

'Come to Rosebank one evening,' I say to Felix, covering the mouthpiece.

'To meet your husband? I don't know' She looks away. 'I might have to go back to Yorkshire to sort out the roof.' She picks up her handbag and nods a farewell, ignoring my hand signals to wait.

'Please?' I call to her.

'Hello?' I hear Tom say. 'You still there?'

'Just a second.' I stuff the mobile into my bag and run after her. 'Please say you'll come.'

She halts and looks at me hard, as though she's weighing me up. Suddenly her face softens. 'Tomorrow evening?'

'Great!' I pull out the mobile again. 'Sorry about that.'

'Minna? What on earth's going on? Where are you?' Anxiety oozes from the phone.

Felix waves a farewell.

'I ran into Felix, we had lunch.'

Silence.

'Good news from the Frobishers,' Tom says at last with a forced air of jollity. 'They're staying near Lulworth but would love to pop over. That all right?'

'Brilliant.'

Another pause. I'm still watching Felix as she crosses the road. Will she show up tomorrow? Or was she just trying to get me off her back?

'I hate to nag you but it would really help if you could finish sorting out our finances this afternoon.'

'Sorry, I'm on my way. With you in twenty minutes.'

As I leave Swanham I notice a sign to the Tank Museum at Bovington. I wonder whether they have uniforms on display. I still can't get a picture of Lew in my head. What would he have worn? The steering wheel seems to turn itself in the direction of the museum. I let the car drive me north through unfamiliar lanes and villages. We reach a junction. I come out of my trance. What the hell am I doing? I promised Tom I'd come straight home. But this will only take a few minutes. I'll ring him again when I get there.

I don't think many solitary women visit army museums. An old boy examining a metal beast called a Cruiser Mark III eyes me with polite interest. 'Your dad in the forces, was he?'

'Afraid not; he was only a boy. I was actually looking for exhibits about GIs. There were quite a few American bases in this part of the

102

world, weren't there?' I pat the side of a tank and my bangle clatters on the metal. The old man grins.

'Swarming with Yanks, we were. There's a Sherman Crab in the next room. With a model Yank soldier beside it.'

'Thank you.'

The GI has a pink plastic complexion and eyes the colour of cornflowers. And Lew wouldn't have worn combat uniform like this; he was confined to support duties. They probably gave him overalls.

I slouch back to the car. As I switch on the ignition I remember that Tom and I were supposed to be going for a walk this afternoon, after I'd done the accounts.

'Where've you been? I've been worried sick.' Tom's face is ashen.

'Sorry.'

'You said you were just leaving Swanham.'

'I was. But I got sidetracked.'

'Where to?'

'The Tank Museum.'

'You drove all the way to Bovington?'

'I wanted to see what GIs looked like. But it was mainly tanks.' I roll my eyes, trying to raise a smile. 'As you'd expect from the name.'

He shakes his head. 'I don't know what to expect any more. If I had to think of one place in the whole bloody country you *wouldn't* be . . .'

'I'm trying to widen my horizons.' I put a hand on Tom's sleeve. 'It's great about the Frobishers coming over.'

He looks at my hand in surprise. Has it been so long since I've touched him? 'They're bringing Marina. Is that going to be difficult for you?'

Marina is just a month older than Benjamin would have been. 'We have to face it some time, don't we?' My words sound very rational. He nods. 'When are they coming?'

'Lunchtime tomorrow.'

'Ah.'

'What's up?'

103

'I asked someone else round in the evening. But she probably won't arrive until after they've left.'

'This Felix woman?'

'She's interesting.' I tell him what Felix told me about Lew Campbell.

'You're kidding.' He shakes his head. 'She knew him?'

'I don't know how much she knows about his last hours.'

I can read his face, I know that irritation and amusement are struggling with some other emotion: probably compassion.

'It takes my mind off things. That's good, isn't it?'

'I don't know.' He studies me. 'I don't know what's good and what's not any more.'

'I'll finish the bank statements.'

I sit down at the table and pick up the sheet I was working on before lunch. I half hope I've remembered the sums incorrectly, that the credits column won't be almost empty. But nothing seems to have been paid in to the account for months. My eyes stare right through the figures.

Sixteen

Minna

'So how's it been?' Sara Frobisher's Merlot-pinkened face assumes the look most of our friends have given me since that Saturday night three months ago: poorly disguised concern.

'Fine. This is a great spot.' I cringe at my hearty response but can't stop myself plunging onward. 'I walk for miles every day while Tom works.'

'You look good.' But her gaze is still anxious.

'Thank you.'

'So thin, though,' she can't help adding.

I slice bread rolls in half for the sausages grilling on the barbecue. 'Yeah, well, I can't get too worried about that. You know how I always hated my thighs.'

Tom says there wasn't much in the fishmonger, which is strange because I remember seeing bass and mackerel when I was in town yesterday. We're certainly not short of sausages, though, the good, cheap ones which barbecue so well.

'You make me feel like a pudding.' In fact, Sara looks lush and womanly. Beside her I must resemble a dried-out stick.

Her eyes swivel round to watch Marina as she crawls towards the stone steps leading to the rockery and wobbles on the edge. My muscles twitch; I want to go and swoop her up out of danger's way but I know I mustn't. We hold our breath. Marina pulls a daisy out of the lawn, executes a 180-degree turn on her bottom and comes back towards us.

I feel Sara relax beside me. 'I can't take my eye off her for a second. This morning she managed to get out the front door while Mark loaded up the car.'

'She's pretty fast.' Benjamin would have been crawling now, too. When we arrived I noted the big gap under the garden gate – an easy exit for the cliffs. Then I remembered I didn't need to worry about these things any more and felt like dropping to my hands and knees and crawling over the edge myself.

'Oh, Minna, I hope you don't mind her being here,' Sara says. I see real pain in her eyes and remember why I always liked her.

I turn one of the kebabs on the grill. 'She's my god-daughter. I want her in my life.'

'How can you bear hearing me prattle on about her?'

'You don't prattle.' I put my hand on hers for a second and her eyes fill.

'I'm no help to you.'

'You are. Seeing you today has reminded me of the good stuff in my life.' And it's true. This lunchtime the pain seems slightly less sharp. Then I think of that house in Wandsworth. 'Oh, by the way, why did you send us the house details?'

A moment's silence. 'What?' She's still watching Marina, now heading for a pot full of geraniums, but I can see a crease on her smooth brow.

'You sent us some estate agent's particulars. A semi in Wandsworth?' I put the kebab on a plate for her.

Sara laughs. 'Did I really? I'm rubbish at emailing.' She scrapes fish and peppers off the skewer and forks the pieces into her dainty little mouth. 'Mmm. This is good. You're not eating?'

'I'll just hand these round first. So the email was a mistake?'

She licks a finger. 'That's right. I thought another friend might be interested in that house. Obviously sent it to the wrong address. Sorry.'

She concentrates on her plate. I hand kebabs out to the men and go back into the kitchen to heat the food Sara's brought with her for Marina. If I keep on the move it's hard for Tom to keep tabs on what I'm eating – or not eating. On my way back to our guests I turn the lamb chops on the barbecue and dribble extra marinade on them to stop them drying out. While Sara's occupied putting Marina into her high chair I drip marinade on to my own plate and cutlery so it looks as if I've eaten. I hate these little deceptions but they save the

106

embarrassment of a scene. Topping up Sara's glass, I notice the Merlot isn't the Australian brand Tom usually favours for barbecues. I take a sip from my own glass and find the substitute's thinner and sharper on the tongue.

'How's Tom's work going?' Sara removes a piece of Emmental cheese from her salad. I always forget she doesn't eat much dairy or red meat these days.

'Keeps him busy.' I feel caught out because I really don't know much about Tom's work.

Sara's frowning. 'Jeremy Wilson's got a bit of a reputation, hasn't he?'

'Has he? What for?'

'Ruthlessness.' She drinks her wine. 'I don't know, just wouldn't have thought he'd be Tom's ideal client.'

Our bank statement floats through my mind. Tom's probably keen to get any kind of work he can. 'He doesn't say much about Waymark. Excuse me a second.' I fetch the heated pureed chicken for Marina. 'What about you? Getting much work done?' I ask Sara when I return.

'I'm doing three days a week.' She works in an art gallery staffed by women like *Vogue* models and men who look like they eat caviar for breakfast. 'I'll probably keep it at that for the time being.' Marina smacks a plump fist into her bowl and splatters herself with chicken. Her mother sighs and then smiles at her grin. A lump forms in my throat.

'Do you have a home office?' I'm remembering the laptop sent to her house.

She laughs. 'Not me. Once I'm home work's the last thing on my mind.'

'So you don't even have a laptop?'

'I really don't need one? Why?'

'Just wondering. Sometimes I think I should get one myself.'

Her eyes are still on her daughter, now shoving bits of bread roll into her pink mouth. 'I've never seen the need, but your line of work's rather different.'

'Oh, I haven't thought about work at all. I can't get myself motivated.' I haven't even opened my drawing pad.

'Oh Minna.'

I go inside to put on the coffee.

After lunch Tom suggests a stroll along the cliff top. 'You go,' I tell them. 'I'll clear up here.'

'You sure?' Mark asks.

'Completely.'

'Like me to stay with you?' Dear, kind Mark. Actually, I would like him to stay. 'We could read the papers.' A stack of untouched Sundays beckons on the terrace – all colour photos of flabby politicians on beaches and fast bowlers punching the air in triumph.

Sara has loaded Marina into a backpack. 'Sure she's not too heavy?' Mark plays with the baby's bare toes. I have to look away again.

'I'll take her if necessary.' Tom looks eager to carry the baby. I wonder what his reaction would be if I offered to take Marina on my back. I give a sly smile at the horror that would flicker over his face. Pain forges better people out of some of us; it's reduced me to a wasp.

Oh well, it'll do Tom good to be with someone else for an hour.

Mark and I settle back into recliners. While Mark loses himself in the British summer as related by the newspapers – MPs with mistresses, allegations of ball-tampering at cricket matches, and ludicrous stories involving farmyard animals – Felix's story weaves its way through my mind. I try and picture myself as a thirteen-year-old from a sheltered environment, meeting a man like that.

Beside me Mark finishes a colour supplement and drops it onto the paving. 'Minna.'

Something in his tone makes me lift my head from the article about a supermodel's facelift I've been pretending to read. Is he going to give me the *sorry* spiel? That's what I call it when good friends trot out carefully chosen words of commiseration. I'd hoped Mark knew me well enough to dispense with this. I've known him for ever, years longer than Tom. Perhaps he'll go for the *why aren't you eating* line?

'What is it?'

'God, I shouldn't burden you with this, but I don't know who else to turn to.'

I sit up. 'Now you've got me worried.'

'It's Sara.'

'What about her?'

'There's something going on. She won't tell me. She's always on the phone, or emailing. We never used to have secrets.'

'Ask her.'

He looks down at the discarded newspapers. 'Suppose it's something I don't want to hear?' I stare at him. 'She might be ill or something. Not wanting to tell me.'

Sara's mother died of breast cancer six years ago. Her sister survived the same disease only last year. The specialists told Sara the women in her family carry a gene predisposing them to the illness. Hence the avoidance of dairy and red meat: Sara's read that they encourage deadly mutating cells.

The garden gate clicks. 'Hello?' I turn and see Felix. She looks at Mark and extends her hand. 'Your husband?'

'A friend.' I introduce them. Mark's too wrapped up in his anxiety to be very curious about the elderly lady who's come calling, probably thinking she's a local WI member or something, trying to persuade me to lend a hand at the fête or arrange flowers in the church. 'The others will be back soon. I'll make tea.'

Felix sits at the garden table, chatting with Mark and flicking through the *Sunday Times* book section, while I go to fill the kettle in the kitchen. I'm spooning Earl Grey into the pot when I hear voices, a baby crying. The walkers have returned. Sara looks tired, a little flustered. What's been said? I put cups onto a tray and take them out to the terrace.

'I'm afraid we're going to have to make a quick getaway. She's hungry.' Sara stuffs feeding pots and spoons into Marina's changing bag.

'Feed her here.' I spot more jars of food in the bag.

'It'll be easier at home.'

'But if she's that hungry?'

'She'll sleep in the car. She's exhausted.' Sara kisses my cheek. 'Lunch was a triumph, thank you.'

'It was great to see you.' I hug Mark and the contact lasts a second longer than usual. The scent of his aftershave, all basil and citrus, makes me want to weep. I haven't been this close to Tom in months; at night we cling to our separate sides of the bed. 'Keep in touch,' I say under my breath, as Sara walks to the car. 'And don't panic. It's probably not what you're thinking. Talk to her.'

Tom whispers something to Sara. She nods, glancing back at her husband.

We wave them off and I turn back to Felix, who's inspecting the mixed borders. 'I don't know what my mother would say about these pink geraniums.' She nods at the terracotta pots. 'But I think the garden's going to look very good when it's matured.'

'We like it,' Tom says. 'Especially at night when the stocks and tobacco plants smell strongest.' He picks through the newspapers. 'I think I might catch up with the business sections indoors,' he says, without making eye contact with me. 'Excuse me.'

'Here.' I pass him a cup of tea as he goes by. 'Have a nice walk with Sara?' And I emphasize the last word ever so slightly to see if her name elicits any unusual reaction.

'Yes thanks. Although Marina was fractious.' He takes his tea inside. Felix has turned to stare at us and her gaze is probing.

'I turned up too early,' she says.

'No you didn't.' I pull out a chair for her.

'Funny.' She smiles. 'I stay away from this place for more than sixty years, then I'm back here twice in a week.'

'Do you mind us being here?' I ask.

She looks surprised. 'Not at all.'

'I'm gripped by your story.'

I can't read her expression.

'I tried getting Louise's number from directory inquiries,' she says, as though in answer. 'But she's not listed.'

'Louise?' For a moment I've forgotten who Louise is. Then I remember the *Herald* piece: Lew's daughter, the child Phoebe was expecting when he came to Fontwell. 'Why do you want to see her?'

Her eyes sweep the flowerbeds for a few seconds before she answers. 'I was wondering if we should show her the cormorant. She might be interested.'

I note her use of 'we' and like the thought that I'm becoming part of this story. And I of all people understand the pull of a memento mori. Don't I sleep with a baby's sleep-suit clutched to me? I remind myself that Louise never knew her father.

'The Swanham paper might give us her details,' I say.

'Worth a try.'

We sit in silence for a minute or two. Somewhere out to sea a motor boat's engine whirrs; funny how clearly sound travels in the evenings.

'Did anyone else find out about Lew while he was in Fontwell?' I think how hard it would be to keep him hidden away, even for a few days.

She was silent and I start to repeat the question.

'I heard you.' Her next words come out slowly. 'Isabel met him.'

'The one who was getting close to the gamekeeper?'

'That's right.' Felix gives a hollow laugh. 'Pity for us she didn't content herself with the gamekeeper, but she got suspicious. She found us in the cave, with Lew.'

'I thought you said . . .?' I'm trying to remember the end of the conversation in the pub yesterday.

'She turned up and changed everything. Typical Isabel.'

'She sounds like a pain.'

Felix runs a finger round the brim of the teacup. 'Years later I found out she'd had terrible depression in her teens. They bullied her horribly at school because she found schoolwork difficult. And, by all accounts, her mother was a complete cow, refused to see her on the few occasions Isabel made contact.'

'Poor thing.'

'Yes. It was easy to look at her and see this beautiful girl – she was dazzling, waves of gold hair, perfect skin, and these slightly slanted eyes. But she wasn't easy to be with. Her moods swung and she'd lash out at people. Even the Squire and David. And she adored them really.'

I fidget in my chair, recognizing my recent self in the difficult young woman.

'She was the last person we wanted to find out about Lew. When she turned up in the cave I knew things would go wrong.'

Seventeen

'How wonderfully cosy.'

A thin torch-beam played on their faces. David blanched under its glare. Felix turned to see Isabel on a rock behind her. Lew's singing must have muffled her approach. She wore a mackintosh and a small navy beret, a little smile playing on her lips. 'Going to introduce me to your new chum?' On her face was a look of complete concentration. Her eyes, usually so sleepy, seemed to glint with interest.

Through the silence Felix heard waves crashing on the rocks, their thump growing more insistent. 'Isabel.' David stood up. 'This is Private Lew Campbell, an American friend of ours. Lew, this is Isabel Parham, my cousin.'

'You're a long way from home, Private.' Isabel shook his hand, then raised her fingers to her hair, twisting a golden lock while she studied him. She shook her head as though trying to snap out of a trance, and turned to her cousin. 'You were missed at supper. I said you were sea-fishing. The Squire seemed to think that a perfectly adequate excuse.'

'How did you know?'

'That you'd taken the rod?' Isabel sprang off her rock. For one who normally moved as though the slightest activity was too much for her, the action was graceful, like a cat jumping from a fence. 'Johnson noticed it'd gone. He's been ranting about it. The Squire told him he could sell the tackle, you see, and keep the money. So I put two and two together.'

'You didn't tell . . .?'

'Johnson? Didn't have to.' Felix's stomach turned cold. Isabel smoothed her hair. 'Come to think of it, he'll be looking for me, too.' She gave a nervous laugh.

113

Lew spoke. 'I'll be on my way.' He drained his bottle.

'You've obviously made quite an impression.' Isabel's pale eyes swept the group. 'Mind you, we don't get many *negroes* in this part of the world.' She looked at him as though she wanted to see how he'd react to the word. But something in the way she referred to his colour made Felix think she wasn't shocked so much as fascinated by it.

He smiled. 'You like a mackerel?' He offered her the one he'd been roasting.

'No thanks, I've eaten.' She caught sight of the beer bottles. 'Wouldn't mind one of those.'

'You want a beer?' David sounded incredulous.

'Why not?' Isabel said. Lew opened a bottle and passed it over. 'Well, isn't this fun?' She sipped her drink. 'Chilly, though.'

'I should get home.' Felix rose. 'Goodbye, Lew. And good luck getting back.'

He stood too. 'Thank you, missy.'

Isabel's stare stayed on Lew. 'David can walk me home when I've finished this and found out more about our visitor.'

'I'll see you in the morning,' David muttered to Felix.

'Night, missy.' Lew's voice had taken on a tight quality. Was he scared of Isabel? Had he noticed the strangeness in her that perplexed David and the Squire and caused the locals to whisper? But then Lew gazed at Isabel and Felix realized she was wrong – there was nothing in his expression suggesting fear: he examined Isabel, unblinking, as though he'd just found something he'd never expected to come across.

Something about the scene made Felix's eyes prickle. She ran across the shingle and climbed the cliff path, pausing at the top to look back towards the cove. Below her the sea roared and snapped as it hit the shore. The smoke was invisible now – it would be impossible to keep the fire going in weather like this.

Isabel had found Lew. Everything had changed. Perhaps now was the time to go to the Squire, to tell him what had happened. But Lew's laughing eyes pulled at her heart and she knew she couldn't hand him in. Anyway, he'd be gone by morning. Something stirred in the long grass at the path's edge. Her heart shot into her mouth. Then there was nothing. Probably a fox. Or a cat out hunting. She forced herself to keep on walking. At least the moon had reappeared from the clouds to light the way.

When she woke in the morning the situation pressed itself upon her sleepy consciousness and she covered her face with the eiderdown to block it out. David, Isabel; too many people knew about Lew. She wished sleep would reclaim her and free her from the worry.

The curtain blew in, knocking a book off the windowsill. She got up to retrieve it and pulled up the blackout. Across the sky grey clouds scurried in from the west. The last of the roses on the trellis had pulled themselves away from their supports and waved in the breeze. A shirt Mrs Derby had left out to dry had wound itself over and over the line. A storm was on the way. She shivered, wishing she could have a fire in her bedroom, but her father had told her there wasn't enough coal – she'd have to gather firewood if she wanted a luxury like that. Perhaps she could look for driftwood on the beach like Sam's mother. Felix had seen her gathering greying branches, her expression defiant but ashamed.

She threw on a wool skirt and long socks and pulled a cardigan out of the drawer to wear over her vest and Viyella shirt. Plimsolls looked strange with the skirt but were more practical than sandals in this weather. Her lace-ups were too small and her father said she'd have to wait until she went to school for new ones.

Downstairs Mrs Derby coaxed the stove to heat water. 'Darn thing, doesn't like the wind in this direction, won't draw properly.' She stood up and massaged her back. 'Weather doesn't do my lumbago any good, either. How's your pain?'

'I haven't got one.'

'Oh.' She nodded. 'Porridge in two ticks, just needs serving.'

Her father looked over the top of his *Times* as she came into the dining room. 'I hear you've been unwell. Better now?' His doctor's eyes scrutinized her.

'Just tired, Daddy.' She helped herself to tea. 'Probably the change in temperature.'

'You'll have to get used to it, winter's on the way.' His eyes turned to the crossword. She bolted down porridge and tea, keen to go and find David.

'I've asked Mrs Derby to go through the uniform list with you,' he said. 'There's a lot to be ordered. It's going to be difficult to get hold of it all. But Isabel Parham told me she kept most of her old uniform and she's happy for you to have it.'

Felix's heart sank. Going to St Agatha's in Isabel's cast-offs, what a start to her school career. She imagined Isabel's lip curling as she handed over the clothes.

'Mrs Derby will need you to help label the garments. And she wants to go through your wardrobe and cupboards to see what we should take when we move out.'

A rope tightened slowly round her throat. She finished her breakfast and muttered excuses. Outside, the wind grabbed her hair and drove it across her eyes, and the cold air sprinkled goose pimples over her skin. She wished she had trousers. Mrs Derby disapproved of girls in slacks and would never agree to make her any, even if they could get the material.

Sam stood in the lane, hands in pockets. He gave a start when he saw her. 'Hello,' she said.

'Hello.' His gaze dropped to the conkers in his hand. 'You off to the beach again?'

'That's right.' She paused, waiting for him to ask if he could go with her, trying to think up an excuse. But he stared at her and said nothing. 'See you later then.'

'Bye.' His tone was flat.

As she walked on she felt something strike her back. She turned and looked down and saw a small stone on the ground. Sam stood in the lane, schoolbooks under his folded arms, lower lip protruding.

'Why did you do that?'

He shrugged. 'You never have any time for me these days.'

'We're just a bit busy.'

'Doing what?'

'Things.'

He blew an explosive raspberry before walking off.

'Sam!'

He stopped. 'What you want?'

'I promise it won't be like this after today.'

'That's what you said yesterday.' He moved away. Shaken, she continued. David was waiting at the end of the Manor's drive.

'Lew's still down on the beach.' He looked grim, tired. 'Isabel's fascinated with him. I left them at nine but she stayed on.'

'Why?' Jealousy stung Felix.

'She was asking him loads of questions about Phoebe.'

'What kind of questions?'

'How he met her. What she looks like, what kind of clothes she wears, how she does her hair.'

'Didn't he mind?'

'At first he looked a bit surprised. Then he leaned back and started laughing.'

'Laughing? At Isabel?' She couldn't picture this. 'How did she take it?'

'She laughed too, said she was being nosy but she couldn't help herself.' David shook his head.

'Has she, you know, fallen in love with him?' Why did the thought make her feel so angry?

'I don't know. But she'll certainly scupper any plans to get him away today. He was already talking about waiting a bit longer.'

'He's completely mad. The police—'

'You don't need to tell me about the police.'

Felix shivered. 'They'll lock him up in solitary for months. Remember how he said they treat the negro soldiers harshest?'

'Let's get down to the beach, see if we can bundle him off now before anyone's around.'

Felix heard footsteps behind her.

Johnson's face had never seemed so gaunt. Dark shadows hung beneath his eyes. He blinked, as though he hadn't noticed them.

'Master David.' He coughed. 'You seen Miss Isabel this morning?'

'No. Why do you want her?'

'I wondered if she needed more firewood. It's cooler today.'

'If I see her, I'll ask.' David nodded at him.

'She shouldn't be out in this wind.' Johnson shook his head. 'She's delicate.'

'She's probably still in her room,' David said.

'She's not.'

David frowned. 'How do you know?'

A blush covered Johnson's pale cheeks. 'The Squire said she wasn't indoors.'

'Oh well.' David looked at Felix. 'If we see her we'll pass on the message.' He set off at a pace Felix could hardly match. She felt Johnson's eyes burning into her. At the top of the cliff a gust of wind nearly toppled her off the path. She clutched David's arm.

Nature was bad-tempered this morning, fizzing the sea as they ran beside it, blowing sand into their eyes. Lew stood at the cave entrance, peering out. David had brought him a razor and he'd shaved and found some way to polish his boots and sponge down his uniform. He looked every inch the soldier, and big as the elements swelling round him. Felix's wish that they'd never met him blew away with the gusts.

He smiled. 'That was a late night we had. Isabel—' He looked down in confusion, not before Felix had noted the dropped 'Miss' from Isabel's name.

David climbed down. 'We need to get you moving, Lew. It's getting too dangerous, too many people know about you now.'

Lew nodded. 'I'll fetch my kit. I've already cleared up the cave.' He paused. 'I did promise Isabel I'd say goodbye.'

'Say goodbye? What do you think this is, some kind of holiday?' Felix had never seen David so authoritative before.

'I guess not.'

'They'll be prowling around within the hour. If we can get you out of the village there's a chance you can cut across country to the main road. Maybe you can hitch a ride.'

Lew put out a hand and touched David's shoulder. 'You kids's been good to me, don't think I don't know the risks you've taken.'

'It was nothing,' said David.

Lew threw on his jacket. 'Let's go.'

Feet pounded the shingle behind them. Felix turned towards the sound.

'What the hell's going on?'

It must have been the first time since she'd left boarding school that Isabel had got up before nine o'clock, but the grey lines beneath her eyes only added to her pale beauty. Again she'd stolen up on them unseen. So much for thinking this place was so safe. She stood scowling at them. 'Did you forget your promise, Lew?'

He shook his head and gave a faint laugh, staring at the ground.

'Just as well I set the alarm clock.' She climbed the rocks and stood beside him. 'So.' She glared at David and Felix. 'Perhaps we could have ten minutes alone?'

Felix's blood boiled. Isabel was brushing them off as though they were in the way, but she was the intruder, not them. What had happened? Had Lew kissed her? Surely not; he was engaged, wasn't he?

'There's no time for this.' David spoke more like a man than a boy of fifteen. 'If the police catch us with Lew we're all in trouble, and as you're the only legal adult you'll be held responsible, Isabel.'

Isabel gave David her slow smile. 'Well you'd never take responsibility for anything, would you? Like father, like son.'

'What do you mean?'

For a second she looked as though she'd said too much. 'That old lecher in Kenya, the man who's never done a thing except sit beside his swimming pool and eye up the tarts. You're just like your daddy – passive.'

Felix realized how little she knew about David's parents: the mother in London who wrote to him once or twice a year, the father in Africa he rarely mentioned.

David screwed up his fists. 'You leave him out of this.'

'Living the life of luxury in the sunshine while the rest of us fight the war.'

'That's rich, coming from you!'

'I've been ill.'

'So's my father, actually. The Squire told me. His TB's come back.'

'Oh.' She looked discomfited. 'I didn't know.' But her confusion seemed to leave her very quickly and she turned and smiled at Lew. 'How was the night? Did you sleep well?' She might have been a society hostess at a country house weekend.

'Yes, thank you ma'am.' He was looking at David and Felix, a frown on his brow.

'I told you not to call me that, it's so fusty. Call me Isabel.'

'Yes – Isabel.' But there was a flicker of something in his expression. Felix thought it was amusement but surely nobody'd dare find Isabel funny? But why were they wasting all this time?

'Lew should go now.' Felix's voice sounded shrill against the waves. 'It's getting dangerous.'

'And what do you know?' Isabel raised an eyebrow at her. 'Oh, by the way, do get your housekeeper to come and collect my old clothes; heard you need them for school.'

Her cheeks felt hot. David pressed her arm, warning her not to respond.

'There's no shame in cast-offs.' Lew spoke gently, as though explaining things to a very small child. 'I grew up wearing my cousin Titus's. Then they got passed down to my brothers. First time I ever wore new clothes was when I signed up with Uncle Sam.'

Felix loved Lew at that moment.

Isabel blinked and bit her lip. 'You don't have to tell me off.' The words were hardly audible.

'Seems like someone's got to.' Something had changed, his tone was more assertive now.

Felix waited for the explosion, not even daring to look at Isabel. But she said nothing. The atmosphere seemed to crackle with tension.

'Hey, listen to me preaching.' Lew guffawed. 'My family'd die laughing.' He glanced at David and Felix. 'Like you say, best I go now. For everyone's sake.'

Isabel moved towards the man and laid her hand on his arm. 'Wait till dusk. Nobody'll see you then. It'll be safer.'

Lew sighed. 'It's gettin' too hot round here, honey. I owe these kids so much, I don't want to get them into trouble.'

'Them! What about me?' Her voice gave a slight quaver.

'Lew's only just met you, he doesn't owe you anything,' Felix reminded her.

'Who do you think you are, Felicity Valance?' Isabel's bottom lip trembled. 'You're a nobody. Your father wouldn't have kept his practice if it weren't for my uncle.' She stopped and bit her lip.

David scowled at her.

'What do you mean?' Felix took a step towards her.

'Well, the villagers weren't awfully keen on having a drunkard as a doctor, were they? Until the Squire went round talking to them all and persuading them to give your father a second chance.'

Something caught Felix in the throat. 'What do you mean?' she repeated. She could barely get the words out.

'When your mother died your father took to drink.' Isabel showed mock concern. 'Didn't you notice?'

Lew was saying something but this time Isabel paid him no heed.

'The good doctor was the joke of the parish. But Uncle hushed all the wagging tongues and had a word with him about easing back on the brandy. At least during surgery hours.'

'Felix.' David was beside her, hand reaching for her arm. 'It wasn't like that, not really. Your father was very depressed after your mother died. Of course he was. It was a bad patch, that's all.'

She shook her head, knew she had to get away from them all. Detaching David's hand from her sleeve she clambered over the rocks.

'Felix!' He scrambled after her. 'Wait.'

'I had no idea.' Those long winter nights spent alone in the surgery the months after her mother died, her father'd spent them drinking? She remembered the empty bottles on the dispensary shelf and turned back to David. 'Does everyone know?'

He dropped his head.

'Your father's a really popular man, Felix. He's saved lives since he's been in the village.'

'But they feel sorry for him.' Felt sorry for her, too, most likely. Poor motherless Felicity Valance, going off to school in another girl's clothes, with a father who liked a drop too much. Her cheeks burned.

'They respect him, the Squire's always saying what good work he does.' They'd reached the cliff path. He put a hand out to her again. 'Listen, Isabel's trying to drive a wedge between Lew and us. She strikes where she sees a weakness.'

Only now did she see the hurt in his face. Isabel's words had cut him, too.

'I want to kill her.' If only she could push Isabel into the sea and hold her head under those grey waves.

'She's not worth hating, believe me, I know.' His voice warbled in the middle of the sentence and he groaned in annoyance, placing a hand to his throat. 'At least I can get away from her at Harrow.'

Felix remembered that this was supposed to be their last few weeks in paradise. 'I wish she'd leave.'

'She'll have to soon. The war's catching up with her, too. People aren't prepared to see an able-bodied girl pouting at the gamekeeper.' He dropped his head. 'I shouldn't say things like that about her, she is my cousin after all. And she's had her troubles, these last months.'

'Her mother not wanting to see her?'

'The Squire was furious when he found out she'd made that trip. Told her she was setting herself up for heartbreak.' He forced a smile. 'Come on, let's say goodbye to Lew.'

She allowed him to lead her back to the pair.

'You all right, missy?' Lew's eyes were soft as he looked at her.

'Yes, thank you.'

'What a fuss about a few home truths.' Isabel kept her gaze averted. 'About time you found out about your beloved Daddy.'

Blood boiled in Felix's veins. 'Who the hell do you think you are?'

Isabel's head shot round.

'You think you're so grand, don't you? But you've done nothing with your life.'

'You can't talk to me like that.' Isabel's fair skin seemed to grow even paler. She glanced at David as though appealing for his support. He folded his arms and said nothing.

'I'll say what I want.'

'Oh, you're so brave now. Just ten minutes ago you were worrying about the police.'

'I'm worried about Lew.'

'If you're so bothered, why don't you go back to the village and see what they're doing?'

'What do you mean?' David spoke.

'I saw the Keystone Cops talking to Mrs Fuller. Apparently a land-girl at Upper Farm claims she saw Lew there two days ago.'

'Why didn't you say so before?' David asked.

'Told you, Lew's better off waiting till dark. No need to panic.'

Lew buttoned his jacket. 'Panic or not, I'm out of here.'

'You can't get down the path, the police are still in the village.' Isabel said. 'They asked me where I was going in the rain.'

'What did you say?'

She gave a half-smile. 'Said my uncle'd sent me out to find my cousin for lunch. They asked if I'd seen their fugitive.' She gazed at Lew. 'I told them they were wasting their time.'

'Lew could get round the rocks into Gull Cove,' Felix suggested. 'There's a path up the cliffs from there.'

'The tide's all wrong.' David shook his head. 'Look how high it is.'

Felix thought of something. 'Why don't I go and spy on the cops? Shout down when they've gone? Then we can take Lew back to the shed till night. Easy to get him out of the valley from there.'

'They'll know something's up if they see you coming and going.'

'I can climb up the cliff. They won't see me that way.'

David's eyes widened. 'Are you mad?'

'Don't do it, missy.' Lew took her shoulder. 'Let me take my chances, but don't you go climbing up there.'

'I climb like a cat,' she told him. 'Just like my name.'

'But you've never done anything like this before.' David folded his arms.

Felix walked to the cliff and examined it. At this section of the beach it was lower – only the height of three houses one on top of the other. The first fifteen feet sloped up gently. Then there was a section with plenty of footholds. The tricky bit would be a twenty-foot section two-thirds of the way up. She scanned the red and grey face and thought she could see small grooves she could use to hold on.

'I don't want you to take the risk.' Lew grasped her shoulder again.

'It's fine.' She shook him off and fastened the buttons on her cardigan and started to climb, finding easy purchase on the lower rocks.

'Take it easy, Felix,' David said.

The steep section was now only two or three feet above her. Felix raised her hand, found a depression she liked, moved her right foot and pushed her toes into a crack. Below her she heard raised voices, shouts. She paused, checked her grip, and turned her head to listen.

'You're mad, Isabel!' David yelled. 'You can't climb up there!'

Felix's left foot slipped. She jabbed at the rock with her toes, found another foothold.

'If she can, I can,' Isabel said.

'But Felix is always climbing.'

'Just watch me.'

Under Felix's right hand small fragments of rock crumbled and dropped. She moved her fingers, found another crack. Isabel would give up after the first five feet when she saw how sharply the cliff rose. Felix continued her ascent. Their voices dropped away until she heard only the swoosh of the sea.

Suddenly Isabel screamed. Felix looked down and caught a flash of something white falling, heard stones pattering down to the shingle. Then silence.

She began to climb down, heart pounding, reminding herself not to rush, no matter what had happened to Isabel. Reaching the easy bit she let herself drop to the shingle. Where were they? She ran to the rocks. The three of them sat together; Lew was clutching Isabel's hand. She looked up as Felix reached them.

'I'm sorry.'

Felix couldn't believe her ears. 'What happened?'

'I fell. I thought I was going to die.' She swallowed. 'Lew caught me, saved my life.'

'Don't know about that, you'd probably just have broken a bone,' he said.

'You're a fool, Isabel.' David stood.

'I know.' She put a hand to her mouth and her shoulders shook. Isabel, crying? But then Felix saw it wasn't tears. 'Sorry. Not laughing, not really. Just can't help wondering what I must have looked like, flying through the air with my skirt round my waist.'

Lew pressed her fingers. 'Why'd you do it?'

She shrugged.

David touched Felix's arm. 'Let's go back for lunch.'

'What about the police?'

'They'll just think we're coming in to eat.'

'But suppose they come down here?'

'They won't see Lew and Isabel if they keep their heads down. The cave's invisible unless you know where to look.'

'Will Isabel be all right?'

He sniffed. 'She'll be all right.' He shook his head. 'I'd never have dreamed she'd have the nerve for something like that. C'mon.' They walked towards the cliff path.

Felix felt deflated. How was it that Isabel, having fallen six feet into Lew's arms, received as much – more – admiration than she did for climbing almost to the top? Would it always be like this? Her arms ached. She realized what a strain the climb had been.

'Lew'll have to stay put a little bit longer.' David gave her an admiring grin. 'There's no way he can climb the cliff like you did.' They continued the ascent of the path in silence, Felix glowing with the warmth of his praise. Still silent, they reached the top and descended into the village. No sign of the MPs. Perhaps they'd given up looking for Lew. David seemed to read her mind. 'I don't think those chaps have gone far; they're probably in one of the cottages, asking questions or begging a cup of tea and a sandwich.'

'Should we run down and get Lew out while they're distracted?'

He shook his head. 'Too risky. Let's wait and see what's happening this afternoon. If they're still prowling around we'll wait until night. Come and find me after lunch.'

She waved and walked away. When she reached Rosebank she demolished two helpings of bubble-and-squeak and a large bowl of stewed pears. 'I might read a book in my room,' she told her father.

Eighteen

Minna

'So Isabel was jealous when she said all those terrible things?' I ask Felix.

'So she said.' Felix laughs. 'But nobody could have been jealous of me. I was small, skinny, scruffy. Isabel could have been in the pictures.'

'Even so . . .' My attention switches to Lew. 'Did you see him again after lunch?' I ask, just as thunder rumbles overhead. Perhaps Lew had attempted the cliff climb himself, desperate to escape. Does Felix feel guilty for planting the idea in his head?

A breeze blows the remaining sheets of newspaper off the table, catching a teacup. I grab it just before it drops onto the paving stones. The sheets tangle themselves in geraniums and foxgloves.

'I should leave you in peace.'

Perhaps she didn't hear my question.

'Come inside and have another drink before you go.'

'I don't drink.' Lightning forks across the sky. 'But perhaps I could wait twenty minutes until this passes over.'

I lead her inside. Tom's working away on his laptop. 'Would you like a glass of wine?' I ask as we pass his office.

He turns his head and smiles at us. 'I had enough at lunchtime.' But in fact he only had a glass or two.

Felix and I sit in the conservatory with a bottle of mineral water.

'I like what they've done with this side of the house.' Her eyes travel over the new flooring and paintwork. 'My mother had great plans for the conservatory, but once she'd gone nobody really bothered with the plants and it just became a dumping ground for things we didn't know where else to store.' Outside the sky is charcoal-grey. The newspapers are now trying to suffocate the delphiniums. The back door slams and Tom comes out, probably looking for the sports sections. He sees the sheets dancing round the flowerbed and hunts them down. He's just about to grab a colour supplement when it whirls from his grasp and tumbles over the lawn. Felix gives a grin of sympathy. I find myself watching Tom as though he's a character in a film. He's good-looking in a quiet way and his figure is still athletic enough to make his dash across the garden graceful.

He retrieves the supplement and rolls it up, hitting his thigh with it as he walks back into the house, as though chiding himself.

'Why don't you two get on?' Felix's startling eyes bore into mine and I find myself studying the stem of the wineglass to avoid them.

'We lost a child.' I hear my flat tone and shudder. Will my voice ever express emotion again?

She says nothing.

'We don't seem to be able to get past it.' I correct myself. 'At least, I don't.' Tom has perhaps found his own way of moving forwards.

Her gaze is still on me. 'Sometimes loss does that to you. How old was your child?'

'Five months. It's as though the whole world has lost its point. Tom has his work. I haven't been able to do anything since the accident.'

'When did it happen?'

'Four months ago.' The wind drives a branch of the rose against the pane and thorns scrape the glass. Thunder still rumbles to the east.

'That's not long. For a big loss like that you'll feel at sea for a long time. Even a much smaller loss can do that to you. After we left Fontwell David went to live in Dorking with his uncle and I went to boarding school. I went into a kind of catatonia for the best part of a year. I couldn't seem to feel any emotion at all.' Her hand touches mine briefly. 'It's not the same, I know. I don't mean to devalue the death of your baby.'

'You're not.' The words catch in my throat. 'Tell me about leaving here. It must have been terrible.'

'It felt like being thrown out of Eden.' She blinks. 'And at the same time it was almost a relief that it was time to go.'

'A relief?'

'Life had become very intense.'

The wind's murmur rises to a more insistent moan.

Nineteen

Felix 1943

An early mist still covered the village, so only the nearest objects were visible. The frost was starting to disperse, leaving leaves wet and slippery. Felix could make out Sam's cottage across the lane but the church steeple was still shrouded. Her father shivered. 'A funereal day.' He'd already been to the graveyard to put the last of the dahlias onto her mother's grave.

Felix carried her bags and boxes out of the house. Mrs Derby was checking the rooms for anything left behind. The doctor went back inside and brought out a box of bottles from his dispensary. 'No point in taking out-of-date medicines with us. I'll leave these in the drive.'

'Let me.' She held out her hands for the box.

'No thanks, I can manage.' He jerked the box away from her

Still no sign of the truck. Felix longed to see the beach one last time. She started to walk away, expecting them to call her back. Silence. She reached the end of the lane, passed the Manor gates, the telephone box, the village shop, boarded up and dark. Fifteen minutes to reach the beach, fifteen minutes back. She ran through the mist, relying on memory to tell her how the path bent and twisted. Her feet felt the dip at the top of the cliff and she slowed her pace.

Fog hid the sea, the only indication of its presence a gentle murmur. Autumn storms were only a memory now; the sombre serenity of winter had replaced them. She walked down to the water, the crunch of her feet over pebbles turning to a crackle as she reached the fine shingle. She lowered a hand and a wave wet it.

In the last week she'd started dreaming that Lew had come up to Rosebank to ask why she didn't go down to the rocks any more. 'I'm scared of the dark,' she told him. He said nothing in answer but stared at her, accusation in his dark eyes. Sometimes he brought one of the fishing rods with him and sat dangling it off her bed. 'Mighty big fish I'm pulling in,' he said. 'Hope you've a pan big enough to cook him in.' And Mrs Derby came into the bedroom and told Lew off for sitting on a white girl's bed. 'Don't you take that tone with me, ma'am,' he said. 'My uncle's a pastor, you know.'

Her ten minutes were up. She turned her back on the sea and ran to the cliff, stopping only to scoop up a pebble, any pebble. Her fingers touched a small, smooth stone and she dropped it into her pocket.

She wanted to turn round for a final glimpse of the beach but there would be nothing to see.

She ran faster than she'd ever run before, reaching the pile of boxes and trunks outside the house just as the truck arrived and Mrs Derby ran out to help Father load them in. The noise muffled the horses' hoofs and it was only when the Squire's hay wagon was level with Felix that she looked up and saw Isabel sitting with the driver. Isabel wore a mink coat and hat. As she saw Felix a faint blush covered her white cheeks and she looked away.

Mrs Derby pulled Felix into her arms. 'Goodbye, my darling.' Felix breathed in her scent of bread and milk and coal dust. The driver jumped down to load her bags and helped the housekeeper up beside Isabel, who moved to leave a space between them, eyes averted from Felix. Where was David? Gone on ahead with the Squire, perhaps, to the house they'd rented in Dorking in Surrey, a town where the Squire had once lived as a child. David would start school at the same time she did. When would she see him again?

'Hello!' Sam ran up the lane and waved at the wagon. 'We're going to a house with electric lights!' he shouted. Sam's mother was very sick now. The doctor had been seeing her almost every day, visiting her in the cottage so she wouldn't have to expose her bad chest to the November air. The family was moving to a council house in Swanham.

Felix's father was scribbling something on a piece of writing paper, using a suitcase as a desk. He took the sheet and pinned it to the front door. Felix walked up to peer at it.

PLEASE TAKE CARE OF THIS HOUSE. WE ARE GIVING IT UP FOR THE SAKE OF OUR COUNTRY. WE SHALL RETURN TO OUR VILLAGE WHEN PEACE COMES.

We shall return.

Felix ran round to the back of the house, praying the door would still be unlocked. It was. No time to get upstairs to her bedroom. 'Felix!' Her father was calling from the front. She shot into the dispensary and pulled the cormorant sketch out of her pocket and reached up to slide it onto the bottom shelf.

'You belong here,' she told it silently. 'I'll come back and get you as soon as I can.'

She ran back outside.

''Scuse me, miss, but we're waiting for you.' The sergeant helped her up into the back of the truck, where she sat with her father and Sam as they made a last slow sweep through the village. A feeble sun broke through the haze just as they were climbing the steep section of road by Upper Farm, and she leant out and looked back, catching a glimpse of the church tower for a second before they passed over the brow of the hill.

Part Two

Twenty

Minna

Felix's story is emerging all out of order, as though someone has muddled up the chapters in a book. But I'll encourage her to tell me about St Agatha's. Perhaps we can work back to Lew's death from there.

'Then they sent you away to school?' I used to lap up boarding school stories, but I suspect Felix's account of her time there won't include jolly accounts of midnight feasts and pranks.

She wrinkles her nose. 'I started in November. St Agatha's. Ghastly place. The very first thing I did was work out possible escape routes. Just in case.'

'It must have been a bit of a culture shock after having private lessons.'

'David and I loved our sessions with Mr Stewart, just the three of us, all cosy in the library.' She tells me about their lessons: how they studied in the wood-panelled room, a fire burning in the grate. He'd allowed them to learn pretty well whatever they liked: David would draw and label the bones of a bird while she copied the image of the north face of the Eiger from a mountaineering book and described its geological features. A kitten from the stables would wander in and lie on the hearth rug, playing with its fringed edges. Mr Stewart would recite a mildly racy Latin poem about cats.

Occasionally his conscience pressed him to set them algebra or even Greek, but these episodes were short-lived.

'St Agatha's wasn't nearly as accommodating. As I said, I took any opportunity to escape. When I went back to school after Christmas I found out about Isabel's wedding. I wondered if David might be there.' She sips her water.

'You hadn't heard from him?' Surely he'd have sent a Christmas card at least to such a close friend?

'No.'

I'm surprised. How could two such close companions break off contact like that? But perhaps a few weeks' silence when they'd just started new boarding schools wasn't so surprising.

'I really wanted to see him so I decided to run away for the day.'

Felix 1944

St Agatha's girls were allowed to read *The Times* so they could keep up with war news. Felix, being Middle School, was only allowed the newspaper when the Upper School girls had finished with it. And usually she was still wading through hours of prep, unused to conjugating *être* and grappling with logarithms. Now she was paying the price.

'It's not so much that you're dim-witted, Felicity,' the maths mistress told her. 'Just behind.' Girls tittered around Felix in the classroom.

One Saturday morning in late January she finally managed to subdue the equations she'd been set and reclaimed the previous day's newspaper. She flicked through greasy pages, already thumbed by a dozen girls. And there was Isabel's wedding announcement in the court and social section. Felix blinked and read it again, all in black and white: Isabel was going to marry a Sir Reginald Barrington the following Wednesday afternoon.

Wednesday afternoon. Double hockey. Home matches for every year. Felix had missed so many PE lessons she doubted the teacher even knew she existed. For days each month she retreated to the sanatorium with a hot-water bottle and an aspirin. She had the perfect excuse. 'I've never known a girl suffer so badly with period pains,' Matron had told her. Matron was kind but the sports mistress already suspected a lack of team spirit.

David was sure to be at the wedding. She said nothing to anyone about the forthcoming nuptials – one of the advantages of not having any friends was that she could keep secrets. It was easy to feign hormonally-induced lack of appetite at lunch: a plate of mutton stew resembling a flooded cemetery. Felix put down her cutlery, and got up to scrape the meal into the swill bucket.

'You'll be given lines for that,' warned the prefect.

'Stomach cramps.'

'Merchant seamen died to bring you that meal.'

'No, an ancient ewe sacrificed herself.'

The prefect glowered.

Felix went upstairs to the sanatorium and presented herself to Matron. 'I'm feeling a little faint,' she said. 'May I have a hot-water bottle and an aspirin?'

Matron'd had a week of measles, her beds were full and her assistant had joined the Wrens. 'Help yourself.' She nodded towards the sink where rubber bottles dangled from a shelf like limp orange flatfish.

Once Matron had bustled out with a thermometer, Felix bolted for the stairs, only to spot her housemistress at the bottom talking to the French mistress. Damn. She watched the pair, praying they'd walk outside to see the match. The French mistress's hands waved and the housemistress's tongue made tsk-ing noises. Probably complaining about the rations again.

She walked back into Matron's office and pulled up the sash window. A drainpipe dropped to the flat roof above the bicycle shed. Nobody was around. Felix spat on her palms and swung out of the window, sliding down the pipe until her feet found the roof. A quick glance assured her she was unobserved. She rolled onto her stomach and lowered her feet over the side, dropping to the flowerbed below. A roar from the other side of the building told her the home side had scored. Good. Nobody'd be watching the gates.

As she walked out, a wad of banknotes crackled in her mackintosh pocket. Ever since she'd arrived at school, Phoebe's money had been hidden under her mattress. Thank heavens they hadn't found it. They might think she'd stolen it or was trading on the black market. And she couldn't exactly tell them how she'd come by the notes, could she?

She estimated she had until teatime before she was missed. If she couldn't find her in the sanatorium Matron would assume she had felt better and had gone out to support the school team like the good St Agatha's girl that she wasn't. The other girls would think she was still lying down with a hot-water bottle clutched to her stomach.

She'd hoarded her tuck money for emergencies and used it to buy a return to Paddington. There was enough left over for a sandwich from the station buffet to make up for the lunch she hadn't eaten. She sat in the scruffy carriage wishing she'd thought to take a mountaineering book with her. Train journeys were perfect for reading about the Himalayas without ignorant girls jeering at her.

The wedding ceremony was to be held in Holborn at a register office. From eavesdropping on the older St Agatha's girls Felix had discovered that this was usual practice where one of the parties had been married before. Interesting. Did Isabel mind not marrying in a church?

Felix couldn't afford a taxi and didn't know the London transport system well enough to trust herself to the labyrinth of the Tube, so she asked directions at Paddington and started to walk east.

A cold breeze rubbed at her face. She wished she'd worn her winter coat, rather than the mackintosh, but it'd be worth the discomfort to see David.

She hadn't visited London since the Phoney War. The newspapers hadn't shown the full devastation of the Blitz, how much of the city had been destroyed. She stood at the station entrance and blinked at the exposed upper storeys of houses and shops whose walls had been torn away.

'C'mon, miss, get a move on,' someone shouted at her. She followed the flow, hoping she was heading in the right direction. Young doctors stood smoking on the steps of St Mary's hospital, weary-eyed and pale. Fleets of ambulances waited outside. Felix walked on to Edgware Road, shocked at how many windows were boarded over, how filthy the brickwork was, how pockmarked the buildings from shrapnel. Housewives dragged weary children and empty shopping bags from one shop to another. She halted at

Marble Arch and asked a middle-aged woman the way to Holborn. She pointed out Oxford Street and told her to walk its full length.

Felix peered into shop windows, seeing only empty shelves or a few dusty goods. Perhaps London wasn't the golden city Isabel had longed for. Oxford Street seemed to stretch on for ever. At the cross-roads with Tottenham Court Road and Charing Cross Road she halted, convinced she was lost. She headed south, realized her mistake and stopped outside a tobacconist's, where a Canadian soldier told her to retrace her steps and turn right into New Oxford Street.

The registry office was in a side street off Holborn and she only found it after asking directions three times. The building presented a sooty façade to the public. It looked like the kind of place you'd visit to apply for an identity card or a ration book, rather than to be united in blissful matrimony. She'd always pictured Isabel marrying in a cathedral, with bells pealing, and fleets of shiny cars and carriages. A couple of taxis waited outside, drivers leaning against bonnets to smoke cigarettes. Someone had swept up the glass shards into a pile to form a path from the kerb to the steps, but dust coated the pavement. A soggy sheet of newspaper flapped in the gutter.

She straightened her mackintosh over her knees and walked up the steps, trying to look as though she were supposed to be there.

'Can I help, miss?' The man on the front desk didn't seem surprised to see a schoolgirl.

'The Parham-Barrington wedding?' she managed to mumble.

'Room 3, just down the corridor. If you hurry you'll just make it in time.' She had no intention of witnessing the nuptials – she wouldn't have put it past Isabel to have her thrown out. Instead she sat on a shiny wooden bench outside the door and opened the *Evening News* she'd bought at the station. Registry services obviously didn't last long; she'd only just started reading about a draught horse that had survived the bombing of Chiswick Dairy when the door creaked and she heard a low murmur. Isabel hurried out on her husband's arm. Felix had pictured her in a sweeping ivory gown, trimmed with jewels, but she wore a cream suit that finished just on her knee, with a little pillbox hat on her fair head. In her arms lay a bouquet of white lilies so perfect Felix thought they must be silk until their exotic scent reached her.

Isabel's face was pale like the little clouds that hovered offshore on summer afternoons. Felix scanned her for traces of guilt. She'd dallied with Johnson and Lew but now she was marrying this Sir Reginald. Nothing. But nor was Isabel's expression that of the radiant brides in the pictures, all sidelong loving glances and little blushes. Her eyes were lowered and her hand drooped limply on her new husband's arm. Felix remembered how Isabel had touched Lew's shoulder, how her face had glowed every time he'd looked at her.

She couldn't see David among the guests. She'd come all this way for nothing. Perhaps Isabel didn't want any reminders of her misadventures at the seaside? The Squire followed the bridal pair, looking paler away from his house, as though she were watching him in black and white. Felix didn't know any of the other guests, all of them middle-aged and stolid: not the glamorous friends Felix had pictured Isabel summoning. Their clothes looked drab in the grey light, despite the women's jewels. Nobody wore uniform. Felix felt cheated: where were the young officers and debutantes?

Her scrutiny turned to Isabel's husband. She'd always imagined someone like Errol Flynn or Laurence Olivier, but Sir Reginald was short, only just matching his bride for height. His lips were thin and his eyes very pale. Wispy hair was combed carefully over a high forehead. What a contrast with Lew's strong cheekbones and full mouth.

Where would they all go now? Surely there'd be a reception, war or not? She looked at her watch. Half past three. If she didn't leave now she'd miss her train and they'd kick up a stink at school.

She brushed past the lingering guests, careful to keep out of the Squire's sight, and went down the steps to the street. Nobody seemed to notice her. A taxi driver was opening the door for Isabel, her husband was motioning her inside. The car started and the bridal pair drove towards Felix. She opened the newspaper and hid behind it. As they passed she glimpsed Isabel, brow resting on one hand.

Felix watched the car until it turned the corner into Queensway and vanished. Phoebe's money seemed to weigh heavy in her pocket.

The Squire stood looking in the direction the taxi had taken, his face expressionless. Now was her chance, he'd always liked her and he'd been close to her father. But how on earth would she phrase what she wanted to tell him? He'd think she was mad, ranting on about coloured GIs on the beach. He'd tell her father, the school. They might think she'd stolen the money. They might call the police. If only David had been here. He would have known what to do with it.

Felix turned and trudged away, half tempted to toss the notes into a bombsite for the benefit of whoever found them.

Twenty-one

Minna

I frown. Something doesn't add up. 'When did Lew give you the banknotes?'

'On the beach.'

'Only you didn't mention it before.' Perhaps old age is playing tricks with Felix's memory.

She looks away. 'I must have forgotten. He thought the money would be safer with us. He knew we understood how important it was for Phoebe. And the baby – Louise, I mean.'

Louise. We keep coming back to this unseen woman.

'So what did you do with the cash?'

'Hid it under the mattress again when I got back to school.'

'By then Phoebe must have known something'd happened to Lew.'

'Lots of soldiers were missing in action for months. She must have been hoping he'd been taken prisoner and would reappear in due course.'

'Wouldn't she have contacted the base?' I ask.

'She may have done but they probably wouldn't have told her anything. She wasn't married or officially engaged to him. All the time I kept hoping I'd find a way of making contact.'

Felix 1944

The weeks limped by until the Easter holidays arrived. For the first time Felix travelled to Yorkshire – in an unheated train with a lavatory so noxious she crossed her legs and prayed the train wouldn't be delayed.

The house in Harrogate was larger than the one they'd left. It had electricity and looked out over an expanse of park, now dug over for vegetables for the war-effort.

'If your mother could have seen this . . .' Felix's father sat in a leather armchair and raised his eyebrows at the high ceiling with its moulded cornice.

'Mummy loved Fontwell.' The afternoon she'd died she'd begged Felix to open the curtains so she could look out over the valley towards the church. The candles were still blooming on the chestnuts and the hawthorn was out.

Her father nodded and a faraway look passed over his face. Felix could have kicked herself; talk about tactless. The doorbell rang.

'Ah.' He looked furtive. 'That will be Mrs Murdison.'

'Mrs Murdison?'

'One of the local matrons. She pops in.' He grimaced. 'Seems to think I'm not capable of looking after myself.'

'I'll put the kettle on.' The kitchen was warm and she felt overheated in her serge gymslip. None of her out-of-school clothes fitted her any more and they didn't have many clothing coupons. She wondered whether the trunk of Mummy's clothes had come north from Dorset. Perhaps she could wear one of her skirts or summer frocks? Or would that upset her father? She almost wished she was back at the hated St Agatha's, where she didn't have to worry about emotions and could seal herself in her own little world of memories. She'd taken home the wad of money, still hoping some way of getting it to Phoebe would present itself, however unlikely this seemed.

When she came back in, Mrs Murdison, a tall thin woman with round spectacles, was sitting on the sofa. 'So you're Felicity.' She looked her up and down.

'How do you do.' Felix shook the skinny hand.

'Nice for your father to have you at home to look after him.' Mrs Murdison gave an approving nod. 'He was telling me you were friendly with the Parhams when you lived in Dorset.' Her eyes glinted.

'Yes.'

'Isabel Parham certainly made a good marriage.'

Felix thought of Isabel's bridegroom and repressed a shudder.

Mrs Murdison leant forward. 'And you've heard about the baby?'

'No.' The doctor leaned forward.

'A good friend who lives in Belgravia told me Isabel – Lady Barrington – is expecting in July.' Mrs Murdison smiled behind her hand. 'Poor Isabel, she must know people have calendars.'

Her father gave an embarrassed glance at Felix. 'Isabel Parham was a patient of mine.'

Mrs Murdison turned pink. 'Oh, of course, you wouldn't be able to say anything, patient confidentiality and all that.'

'I think I'll go and change,' said Felix.

In her new bedroom she put on a cotton frock that was too short and too tight. Was calamity about to hit the Parham family? The night they'd cooked the fish on the beach – how long had Lew and Isabel been alone together after David had left? Lew had seemed so upright, so honourable.

Felix had heard girls at school muttering about mistakes their elder sisters had made. Girls thought they could get away with more these days, leading freer lives away from parents' watchful eyes. And their younger sisters listened in enthusiastically to conversations, passing on snippets when they returned to school. Felix had learned a lot in the last term. She knew less shame attached itself to one-night stands in wartime. Even girls from very smart homes did it – *especially* girls from very smart homes. They met officers at night-clubs and took them home to their parents' deserted townhouses.

And it wasn't as if Isabel were whiter than white. There'd been Johnson, too. That flush on his face when he looked at her. The expression on hers, contemptuous, knowing . . .

On the other hand, the baby could be Sir Reginald's. Just because you had a title didn't mean you were above doing that kind of thing. When exactly had Isabel first met her husband?

But Felix's mind kept returning to Lew.

She waited a few days to ask the question on her mind. Luckily she had a father who didn't mind frank discussion. 'If a negro man and a white woman had children, what colour would they be?'

He put down his paper. 'Good God, Felicity, whoever do you know in that situation?'

'Nobody. But there's no law against it, is there?'

'Unless you live in Germany or parts of the Deep South of America. Miscegenation, they call it. But mixed-race children are usually a rather attractive coffee colour.' He frowned at her. 'Be careful who you talk to about things like that. Some people are a little peculiar on the subject of race – they spout all kinds of rubbish.'

The birth announcement appeared while she was back in Harrogate for the summer holidays. 'BARRINGTON, Sir Reginald and Isabel, a son, Justin'. Would they have announced baby Justin's arrival if he was the colour of coffee? Perhaps they were going to brazen it out. Felix needed to see the baby. Why shouldn't she know? If it hadn't been for her and David, Isabel would never have met Lew.

'I'd like to go back to school two days early if you don't mind,' she told her father. 'A friend's asked me to stay. She lives in the country, near school.'

He looked up over his newspaper. 'Her mother hasn't written to me.'

'The letter must have got lost in the post.' Damn, she hated lying like this. But he'd never allow her to go to London.

He said nothing for a while. She crossed her fingers. 'Well I'm glad you're making friends. And you're old enough to be trusted to be sensible these days.'

She turned away quickly so he wouldn't see her cheeks reddening.

She'd salted away her pocket money since the last covert trip to London but not much had accrued. She had exactly four shillings. And she didn't have a clue where she was to stay when she got to London. Or how she was to eat. London grocers wouldn't accept her ration books.

The mention of flying bombs in the news next morning gave her an idea. Morning surgery had finished and she found her father sitting at his desk writing up his records.

'Are Londoners spending the nights down in the shelters again?' she asked in as casual a tone as she could manage.

'Suppose they must be.'

'Do they feed them down there?'

'I've heard rumours of tea and buns.'

Free food and accommodation in a shelter, with flying bombs overhead. Compared to staid old Harrogate with its stern-faced women queuing for their butter ration, it didn't sound bad. For the first time she was glad Mrs Derby was no longer around with her sharp questions. The housekeeper was now living in Bexhill with a dentist's family.

The doctor frowned, very slightly. 'Do take care, won't you, sweetheart? I'm sure Mrs Murdison would think me very reckless, letting you go off at a time like this.'

'What business is it of hers?' she muttered under her breath.

'Anyway,' he continued, 'I'm sure your friend's family will take good care of you. What's her name, by the way?'

'Phoebe Lewis.' She looked down at the carpet.

He shook his head at the card in front of him. 'You know, Mr Crabbe would do so much better if he'd only agree to eat a couple of pieces of fruit a day . . .'

Felix took a small suitcase with essentials in it, telling her father that her uniform and other things could be sent on for when school started officially.

'I'll miss you,' he mumbled on the platform, giving her a clumsy kiss and pushing a ten-shilling note into her hand. She tried not to wrinkle her nose at the smell of stale brandy on his breath. He'd bought her a *People's Friend* to read. 'Work hard at your algebra and Latin and make sure you drink at least two pints of water a day to keep your bowels open.'

The woman next to Felix clicked her tongue.

'See you at Christmas,' Felix mouthed at him through the

window, feeling a pang as the train pulled out of the station and his figure grew smaller. He'd already told her he wouldn't be able to have her in the middle of term. There was nowhere else she could go. She'd thought of asking if the Squire might put her up in Dorking for the short half-term holiday, but it seemed presumptuous when they hadn't heard from any of the family for so long.

As she came out of the station at King's Cross the streets seemed even more run-down than they had back in January. Her funds wouldn't run to a taxi so she headed south by foot to Belgrave Square. She didn't have an *A–Z* and hadn't liked to take her father's copy in case the theft alerted him to her plan, so she'd memorised the route. West along Euston and Marylebone Roads. South to Oxford Street and Mayfair. Over Green Park and past Buckingham Palace. Then make for Grosvenor Place and take one of the left turnings that should lead her to Belgrave Square.

This time she'd prepared herself for a long walk. To her disappointment the sirens didn't sound as she trudged along the shabby streets. She wished she'd bought something to drink and was grateful when she found a drinking fountain in Green Park. At Buckingham Palace she paused for a few minutes in the shade of a chestnut tree to gaze at the Standard flying on the flagpole and marvel at how close she was to the King and Queen. By the time she reached the battered splendour of Belgrave Square she was panting and the suitcase handle had carved a red welt on her palm.

She had no idea which house was Isabel's and sat on one of the doorsteps to work out a plan. If she'd had any forethought she'd have looked her up in a telephone directory but there were no public call boxes in sight and she couldn't face trekking off to a library or post office. Her head ached. What an idiot she'd been. What were the chances of actually seeing baby Justin? The best thing now would be to travel on to school. They'd be surprised to see her but she could think of some excuse for turning up early.

A delivery boy on a bicycle slowed and jumped off. When she asked him where the Barringtons lived he eyed her shabby sandals and Aertex shirt and nodded across the square. 'Red door.'

It was the middle of the afternoon. Would Isabel, or her nanny – surely Isabel would have a nanny – have completed the post-lunch walk everyone with babies seemed to take? Where would the infant be now – in a pram under a tree in the gardens in the middle of the square? Back in his nursery for the afternoon feed? She walked through the gardens, now planted with runner beans and potatoes, and peered at the red front door.

A siren screamed, and as though in answer a barrage opened up in St James's Park. The people in the gardens tutted and rolled their eyes, gathering up magazines, knitting and small children. Nobody seemed to hurry. So this was it – her first air raid. Perhaps she'd see some of those pilotless planes everyone was talking about. There'd be a shelter somewhere nearby. She looked for a sign. Nothing. She should ask. Little country mouse up for the day, not knowing how things worked. She spotted a girl of her own age tugging at the lead of a cocker spaniel. The girl looked at Felix's scuffed sandals and raised an eyebrow.

'Come on, Wilberforce, let's get you down into the cellar.'

The siren sounded more insistent now and the square had emptied.

Hearing an explosion a few blocks away, Felix ran down a side street, past a row of shops, looking for a shelter.

'We're all going to die!' A drunk leered out of a doorway, breathing spirits into her face. She ran into an alley, tripping on an uneven paving stone and throwing out an arm to right herself, clinging to her suitcase. From overhead came a rumble. Felix looked up and saw the silhouettes of the planes. She hurried back to the square. Surely Isabel would have to let her in?

A few streets away something thundered. A series of lesser crashes followed as masonry hit the ground. The pavement rocked.

She reached Isabel's red front door and sprang up to the doorbell, hammering on the knocker at the same time.

No answer.

Overhead engines whined closer and closer. She was going to be sick. She picked up her case and ran down the steps to the pavement and down again to the basement. Perhaps the family was sheltering below street level and couldn't hear her.

She put a hand on the basement door handle. The pavement shook again and an explosion cracked through Felix's ears. The door swung open and she fell inside, still clutching her suitcase. She slammed the door closed and dropped to her hands and knees, crawling over the black and white tiles until she reached the kitchen table.

Her heart stopped racing. A bomb might land on top of the house – she'd heard that no building could withstand a direct hit – but she felt safer. A tap dripped into an enamel sink, comforting, everyday. A clock ticked. Felix noticed that she'd scraped her right calf. The bleeding'd stopped now. Overhead a fresh wave of explosions rumbled. Then the whining engines faded. The barrage continued for a few more minutes before ceasing.

Another siren. They'd be coming out of shelters and cellars. What would Isabel say if her servants discovered Felix cowering down here like a frightened animal? She stood, shaking brick dust out of her hair, ashamed. She'd come to London to see the baby and that's what she'd jolly well do. And while she was here, why shouldn't she take a look at Isabel's posh house? Interesting to see if it was grand enough to make up for Sir Reginald.

She hid her suitcase under a pile of newspapers in the pantry. There'd be photographs of the infant somewhere in the house. If she was quick she could find one and get out before everyone came back.

Slipping off her sandals and holding them in one hand she tiptoed up the steps and into the hall. Most people had released their servants for war service, so she counted on there being only a couple of domestics in the house. This should be a quiet time of day for them: lunch was over and it was too early for afternoon tea. Or so she recollected from her observations of the staff at Fontwell Manor. She put her ear to the second door she came to. Silence. She opened it to reveal the drawing room, shuttered and gloomy. Two photographs on the Bernstein, both wedding portraits from that day at the register office.

She ran upstairs to the landing. One of the doors was slightly ajar – she caught sight of a dressing table laden with scent bottles and powder boxes. There on the dressing table, among the Mitsouko and Jean Patou, was a silver-framed picture of an infant, with pale skin and fair hair.

What a fool she'd been to imagine anything else. Looking down, she noticed that her grazed calf was bleeding again. She decided to see if Isabel had a clean handkerchief in her chest of drawers. She pulled open the top drawer. The edge of a leather-bound book protruded. Felix's heart fluttered as she pulled it out.

Going through someone else's diary was the very worst thing you could do. She thought about it for a few minutes. She wouldn't really read the entries, just see what period they covered.

The first date was only a month back.

Last night I picked up his razor. I told him I'd cut my wrists
if he didn't let me go to the seaside. Or the country, at least.
London is killing me. And he hates me. He told me not to
be hysterical. I scratched my skin with the blade and a little
blood came out. He grabbed the razor and slapped me
round the face. The doctor came and gave me something to
calm me down. I slept for nearly 24 hours and felt very sick
when I woke. Haven't seen Justin for two days. Nanny says I
upset him.

Felix skipped through the next few pages: people to dinner, an unsuccessful attempt to grow lettuces in the gardens across the road, Isabel couldn't bear to pull out the last of the roses from the small garden at the back of the house, they reminded her of Fontwell. There were excursions with nanny and baby to various London parks, and descriptions of the resumption of air raids. Isabel found the capital dingy but was relieved to find such a choice of wonderful hairdressers.

The last entry looked more interesting.

I tried to see her again. I took a photo of her grandson with me. But the windows were boarded up and the roof had a hole in it. Perhaps she's dead. Or injured. Why do I care? She rejected me. I should forget her, just as the Squire said. I wish I could live with him again. But Reginald says that wouldn't do – I'd be letting him down if I move out. Oh Lew. You were just a boy from the Georgia countryside, never been anywhere before you came to England . . . When I left Fontwell I picked the first man I could find. I was so sad, desperate, really. You told me to respect myself. You wouldn't even kiss me, said it wasn't right because you belonged to Phoebe. If things had been different perhaps I'd have become a land-girl as Felicity Valance suggested. Little Felix, with those blazing eyes and cat's grace. What a bloody mess. Why did I choose him? It's as though I found the one person most guaranteed to make me feel disgusted with myself, as though I was just as bad as my mother thought me. It makes me want to scream.

Felix slammed the book shut, dropped it onto the bedside table and ran out of the room. She retrieved her suitcase from the basement, before running out into the darkening street.

A policeman directed her to Paddington, assuring her it was unlikely there'd be another raid that night. 'Random day raids, that's what we get now,' he said. 'You'll be safe at Paddington. Find the WRVS ladies and they'll make you some cocoa. Maybe even find you somewhere to sleep.'

Twenty-two

Minna

Tom pops his head round the conservatory door. For the last hour I've been aware of him moving round the kitchen, washing up and tidying after the barbecue. And my conscience has pricked me. Not enough to tear me away from Felix, though. 'I'm turning in.' He nods to Felix. 'Nice to meet you.'

She fastens the buttons on her cardigan. 'I'm going too.'

'No.' My tone sounds strident. They both blink at me. 'Not just yet.' Felix sits again.

'I'll leave you to it.' Tom disappears.

'Sorry.' I feel my cheeks redden. 'I don't mean to sound pushy. But we seem to have missed a whole chunk out of the story.'

'It's painful.' Her sigh is just audible above the wind. 'It's something I've kept hidden for so many years. I never expected I'd have to revisit it.'

'Until Tom and I found the body.'

Our eyes meet. 'Yes. You became part of the story.' She clasps her hands. 'All right, I'll carry on from when we left Lew and Isabel together on the beach that lunchtime. We knew the MPs were still asking questions. I stayed home that afternoon.'

Felix 1943

The knock on the door came as Mrs Derby was pulling down the blackout. 'You get that for me, pet.'

The mismatched MPs stood on the doorstep.

'Can we come in, miss?' Hardy asked. Felix stood back to let them into the hall. 'This afternoon we heard more rumours of the negro soldier walking round this valley. You seen anything when you were off fishing?'

She shook her head. Mrs Derby came out of the kitchen. 'Her father's out. You shouldn't go talking to her without his permission.'

'This is serious stuff, ma'am. We need our soldier back.'

Mrs Derby shook her head. 'Good heavens, as I said, we've seen nobody that exotic in these parts for a good twenty years. Not since Bailey's circus. On Swanham Common, that was. Back in '23 they had a fakir who walked on a bed of nails.'

'Why do you want him back?' The words came out before Felix knew she'd said them. 'So you can torture him? Beat him up? Lock him in a cell?'

'Felicity!'

'It's all right, ma'am.' Hardy smiled at Felix. 'We don't mistreat our soldiers, miss. Whatever colour they are.'

'That's not what I've heard.'

They looked at one another. 'So you have seen him?'

Felix stared at the badge on his cap until the edges blurred. They couldn't torture *her*, could they? She was a British subject. The telephone rang.

'Well, I'll be blowed, they must have fixed the line.' Mrs Derby made for the study. 'You'll excuse me, might be a patient calling for the doctor.'

Laurel waited until she'd closed the door. 'Miss, every day that passes makes things more difficult for Private Campbell. You'd be doing him a favour.'

'Really you would,' Hardy said. 'You don't want him harshly punished.'

'Thought you said you didn't do that?' she flashed.

'Soldiers need discipline. Especially in wartime. But we need Private Campbell. He's too useful to harm by mistreatment. We need every man we've got right now.' Laurel's eyes claimed hers, wouldn't even let her blink. 'You know what's at stake here, miss.'

'You just make the black soldiers drive jeeps and cart supplies around. You don't even let them fight.'

His eyes stayed on hers. 'You think there's something ignoble about driving jeeps and supplies? You've seen what happens when armies run out of food? When men can't get kit they need?' He shook his head. 'Every soldier counts. Whether he's shifting boxes of dried milk or bayoneting Germans. In Italy American negroes are fighting Germans. It's not impossible for Private Campbell to do something similar. But he needs to come back.'

She clutched the banister.

'We won't hurt him. We'll have to discipline him, you understand that?' His gaze didn't falter. 'But the longer he stays away the harder it will be for him.'

'He was on his way back. He hurt his ankle. It was an accident.' She was gabbling now.

Laurel nodded. 'We know he's a good man.' His voice was low, respectful.

'I promised I wouldn't tell.'

'It's for his own good.' Hardy folded his arms. Felix heard the clock tick on the wall.

'This is your chance to be a true friend to him,' Laurel said. 'Think of the career he might have with us. Think what he's throwing away.'

'He's on the beach.' She heard the words as though they were coming from someone else. 'In a cave at the far end.'

He smiled. 'Thanks, missy.'

'You promise you won't harm him?'

'I promise.' He stepped forward, put his hand on her shoulder. 'You're a good kid.'

Felix watched the door close, spun round, ran towards the kitchen.

'Where are you going?' Mrs Derby came out of the study.

'To feed David's owls.' Felix flung herself out of the back door, running as she'd never run in her life. She had to tell Lew what she'd done, reassure him and David it was the right thing. The lights of the MPs' motorbike preceded her. She'd cut through the woods, reach the cliff path before them.

Twenty-three

Minna

'You told them?' I pray I don't sound accusatory. I can understand Felix's choice. The military police were on Lew's tracks, it would only have been hours, a day at most, before they caught him anyway.

She nods. 'God help me.'

'Seems sensible enough to me. Especially as the weather was closing in.' I frown as I work it out. 'So the police got to the beach and Lew tried to escape?'

She says nothing.

'So it wasn't your fault.'

Still she's silent.

'You did what you did for the best.'

Her head drops. 'David never saw it like that.'

'He blamed you?'

'He hated me for what I did.'

'He was only a boy.'

She lifts her face and I see how the memory of David's blame haunts her. 'He didn't speak to me again for years. Even though I tried to help Lew out of the water.'

Now I'm really thrown. 'You saw it happen?'

A nod. She reaches for her glass of water and gulps it down like a defendant on the stand who's broken down under cross-examination.

'I don't understand why you kept quiet about it.'

Her hand clenches the glass. When she looks at me I see a scared girl, not a woman in her seventies.

'I was frightened.'

Felix 1943

Felix's heart pounded so fast it seemed it would burst out of her throat. She dashed across the beach, shingle flying up to sting her calves. Laughter reached her. 'Lew!' she yelled. The voices paused. Lew's head poked over the top of the rocks. The expression on his face told her he knew this was serious.

'What's going on?' Isabel's head appeared over the rocks, her hair lying loose over her shoulders like a pale silk scarf, blinking as though she'd woken up. But her eyes were sharper than Felix had ever seen them before. 'Someone's coming, aren't they?'

'The MPs. They'll be here in a few minutes.'

Isabel was watching her, eyes narrowed. 'You told them, didn't you? You sneaked on him?'

'It's all right.' Felix looked at Lew. 'They've promised to treat you fairly.'

'You little bitch.' Isabel's voice was icy. She gave Lew's shoulder a push. 'Run.'

'No, stay, it's better that you let them take you,' Felix pleaded. Lew looked from one to the other.

'Why'd you tell 'em, missy?'

'They said it would be all right. If you come back with them now, they won't treat you badly.'

Lew frowned. 'Maybe you're right. They'll catch me sooner or later.'

'They say you should look to the future, to what you might do in the army.' Felix grabbed at his arm. 'Think about it, Lew.'

'I still think you should run.' Isabel sounded desperate. 'Hide out for a while. Perhaps the Squire could help get you out of the country, to Ireland or somewhere.'

'Ireland?' Felix laughed. 'Are you completely crazy? What would Lew do in *Ireland*?'

Further up the beach shingle crunched. 'They're here!' David said.

'Go!' Isabel said.

Felix saw pinpricks of light: the beams of the MPs' torches.

Lew scrambled at the rocks behind them, a fearful instinct suddenly seeming to propel him away from the police as though he were a rabbit evading terriers.

'Don't go!' Felix clambered after him. 'It'll be fine. They promised.' She could see Lew's shadowy figure ahead of her on the boulders but he was already scrambling away from her, moving faster than she could. Then he vanished. She stopped and stared at the darkness. Feet clattered on the rocks beside her. David pulled her down. 'Where is he?' he hissed.

'He just disappeared. One minute I saw him, the next he was gone.'

Isabel's face scowled at her. 'Those cops are right behind us. Get down.'

Felix raised her head. 'No, we should—'

'Shut up, won't you!' Isabel grabbed Felix's torch and turned it off.

Behind them snatches of Laurel and Hardy's conversation reached them: '. . . thought I saw a light . . .'

'. . . didn't see nothing . . .'

Now David was holding Felix down, too, clenching her arm so it hurt. He put a finger to his lips. Felix heard boots scrunching nearer and nearer. They must have reached the cave now.

'Anyone there?'

She tried to wriggle free but David held her tight.

'Don't say a word,' he hissed. The wind had dropped, she could hear what they were saying.

'Shine the light around the rocks a bit,' Hardy called.

'There's some kind of a cave in here.'

'And look – fish bones.'

'So the little girl was telling the truth about our nigger?' Laurel said.

'Yup. But the bird's flown.'

'Damn him.' They poked around for a few minutes.

'Let's get out of here.' Hardy sounded weary.

157

Felix heard them scrunch away.

'*When it rains five days and the skies turn dark as night*,' Laurel sang as they went. '*Then trouble's takin' place in the lowlands at night.*'

'Didn't have you down as a blues man . . .' Their voices faded.

Felix managed to squeeze herself free. 'Where's Lew? Can you see him?'

'I don't know.' David pulled her up. 'Come on.'

'Give me back my torch,' she scowled at Isabel, who thrust it at her.

Her clothes were sodden, cold and heavy like chains around her body. She shivered and followed. 'Lew! Lew! They've gone, where are you?'

David scaled a large rock and stopped. 'There he is! In the water!' David vanished over the other side.

'He can't swim. Oh God!' Isabel put a hand over her mouth.

'Hang on.' Felix clambered over the wet stone, plimsolled feet curling their way into holes and fissures. No way of telling where seaweed lay, slippery and treacherous. She slipped several times, only regaining her balance by clutching at the rock, tearing her hands on sharp edges. Her feeble blackout torch was next to useless, she stuffed it into her pocket. Waves roared at her, their coldness thumping the breath out of her lungs. Her lips tasted of salt. She saw David, leaning over a large dark pool, stretching out and grabbing at a formless black shape below. He turned his head slightly as she half scrambled, half fell to him.

'He's heavy, I can't hold him.' She threw herself down beside him and took hold of Lew's sodden coat.

'Don't let yourself slip in, missy,' he shouted. A mist seemed to cover his eyes and he shivered.

'I won't, Lew.'

'You think you're falling, you let go, you hear?' But his words were faint now, hardly audible over the roar of the waves.

She nodded. 'I'm sorry, Lew, I'm so sorry.'

'Not your fault.' A wave broke into the pool and onto him and he slumped down beneath the surface. She could only see his cap now.

'Pull him out!' Isabel screamed behind Felix.

'He's heavy.' She reached down further and managed to put her hands under Lew's arms, taking some of his weight from David.

'After three. One, two, three,' David said, his voice strained.

Lew's torso started to rise from the water. Another wave broke and lifted him up towards them. Felix's arms trembled with the strain. Together they wrenched him out of the water and laid him on the flat rock, both panting from the exertion. Behind them Felix heard a moan – Isabel had reached them.

David dropped his head to Lew's chest. He listened for a moment then raised his head very slowly. 'He's gone.'

'He can't have!' Isabel screamed.

'He was under too long.'

Felix put a hand to Lew's neck and felt for a pulse under the cold skin. She sprang up. 'I'm going to get my father, he'll save him.'

David pulled her back. 'It's too late.'

She couldn't bear to look at Lew's face. 'We can't leave him like this,' she whispered.

'He's dead.'

'No.' He couldn't be dead, he couldn't. Not after he'd sat on the sand with them and told them to enjoy life. Not after he'd drawn the cormorant and sung to them of cornfields and the moon.

David pulled at her shoulder. 'Come on.'

She touched Lew's cheek, just to check, but it felt like stone on winter mornings. 'We have to tell someone.'

'Let the sea take him.'

'He's got family in America, a mother, a father; they'll never know what happened to him.' Felix pictured an old dark-skinned woman waiting for a telegram, a letter, jumping up each time someone knocked on the door, hoping they brought news of her son.

'Shame you didn't think about that before you blabbed,' Isabel spat.

'We've got to tell them what happened.'

'They'll see his dog-tags and track down his family. If they find us with him we're all in trouble,' David said. 'They'll think you came down here to warn him they were coming.'

'They already know we gave him food and shelter.' She let him hoist her to her feet.

'Isabel might have done a little more than that.'

'Shut up.' Isabel was shivering. 'Shut up, both of you.'

'We should take his money,' David said. 'He meant it for Phoebe. If they find it on him they won't know it was for her.'

'How can you even think of that now?' Isabel hissed.

'He's right.' Felix stooped down and fumbled in Lew's jacket, finding a bundle of notes, damp but still recognizable, in one of the pockets. 'It's the only thing we can do for him.'

The wind calmed, soughing instead of roaring, and the clouds moved to reveal a silver slash of light above the sea's dark mass, as though heaven were opening to hurl down retribution on Felix. She thought of Lew's body bobbing as the waves broke into the pool and doubled over, retching. David pulled Isabel up; they were already moving away, leaving Felix alone on the shingle. She opened her lips to beg them to wait for her, then closed them again.

Twenty-four

Felix 1943

Felix came down to breakfast next morning at half past eight, praying her father would have finished his meal.

'Felicity?' She cursed silently. 'You're up very late, child. Did you sleep badly?'

'Yes.'

Her father's eyes were on her, concerned and kind, as though she were one of his patients. 'I'm going to increase your iron tablets. You may need extra now you're entering puberty.'

She looked down at her shoes, still scuffed from scrabbling over rocks last night.

'Mrs Derby said you went flying out of the house yesterday evening. Like you had dogs on your heels, she said.'

'Forgot to give the owls their water.' How quickly lies came to her these days.

Someone pounded at the door at the same time as the telephone rang.

'Good Lord, is there never a moment's peace? It can't be Mrs Fuller, I only saw her yesterday. Mr Day's bunions, perhaps? Mrs Gant's septic finger?'

Mrs Derby was answering the telephone. 'Hang on, I'll fetch the doctor,' they heard her say.

Felix stood up. 'I'll open the door.' He nodded thanks as he rose to take the call.

Laurel and Hardy stood outside.

'Oh.'

'Morning, miss. We need to ask you a few questions.' Hardy looked tired.

'Were you on the beach last night?' Laurel asked, his eyes boring into hers.

She shook her head.

'See, we went down there looking for our man after you told us he was there. We thought we saw a light but we found nobody.'

'Perhaps he heard you coming and ran away.'

'Over the rocks?'

She shrugged.

Laurel shook his head. 'That crazy devil – beggin' your pardon, miss. He sure didn't mind risking his neck.'

'I just wanted him to be safe,' she said.

'We know that, missy.' Laurel's hand touched hers. 'He brought it on hisself.'

She couldn't speak.

'We'll keep looking. You take care of yourself.'

She heard her father opening the parlour door. 'I will.' She forced a smile and closed the door.

'Who was that?'

'MPs.'

'Still looking for their man?' Her father sighed. 'You'd think they'd try somewhere else, he's obviously not here.' If only she could tell him what had happened, have him make it right for her.

'I must make my house-calls. At least the phone's working again.' He yawned. 'Last night was hard. Been up since two in the morning.' He picked up his bag and patted her on the head.

Had he been out with a patient? She hadn't heard him leave, but when she'd finally slept it had been a deep, exhausted slumber. Mrs Derby took the broom out of the cupboard and started to sweep the hall. No chance of leaving the house unquestioned and Felix couldn't bear to talk to anyone except David. Surely she could make him understand why she'd told Laurel and Hardy? She ran upstairs, opened her sash window and swung herself out onto the wisteria in the familiar fashion. One of these days she'd be too heavy, already she could see how the branches were pulling away from the masonry. But, of course, by the time that happened she wouldn't be living here any more. Her legs were so leaden and cold she could hardly move them across the lawn to the drive. It took her nearly

162

twenty minutes to reach the Manor. She paused at the gates and decided to go to the back door, in case the MPs were still hanging around.

She knocked softly and footsteps came towards her. David's eyes narrowed as he saw it was her. 'What do you want?'

'I came to explain.'

He folded his arms.

'They said it was for the best, the longer he stayed out the worse he'd be punished. I didn't think it would end like that.'

'You obviously didn't think at all,' he said.

'If he hadn't run away from them he'd still be alive now.'

'You mean it's my fault?'

'No!' She heard the wildness in her own voice. 'Of course not.'

Someone called inside the house. 'I've got to go, Isabel's ill. The shock.' His expression made it clear he blamed her for that as well.

'Has she said . . .?'

He shook his head. 'But they just sent for your father. She tried to take an overdose. The Squire's terrified he'll have to get her certified.'

Felix looked over her shoulder, even though she knew her father would go to the front door.

David seemed to find it hard to meet her eye. 'Felix,' he said at last, very quietly. She stared at him, knew what he was going to say, knew she couldn't bear it. 'We need to stay apart.'

'Why?'

'We need to keep our heads down, make them forget about us. If they find Lew's body, it's going to be hard to explain what happened. There'd be an inquest. We'd be questioned in court.'

'Suppose Sam talks?'

'He just thought we were fishing down there. He never saw Lew.'

'He knew we were leaving him out.' She remembered the boy's sullen face.

'Sam won't blab.'

Unlike you, she finished for him.

'You must never, ever, say a word about Lew. Promise you won't?'

She lifted her gaze. 'But the police already know I was with him.'

'But they don't know all of it. They don't know that Isabel was down on the beach, too.'

'I promise.'

'Make sure you keep your word this time.'

'David!' The Squire's roar filled the passageway. 'Come and get some water for Isabel, won't you?'

'I've got to go.' He bit his lip. 'I thought you were such a good friend.'

Her lips opened to plead, but not a sound came out. He turned away. She walked back towards the gates, crushing dead leaves under her feet

Twenty-five

Minna

The storm is dying away now, leaving a pitch-black sky, no moon, no stars, just darkness. I switch on the lamp. I'm not wearing a watch and I've no idea what the time is, but it must be late. Above me I hear water running through pipes. Tom is getting ready for bed. I can't bear to be left alone with him. Felix mustn't leave me.

'David was incredibly unfair.'

'Probably no more than I deserved.'

'Hardly. You couldn't have foreseen any of it.' I can't see the expression in her eyes. 'And you kept quiet about Lew?'

'I didn't say anything. I tried to forget. Sometimes I succeeded. But then he started turning up – mostly at night, in my dreams, but sometimes I thought I saw him in broad daylight.'

Once or twice over the past few months I've run in from the garden, convinced I hear Benjie crying inside, so I don't see anything odd in what she says.

'It became quite distracting.'

Felix 1944

Lew sat on the desk in front of Felix and started singing about the moon rising high. Although she tried hard to block him, the deep notes blanked out the teacher's explanation of the Latin on the blackboard.

'Perhaps Felicity Valance would like to explain the ablative case to us as she doesn't need to listen to the lesson.' The scowling teacher folded her arms, raising a thin eyebrow at Felix. The class sniggered. Felix felt her cheeks burn.

Go away, she told Lew silently. *I can't deal with you* and *Latin*. He nodded and slid off the rock into the water, easy as a seal.

Felix tried to shake off the shingle she felt under her feet and block her ears to the hiss of the waves, so loud she almost wondered the rest of the class couldn't hear it.

When the lights were switched off at night Lew returned.

'You make a terrible racket at nights,' the prefect told her next morning, face tight with disapproval. 'Calling out and moaning. Perhaps you need to see Matron, Felicity.'

'Sorry.' Felix liked Matron and her collection of pills and potions, but she couldn't imagine the stout middle-aged woman in the white apron would have anything to take away guilt.

Occasionally her father wrote suggesting she bring another girl home for the holidays.

'I prefer coming home by myself,' she replied. 'I have enough of them during term-time.'

'You're not enjoying boarding school much, are you?' he asked in his next letter.

'I don't mind history and geography.'

You had to be careful what you wrote because the teachers read their letters before they posted them.

'I thought it was for the best,' he wrote back. 'I'll think about alternatives, but it may take some time.'

Her heart gave a thump of joy, snatching at the prospect of release.

When she next went home she noticed he'd stopped drinking. The whites of his eyes, which she remembered as yellowed or blood-shot – sometimes both – cleared. She often heard him whistling in the mornings. At first she put it down to the success of the D-Day landings; everyone looked brighter after June 1944. But as the war dragged on without the prospect of an end her father's good humour continued. A woman? If the new love of his life was Mrs Murdison she'd have to run away from home.

A week after her return he sent her out with half a crown and the ration books to find something for tea. 'There's someone I'd like you to meet.'

Felix tramped the streets of Harrogate in search of cake, finally settling for some scones in a baker's shop half a mile the other side of town. She went back home to the kitchen to put them on a plate and knocked on the drawing-room door, heart pounding.

A small plump woman with a wide smile sat on the sofa beside her father. 'Lovely scones!' she said. 'Ooh, what a treat.'

Rebecca Wheatley, who became Felix's stepmother in 1945, brought her closer to her father than they'd been since Felix's mother died. So close, Felix sometimes wondered about confiding in her about Lew. But she'd made her promise to David and she intended to keep it.

Becky moved into their house in Harrogate and it became a changed place, softened with bright rugs and carpets she had brought from her old house, and repainted in warm colours. 'I'm sorry to say this,' she said, stripping faded brown wallpaper from Felix's bedroom, 'but like most men your father's completely clueless about interiors.' She sat back on her heels to examine the exposed wall, brow furrowed. 'I thought lavender paint for this room. And how about some new curtains?'

'We'd never get the fabric, would we?'

'We can take up the pair I brought with me from my old dining room. They're plum velvet. Lovely.'

Two years passed. Her father was muttering about Fontwell. The enemy was finally defeated and now he wanted his house back. High ceilings and electricity weren't sufficient to dampen his nostalgia for the valley. 'Yorkshire's all very well, but it was only ever going to be temporary,' he explained to Becky.

'I wouldn't mind living on the south coast,' she said. 'I went to school in Poole.'

'Won't you miss this?' Felix glanced at the newly painted walls.

Becky shrugged. 'Easy enough to start again.'

'And you'd like to move back home, wouldn't you sweetheart?' Her father turned to Felix.

She forced a smile.

Becky was watching her. 'You know, I think Felix needs time in London.'

'London?' The doctor made it sound like Gomorrah.

'It's perfectly safe now. You'd like it, wouldn't you, sweetheart?'

'Yes.' Felix's enthusiasm for the idea surprised her. 'Perhaps I could do a course or something.'

'I wanted you to go to university,' her father said.

'I want to work. Secretaries earn good money.'

He looked at her for a few moments. 'I remember how you loved those old mountaineering books. I used to dream of sending you to Switzerland, to finishing school. You'd have been able to ski and climb. But the war put a stop to that.'

'The war put a stop to a lot of things.' She sounded terse.

He looked at Becky and shrugged. 'It's your decision.'

Twenty-six

Felix 1947

Felix's right hand lurched at the windowsill and missed. For a second she thought she'd lost her grip and braced herself for the twenty-foot drop to the street. What would her father say when he discovered she'd plummeted to her death just because she'd forgotten her front door key again? How damn silly could you get? Her left hand clutched the drainpipe and she retained her position on the wall. She moved her right foot up a brick, inserting the toes into the gap where the concrete had been blown away. Thank goodness for wartime masonry damage.

Now her fingers could reach the sill. She let out a breath. She moved the pot of geraniums to one side. A quick rest and she'd pull herself in.

Below her, footsteps rounded the corner. The landlady. Blast it. Another roasting if she was caught climbing in. No time to catch her breath. She willed her arms to pull her up and wriggled through the window, landing head first on her bed. Thank God. She glanced out of the window. A young man stared up at her. Her eyes widened.

'Felix by name and Felix by nature. What on earth are you doing?'

'Locked myself out.' She was surprised she could speak.

'And you don't believe in knocking on doors?'

She grinned at him. 'The landlady gets ratty.' She remembered that Mrs Auden had sharp ears and winced. But no reproving head appeared out of the ground-floor window.

'How did you do it?' David asked.

'Climbed up on to my bike seat,' she nodded at her bicycle, leaning against the wall. 'Then onto the ground-floor windowsill. Onto the porch and across to this window.' Were they really talking like this, like friends? He hated her, didn't he?

'A cat couldn't do better.'

'Come up.' She expected him to make excuses.

'Love to.'

She closed the window and leant against the peeling wallpaper until her heart stopped racing.

London, two years after the end of the war, still surprised her with its rubble and scorched bricks. If anything, its inhabitants looked even more threadbare and weary than they had when she'd made her secret visit to Isabel's house. Felix had now settled into the lodgings Becky had organized for her in a house off Goodge Street.

'It's Fitzrovia,' Becky told her, looking proud. 'A literary area. You'll probably meet poets and novelists.' A couple of weeks at her new address were enough to show Felix the reputation was exaggerated. Jowett Street gave off a cheerless air – dustbins left out on the pavement, window-boxes grown straggly and dusty. The red-bricked Victorian villas and mansion blocks were handsome enough, or would have been if anyone bothered to polish the windows and sweep the steps. But even Mayfair and Belgravia looked down-at-heel these days, with their boarded-up windows and missing iron railings. The war was over, but London seemed unable to throw off its gloom. David knocked on the door and she opened it.

'It's been a long time.' Her voice sounded shaky. She prayed David didn't notice.

'Too long.'

'Come in.' The warmth of the rooms brought out the peppery smell of the geraniums on her windowsill, her Bronnley soap and the whiff of milk she should have washed down the sink this morning.

'Sorry, it's such a mess,' she said. 'Never seem to have enough time to tidy up.' She could see him frowning at the heap of newspapers on the floor and her unwashed breakfast crockery on the table. 'Just let me sort this out.' She picked up the tangle of coral-pink underwear and stockings from the living-room floor.

He walked to the grimy window and looked out. 'I walk down this street quite often when I'm in town.'

'I'm doing a secretarial course.'

'How do you like that?'

She wrinkled her nose. 'Some of the girls are fun. I heard you were studying medicine, are you enjoying it?' Now they sounded like people who'd only just met.

His face lit up. 'Loving it. And what's really fun is that a great friend from school is reading Greats at the same college.'

'I always thought all that animal-tending would lead to great things.'

'It was useful for teaching me basic medical and anatomical stuff.'

'What happened to your animal hospital?' She'd often wondered.

His face closed in. 'I released the owls in Surrey. Never saw them again. The hedgehog died on the journey, dehydrated. The rabbit was still too lame to release so I took it to Harrow in a hutch. One night someone let it out for a joke. The housemaster's Jack Russell killed it.'

'You must've hated that place.' Felix couldn't imagine how he could bear it. She'd loathed St Agatha's and she'd always figured herself the tougher of the pair.

'I detested every second of it, at first. If it hadn't been for making friends with Charlie – he's the chap who went on to Cambridge with me – it would have been grim. But Charlie's such good fun.'

'I went to Isabel's wedding. I thought you might be there.' His eyes widened. 'She didn't see me, I hid behind a newspaper.'

He shook his head and a grin spread across his face. 'You've got some guts, Felix.'

'I ran away from school. They didn't even notice I'd gone.' She told him how she'd slunk into school at supper time, taking advantage of the jubilation over a sports victory to reach her dormitory unobserved.

The grin had become a beam. 'I take my hat off to you. I got tonsillitis that week and ended up in hospital. Else I'd have been at the register office, too.'

'Shame,' she said lightly. She wouldn't tell him about the wad of notes she'd taken to Holborn with her. She didn't want to talk about Isabel and her affairs; she wanted David to talk about them, about Fontwell.

'What did you think of Sir Reginald?'

She struggled for diplomatic words.

He laughed. 'I feel the same way. I'm not sure the marriage is terribly happy.'

'Let's have a drink,' Felix said. 'I've got some bottles of beer somewhere. Don't tell my landlady.'

'Promise.'

She retrieved them from the cupboard while he sat on the sagging sofa she'd tried to disguise with an old shawl, à la Becky. 'This is cosy.' He almost sounded envious.

'Sorry your glass is chipped.' She found a mug for her own drink as she only had one glass.

'I hadn't noticed.' He took a long sip. 'This is great, just what I needed.' His voice dropped. 'Felix?'

'What?'

'I'm sorry about what I said to you that terrible night in Fontwell.' His eyes seemed to plead with her. 'I hope you can forgive me.'

Her cheeks burned. 'Expect I deserved it.'

'No, you were right to think Lew would be safer handing himself in. I don't know why I felt so strongly that he should make a run for it. He suddenly looked so scared, like a hare running from dogs.' He shrugged. They fell silent.

'The MPs seemed like decent men.' She could still see Laurel and Hardy's faces.

'I'm sure they were. If they'd arrested Lew they'd have done their duty, nothing less. I was awful, saying what I did. Must have been the strain of the moment. And worry about Isabel.' He finished his beer and gave her a sidelong look. 'Are we friends again?'

'Of course.' She extended her hand, hoped her wretched eyes wouldn't let her down.

He squeezed her palm. 'Thank God.' He sighed. 'Let me buy you supper to celebrate. There's a Cypriot place a few blocks away that isn't too awful.'

Out to dinner. She'd been in London for months now and had never been out to a restaurant, except the Lyons Corner Houses she sometimes visited at lunchtime. Her mind went to her wardrobe and the very few garments hanging in it. Felix had discovered a love of clothes, but it wasn't one she could do much to fulfil while rationing and shortages continued.

'It's all very casual.' He hadn't lost his ability to read her mind and put her at ease.

'I'll just change.' Her stomach was doing strange things. This was David, childhood friend, the boy who'd seen her muddy and dishevelled. Why did she feel she had to brush her hair and put on lipstick?

'Take your time.' He leaned back and picked up the sepia studio photograph of her mother. Hard to believe she'd been dead for nine years now. Felix could close her eyes and be back in her parents' bedroom kissing her goodbye, clutching her father while Mummy's breaths grew more laboured, and finally stopped. At least she'd missed the war; Martha would have hated the death and upheaval.

Felix banished the image and found a clean blouse in a heap beside her bed.

As they walked to the restaurant in Charlotte Street she stole looks at him. His hair was still the rich chestnut she remembered from childhood and his smile was as warm, but she doubted his pockets would now contain birds' skeletons and bits of string. She could imagine what a hit he'd be with the clever and worldly-wise Cambridge females. He probably had a host of girlfriends studying unimaginably learned subjects. David led her past a row of boarded-up cafes and stopped outside the restaurant. He held open the door for her, exchanging pleasantries with the manager, who seemed to know him well.

'So, are you down for the weekend?' she asked as they were shown to a table in the corner.

He paused. 'That's right.'

'What a coincidence you coming down the street like that.'

He fiddled with the cutlery. 'I asked your father where you lived. I thought it was time we made it up.'

'I'm glad you did. Tell me about school.'

'I was a basket case when I arrived.'

'Over Lew?'

He glanced over his shoulder. 'Yes.' He shook his head at himself. 'Crazy, isn't it? I still expect the police to knock on my door and ask why the hell I didn't report his death.'

'So do I.' *And Lew sits on my bed sometimes*, she'd been about to add. But she didn't want David to think she was going daft.

'Funny, we've lived through a world war but a single death pre-occupies us.'

'My friend Charles often says the particular matters more than the universal.' David's eyes took on a dreamy aspect. 'Like war babies – everyone's read about illegitimacy rising since '39, but it's just figures. Till you think of particular children.' He bit his lip.

She put down her fork. 'What?'

'Phoebe was pregnant, wasn't she? That's why he was trying to get the money to her. Say the child was born in spring '44, it would be about three now.'

So that's what Lew had meant by women's trouble. How dense she'd been. Lew had fathered a child, but it was Phoebe's, not Isabel's. She gave a short laugh. 'Funny, Lew was so . . . gentlemanly, in so many ways.' She remembered him talking about his preacher uncle.

'Lew was a good chap, but he was a soldier in wartime, far from home with a girl who adored him. English girls went crazy over the coloured GIs. Hard to resist the attention, I'd imagine.'

Felix chewed her lamb, which had the texture of carpet-backing, and sipped the thin wine. Phoebe would be struggling to bring up her child, not knowing what had become of its father. How had she managed without Lew's money? Felix decided to steer the conversation elsewhere. 'Do you have any idea what kind of medicine you might like to do when you're qualified?'

David's face relaxed. 'Not sure. General practice, perhaps, like your father. But Charles says I should think about specializing.'

Charles seemed to have views on many subjects.

The wine didn't taste so bad after the first few mouthfuls. She held out her glass for a top-up. 'Daddy's always enjoyed general practice, though the National Health Service is changing the way he works.'

David rolled a morsel of bread between his fingers. 'I like the idea of no money changing hands between doctor and patients.'

'Father says there were always ways of looking after poor patients. Look at how he treated Sam's mother. Not that he could save her in the end.' Mrs Fuller had died a year or so after they'd moved away from Fontwell. But Felix didn't want to think about Sam losing his mother, not on an evening like this.

'You heard about Sam?'

'No.' A coldness in her chest told her bad news was coming.

'After his mother died they sent him and Philip, you know, his brother, on a liner to America.'

Felix knew what he was going to tell her. 'U-boats?'

'They were so unlucky – most of the attacks had stopped by then.'

'But Sam . . .?' Her eyes were covered in a film.

'His brother saw him in the water after the boat sank, but he lost sight of him when they were pulled into lifeboats. When a rescue ship picked them up nobody could find him.'

She bit her lip. 'I never taught him to swim. He kept begging me. I just put him off all the time.'

David's hand pressed hers. 'The water was freezing – it would have made no difference. And they had lifejackets. He probably died from injuries.'

She shook her head. 'All the same. I should have taught him.' Felix abandoned her lamb.

'You're not eating.' His eyes were sorrowful.

She turned to her salad. It was a relief to see lettuce – a rare treat in the capital. But she could only pick at it.

David was watching her. 'Would you like a pudding? They do something here that's almost like a pre-war Greek baklava.'

'Almost?' She made an effort to respond to his concern.

'Actually it's like lino covered in axle oil.'

She felt a wave of homesickness for Mrs Derby's bread-and-butter pudding or Becky's syrup roll, smothered in custard. 'Perhaps just a coffee?'

He walked her back through the light streets, blackbirds singing their hearts out in the budding trees. 'Remember Fontwell on nights like this?' she said.

He sighed. 'May was the best time there; May, or early June when the leaves were so green they were almost decadent.'

'We keep talking as though the place doesn't exist any more.'

'Perhaps it doesn't when we're not there.'

They fell silent. She was remembering how at this time of year dog roses in the hedgerows bloomed overnight, how late irises in Miss Foss's garden nodded their heads in the breeze. How the whole valley smelled of freshly cut grass. How the sea still felt wintry this early – you had to wait until July or even August to be comfortable swimming. An image of Sam struggling in cold, inky waters, thrust itself before her and she swallowed. Another ghost.

Outside her lodgings David stopped and placed his hands on her shoulders, drawing her towards him. 'I miss you so much,' he whispered. 'I've never forgiven myself for what I said to you.'

Something was happening to her body, she felt weightless, light-headed. And every vein in her body seemed to tingle. She raised her chin. He kissed her lightly on the lips, dropped his hands, then grabbed her round the waist.

'Why the hell not?' he muttered as though he were justifying himself. There was nothing light about the second kiss.

*

Summer passed. When Trinity term ended David moved back to Dorking, taking the train up at least twice a week to see her. Meanwhile he waited to see whether he'd got into medical school, or whether National Service would claim him first.

Her secretarial course ended but she stayed in London. 'I need to do some job-hunting,' she wrote to her father. 'Better to be on the spot really, in case something comes up suddenly.'

She'd made a friend, Maureen Smith, a companion for lunchtime strolls in the park and mid-week trips to the cinema. If David wasn't in town they sometimes went dancing at the Hammersmith Palais on Saturday nights. If only she could bring David here, but he preferred to stay in her rooms or go to one of the shabby restaurants in Soho or Fitzrovia.

'You've never asked me up to Cambridge,' Felix said one humid July evening when they'd returned from the Cypriot restaurant. 'I'd love to try punting. And don't they have wonderful balls?' She'd seen photographs of the university, thought it looked more beautiful than any other town she'd ever seen.

'Such a romantic.' He twisted a bit of her hair.

'You sound surprised.'

'There's still a part of me that thinks of you fondly in shorts and Aertex shirt.' He ran a hand over her stockings. 'These are beautiful.'

'Took me months to get them. I had to put my name on a waiting list.'

'They're very glamorous, but I almost prefer you in your tomboy kit.'

'Certainly easier for climbing trees.' But she felt a flash of disappointment he didn't think more of the stockings, or remark on the figure-hugging new blouse Maureen had helped her make.

'And rescuing badgers from traps.' They fell silent, probably both thinking of Johnson.

'But you'll manage to come up to Harrogate while I'm there?' She'd promised her father to take a fortnight's holiday in Yorkshire. At the time, she'd looked forward to the break; now she resented time spent apart from David.

He stroked the stocking again. 'Yes.'

'Becky would love to see you.'

'I seem to have committed myself to Charles for the Twelfth.' He shuddered. 'I hate the mass slaughter of grouse. But Charlie tells me I'm pathetic.'

'I like eating grouse,' she admitted. 'Compared with some of the stuff we get it's ambrosial.'

'So do I.' They grinned at one another.

'Living off the spoils of murder, both of us.'

The hand dropped from her thigh.

'Sorry.' She sat up. 'Sometimes I just forget what happened and things just come out.'

'You've nothing to apologize for. We can't be tripping over the most innocent words.'

She reached for the bottle of whisky David had brought down from Cambridge with him and poured them both another glass, drinking hers in a couple of sips. 'Will it always be like this? Perhaps we should just go to the police now and tell them what happened.' Thunder rumbled somewhere in the distance.

'What would we say when they ask us why we waited nearly four years to tell them?'

She shrugged and eyed the bottle again. David followed her gaze. 'Would you like another one?' she asked.

'I hadn't noticed how much we've drunk.' Raindrops drummed against the window.

He went to the mirror to comb his hair back into place.

'Are you going?'

He came back to her and sat down. 'Suppose I stayed?' The question sounded very casual but she knew what he was asking and sat up.

'We'd have to be very careful.' Thank God her father'd given her all those books to read, although the descriptions of the precautions married women could take to avoid pregnancies were vague. Becky's advice had been very simple. 'Wait until you're engaged, dear.' But David had never mentioned engagement.

The wind blew the curtain into the room, knocking a hairbrush from the windowsill and sending it thumping to the floor.

She held out a hand. 'Oh stop talking and let's go to bed.' The rain lashed against the window. The curtains blew in again and knocked the photograph of her mother from the windowsill to join the hairbrush on the floor. David's lips moved down her neck towards her breasts, sending the blood racing round her veins, making her gasp. For a second Lew's face flashed across her mind but she pushed his image away and pulled off her blouse so David's mouth could descend further. And then it was just the two of them, like it was in Fontwell when they ran down the cliff path, hearts throbbing, half with excitement, half with fear they'd miss a step and plummet to the rocks below. And he was pushing himself into her and she was opening her mouth to tell him she didn't like it when it was all right again and she found she did like it. A lot.

But he was already pulling away, muttering something, before getting out of bed and dashing for the bedroom door. She heard the lavatory flush. He reappeared a few minutes later, very pale. 'Felix, I don't know what happened. Probably the chicken in the restaurant.'

She didn't understand enough about sex to know whether or not what they'd done constituted the act itself or some kind of pre-amble. Was she technically still a virgin? 'Have a mouthful of whisky to wash out the taste.'

He shook his head and started to tug on his shirt. 'I think I need to sleep it off.'

'You can't go now, it's still raining.'

'I'll be fine.' He managed a smile. 'Don't want to pass it on to you.'

'I wouldn't mind.' She rose and put her arms around his neck. 'Please stay.'

'Best not.' He kissed the top of her head and was gone.

She sat among the rumpled sheets and listened but she couldn't hear his feet on the stairs or the front door opening. He'd be careful to be quiet because of the landlady.

She got up and poured another whisky to help herself sleep.

Twenty-seven

Felix 1947

'Post for you, Miss Valance.'

Her landlady handed her a white envelope with familiar neat writing on it. Strange. David must have delivered it by hand while she was out with Maureen. It seemed he was taking a short trip to Wales with Charles.

> His father's got a house they haven't visited since
> the war. We're going to see what the damage is
> and spend the summer doing it up. If this National
> Service comes in, it could be our last chance for
> some time. Sorry I couldn't let you know before,
> Felix, this came up suddenly.
> Love, David.

'He's a man.' Maureen caught the nippy's eye and ordered two more coffees. She'd taken Felix to the Lyons' Corner House on the Strand to cheer her up. 'Men do things like that, they're unreliable.'

'Something changed when . . .' The way he'd rushed to the lavatory like that.

Maureen raised her eyebrows.

'It's the only way I can describe it. I'm not sure if he'd, you know, finished, when he sprinted for the door.'

'Finished?'

'Finished sleeping with me.' Felix shuffled on her chair.

'You mean, come?'

Felix hadn't heard the expression before.

'Well you wouldn't know, first time and all that.' Maureen lit her Player's and raised an eyebrow.

180

'It's that bloody Charles.' A tear started to drop from Felix's eye. 'He's poisoned David against me.'

'You're ruining your make-up. Here.' She handed Felix her handkerchief. 'There's only one thing to do in these circumstances.'

'What?'

'Go out with someone else, of course.' Maureen smiled. 'You're not that bad looking, Felix.' She stopped and scowled. 'You should call yourself by your proper name, Felicity's more feminine. True, you're a bit skinny and your hair could do with a trim.'

'Talk about damning with faint praise.'

'Actually I was thinking about this friend of my brother's—'

'No. I don't want to go out with anyone else apart from David.' She screwed her handkerchief up into a ball and remembered her manners. 'Sorry. I'm sure your brother's friend's very nice.'

'He is.' Maureen picked up her handbag. 'Six foot tall. Manager at the Gaumont in Wembley, he could get you tickets for any film you wanted. Your loss.' She flicked her fringe off her face. 'Let's get moving. I want to see if Peter Robinson's got any decent undies.'

A postcard came from David: 'Darling Felix, running out on you like that was appalling. I'm so sorry and hope you can forgive me. I'll come and see you in Harrogate.'

Felix felt a glow.

Becky's eyes scanned her stepdaughter and a frown puckered her brow like a pulled thread on a piece of smooth linen. 'You've changed.' She stood back to examine her. 'More grown up or something. Your face looks different round the chin.'

Felix examined herself in the mirror in her bedroom and saw what she meant. She also noted how her merino jumper clung to her chest, which was surely more generous than it had been a few months back.

David turned up the morning she decided she must be pregnant.

'I missed you.' His kiss on her cheek felt almost defiant. 'Charlie was due to pay a trip to his Ma – she lives five miles out of town –

so I tagged along with him. I'm going to catch a train back south at lunchtime.'

'I missed you too, even though you were a bastard, running out on me like that.'

He blinked at the word. Maureen had taught her some choice expressions. 'I can't explain what got into me. It was inexcusable.' He was thinner, pale too, despite his holiday.

'I thought I'd done something wrong.' She gave herself a mental slap. 'Never show any insecurity to a man,' Maureen always said. 'If you want to keep them interested act like you don't give a damn.' But Maureen didn't know about the baby.

David put his arms around her. 'You? Do something wrong? Never.' She nestled into his hug, cursing the prickling in her eyes. Could pregnancy make one more emotional?

'You left so suddenly.'

'I panicked, wasn't sure we were doing the right thing.' His hand stroked her hair. 'Your hair's very glossy, Yorkshire air must suit you.' He smiled at her. 'I needed to see you. To tell you the truth, I haven't been getting on that well with Charlie. It's a relief to be heading for Dorking.'

'What's happened?'

He bent his head and fiddled with the belt of her skirt. 'He gets a bit possessive.'

She frowned. 'Does he? How childish. It's not as if you're school-boys any more.'

'No.' He smiled. 'We're certainly not. Tell me what you've been up to, Felix.'

'Finishing off at secretarial school – I did quite well in the exams, you know, I . . .' She took a deep breath. 'There's something you need to know.' Was he going to be furious with her now?

'What's that?' He let her go. 'Oh God, you've found another fellow, haven't you?' He bit his lip. 'Not that I blame you one bit.'

'It's not that.'

182

He drew her back into his arms. 'Then nothing else matters, does it? It's you and me against the world, just like it was in Fontwell.'

'That's good . . .' She swallowed, preparing herself.

The doorbell rang. Becky's heels clattered across the marble tiles in the hall. Felix heard a man's voice, low and urgent; then Becky's, surprised. There was a knock on the door and she stuck her head around it. 'Someone called Charles is here for you, David.'

Felix felt an urge to detain her stepmother. But it was going to be fine, wasn't it? David and she were going to face the world, but she wished she'd been able to tell him about the baby before the doorbell rang. Becky brought in a short man with dark hair almost touching his collar. He wore a shirt of the kind Felix hadn't seen for years – the kind she imagined you had to buy abroad. His nails were neatly filed and his hand soft in hers.

'Well.' Charles looked her up and down. 'This is Felicity.' He sounded amused. 'You're not what I was expecting.'

'What did you want, Charles? Thought you were going out for a ride this morning?' David stood. His face was set in an expression Felix hadn't seen before.

'I came to lay my cards on the table.'

'What table? It's over. I told you this morning.'

What was over? Felix looked from one of them to the other.

'Perhaps.' Charles looked over his shoulder and walked across to shut the door. Felix felt an urge to call out for Becky to come back in. 'But I don't see why I should just let you run off with this little piece, after all our history.'

'What history?' Felix turned to David for an explanation. His gaze was fixed on Charles, face paper-white, hands clenched in front of him. She sat down. 'It doesn't make sense.' Was that tight little squeak her voice?

Charles smiled. 'David and I have been lovers since we were fifteen. Until you got in the way.'

'What are you talking about?'

'An innocent. How touching.' Charles looked at David. 'Didn't you tell her?'

'Oh, he told me all the details.' She was damned if she'd let Charles get one over her. She and Maureen had once seen a film about a lioness protecting her family from a hyena. Now she felt the same fury herself: David was hers, Lew's death had bound them. 'I knew him first!'

'*I knew him first*,' he repeated in a falsetto.

'Get out.' David opened the door again. 'You've no right to come here and say these things to Felix.'

'Perhaps I should tell that very respectable-looking Harrogate matron who answered the door that young Felicity is sleeping with a queer.'

'She wouldn't believe you,' she said with confidence. 'They'd think you were ill.' Thank God Maureen'd filled her in about homosexuals. Maureen's friend Dom was queer. Maureen said he was the wittiest man in Soho. Felix still wasn't sure what Dom and his friends did in bed. Maureen said it was best to draw a veil and just enjoy the banter. How ridiculous of Charles to claim that David was queer.

Charles blinked. 'Suppose I go to the police and tell them about a certain happening on a beach in Dorset in the autumn of 1943?'

She looked at David. 'You told him about Lew?'

David sat. 'Yes.' He looked away. 'I'm sorry.'

Felix still stared at him. 'I never told a soul. Not one single person. Not even my father. You said we owed it to Isabel.'

He met her glance for a second. 'God, I wish I hadn't.'

'Too late for regrets, sweetie. Think I'll give the coffee a miss. Remember what I said, Davie, you stay away from her if you don't want things to slip out.' They heard his footsteps pad across the hall and the gentle shutting of the front door.

'Why's he doing this?' She looked at David.

'He's jealous, doesn't want me to be involved with anyone else if he can't have me himself.'

'He's mad.' She heard her own words, firing round the high-ceilinged room like bullets.

Becky reappeared with the coffee tray. 'Has your friend gone?' Her face fell.

'He just had a quick message for me.' Felix could see David struggling to put on a smile.

'Well, that's a shame.' She poured the coffee. 'I'll leave you two with this, if you don't mind. There's a good play on the radio.'

Felix waited until Becky'd closed the door again. 'You really think he'd go to the police?'

'Charlie's blackmailed other people. He'd tell them everything to spite us.'

'How on earth did you get involved with him?' How could gentle David have befriended someone like this?

'He was good to me at school. I couldn't have survived without him. But he wants to control me.'

'Are you really, you know . . .?' She caught a glimpse of his stricken face. 'Sorry, of course you're not.' She couldn't help touching her stomach below the navel, feeling its rounded contour.

David bit a fingernail and couldn't seem to meet her eye. 'I don't know what to do,' he said at last.

'Let him tell.' Her own boldness astounded Felix. 'We'll say we don't know what he's talking about. How would the police prove anything?'

'It's too risky, Isabel would be implicated; her marriage—'

'Oh damn Isabel!'

'I can't let her down.'

'I don't understand why you don't stand up to Charlie.' David had always been so sure of himself, so keen to champion the under-dog. How could he let a man like that get the better of him?

He dropped his head. 'She's family, Felix.'

Isabel, again. 'Don't *I* count for anything?'

'For a lot.' But his head was still bowed.

'So tell Charles to go to hell!' She drank more coffee, feeling proud of her assertiveness.

He lifted his head. 'You don't understand. If you had siblings, you would.'

185

She frowned. 'What do you mean? You haven't got any brothers or sisters either.' He set down his cup. 'She's just a cousin. You don't even like her.'

'You don't understand,' he said again.

'Damn right I don't.'

'Isabel's my sister.'

And questions and protests screamed in her mind, though she didn't say a word, just stared at him like one of Johnson's foxes, stunned and cornered.

The Squire had had two younger brothers. Both had suffered from tuberculosis, requiring residence in milder climates. For years at a time there'd be no news of Ronnie and Gerald, other than requests for money and occasional rumours of affairs and gambling scandals. The Squire, a wilder youth than Felix could ever have imagined, spent a lot of time in London, enjoying all the pleasures of society life. When he found himself the possessor of not one, but two illegitimate children, what easier way to deal with the situation than to give them 'fathers' who lived abroad? Ronnie and Gerald probably never even knew their names had been used for this purpose. Both died without returning to England. Isabel and David's respective mothers – both of them nervous about irate husbands – were grateful for the Squire's continued support, and happy to keep up the fiction. And delighted for their illegitimate offspring to spend most of their time in a remote house in Dorset, far from gossip-mongers.

As she grew up Isabel dug out more information about Ronnie and Gerald, reading the few letters they sent to the Squire and asking him sharp questions. She kept quiet about the defects of her own supposed father, Ronnie, but delighted in sharing an occasional snippet about Gerald's mistresses and business failures with David.

'She liked to tease me about Gerald, tell me how terrible he was, how useless he was as a coffee farmer and horse breeder, how he just collected rich women. If the Squire heard her he'd tell her to drop the subject but she usually waited until he was out of earshot.'

'When did you find out the truth?'

'When I went up to Harrow. The Squire took me to dinner at Simpson's and said he wanted me to inherit the Manor, even if it meant employing every solicitor in London.' He gave a wry smile. 'That was when we still thought there'd be a Manor left to inherit. He was even going to adopt me if that's what it took.'

'And Isabel?'

'He told her just before she got married. As you know, her mother refused to acknowledge her existence. Mine writes me occasional letters, even has me to tea at her flat in Regent's Park when her husband's away.' He grimaced. 'Isabel's mental problems stem from her rejection by her mother. When Lew died she took an overdose of sleeping tablets.'

'I remember.' Felix sat forward.

'Your father saved her life, pumped out her stomach. We called him out late that same night. When you came to see me in the morning we were expecting him back to check on her. He was very sympathetic. Shame she didn't ask him to give her something for the pregnancy,' he went on. 'Then she wouldn't have had to marry Barrington.'

'What do you mean?'

'She was already just pregnant with Justin. He must be Johnson's.'

Johnson after all.

She watched a bee buzzing at the window, trying to reach the flowers and shrubs it glimpsed outside. 'So you and I . . .?' She couldn't bear to ask the question.

He looked her straight in the eye. 'I'm sorry, Felix. But I truly believe Isabel would kill herself if it came out about her and Lew and Johnson. She's still very shaky. I don't think I could have her death on my conscience as well.'

As well as Lew's, he meant.

The clock on the fireplace ticked very loudly.

She rose. 'Probably best we don't see each other again.' Her words seemed to come from somewhere in the distance.

'Probably.' He stood too.

'Promise me you really won't see Charles again.' Somehow that mattered as much as everything else.

'If I saw the little shit I'd probably brain him.' He looked down. 'I thought I loved him once. Until I started seeing you again. I love you, always will.' His arms were on her shoulders. 'You're brave and you're loyal.'

'But Isabel matters more.'

'She's vulnerable. You're strong.'

'And the strong always have to give way to the weak?'

His eyes filled. She pushed him away.

'This is goodbye, don't you care?'

'I'm used to it. It's not the first time you've rejected me, remember?'

He flinched. 'You mustn't think of it like that. Perhaps Charles will go off abroad when the currency restrictions end. Then we could get back together.'

'It would be too late.'

'What do you mean?'

'Nothing. Please go now.' She closed her eyes, only opening them when she heard the front door slamming. She stared at the space where he'd stood.

Becky came in. 'David gone already?'

'He had things to do.'

She sighed. 'I still entertain foolish romantic hopes about you and him. Tell me I'm a silly old fool.'

Felix put a hand to her mouth. 'Oh God, I'm going to be sick.' And she was, all down her shirt.

Becky's eyes opened in alarm. 'Sweetheart! Are you ill?'

'I need to lie down.'

How long could she carry on having conversations, breathing, living, when a boulder had lodged in her chest, threatening to choke her?

'Poor you. Lucky it didn't happen in front of David.' She put a hand round Felix's waist and steered her to the door. 'Leave your shirt outside your room and I'll rinse it for you. I shouldn't think you'll want lunch, will you?'

Twenty-eight

Felix 1947

Felix stole the ergot when Becky went to Betty's Tearooms to meet friends and her father was making his house calls. It wasn't stored with the other bottles in his dispensary, he'd hidden it in a small, dusty cardboard box behind a row of rolled bandages. Nothing apart from this little bottle seemed suitable for what she had in mind. She remembered David telling her about ergot poisoning in cattle causing spontaneous abortion.

She clenched the small brown bottle in her hand, weighing up the consequences. If this went wrong and the ergot was traced to her father, the authorities might accuse him of carrying out the abortion. And then David would find out she'd killed his child. Forget David. She could only afford to concentrate on one thing at a time. She had to get back to the anonymity of London. Her journey back south was still five days away. Felix knew she couldn't wait that long. This had to be done as soon as possible.

Could she invent some excuse requiring her earlier presence in London? A job interview? Her father and Becky knew she was trying to find something interesting for the autumn. Suppose she said a friend had telephoned her while they were out and alerted her to a vacancy?

She slipped the bottle into her dressing-gown pocket and replaced the cardboard box behind the bandages, reaching her bedroom just as Becky returned from her afternoon of teacakes and Harrogate gossip.

Lying and organizing train tickets were diversions which held back the grey blanket threatening to engulf her. As long as she kept too busy to think, she could function.

'You seem restless,' her father said, eyeing her over his mulligatawny soup.

'She's probably nervous about her job interview.' Becky pressed more bread and butter on Felix. 'Not hungry? Tell us more about the company, darling. A shipping firm, you said?'

'Import and export.' Felix pulled words out of her memory.

'How exciting! I wonder if you'll get to travel.'

'Perhaps when the currency restrictions are lifted.' Her father nodded his approval. 'But we mustn't get carried away, Felix mightn't get the job.'

'I expect she will, she's so clever.'

Her father sighed. 'I still think you should have gone to university, sweetheart.'

'Perhaps I should have. Too late now.' She helped Becky clear the table and decided she couldn't bear it any more. Her father picked up his newspaper and ambled out to his study to finish the crossword. 'Have you got five minutes?' she asked, following him.

'Of course.' He pushed the cat off his armchair for her to sit down. 'What can I do for you?' She thought again how changed he was from the gaunt man who'd spent nights in the dispensary at Fontwell with a bottle of brandy. Becky's affection and cooking (even with ever more stringent rationing) had made him glow.

Surely he'd help her? If he kept the stuff on the premises, if he'd really given it to Sam's mother and risked imprisonment and professional disgrace, he couldn't turn down his daughter's plea for help. 'I need help.' The words tumbled out onto the Persian rug.

He raised an eyebrow. 'Are you ill, child? You're pale.'

'Not ill exactly . . .'

'Tell me.' His hand clenched his fountain pen so tightly his knuckles whitened.

She looked at his face, full of concern. 'I'm a bit short of cash and wondered if you could let me have five pounds for the rent?'

Next morning she sat on the train clutching the basket of food Becky had given her. Felix tried not to think about the sardines, the pickles, and the precious sliver of cold beef wrapped up in grease-proof paper. She didn't want another trip to the lavatory, whiffs from which reached her over the smell of soot and hot metal.

The train beat out a rhythm directed at her: *You shouldn't do this, you shouldn't do this, you shouldn't do this.* She stuffed her fingers into her ears to drown the sound.

She took the ergot as soon as she was inside the bedsit, which had grown stuffy during her fortnight away and seemed poky after the space of the Harrogate villa. With no idea how much of the stuff she was supposed to take, she took a teaspoon. The liquid tasted faintly of orange. Perhaps her father had found one of these rare fruits and added its juice to make the ergot more palatable. Nothing happened. She sat on her bed, wondering what to do. She tried to read, threw the book on the floor, paced the narrow room. All the guilt and she'd failed. It was a sign: she'd keep the baby and brazen it out.

A hand squeezed her lower abdomen and twisted her guts. Within twenty minutes she was clutching the bed head and biting her lip, perspiration running down her face, heart pounding while the hand clawed inside her with its iron nails. Her stomach tied itself into knots, driving her out to the lavatory to retch up the Spam sandwich she'd eaten on the train. After she'd run back and forth three times she decided it would be easier to spend the afternoon in there while she shivered and sweated in turn. At six o'clock her uterus gave a spasm that nearly propelled her off the lavatory seat and expelled an object the size of a prawn into the pan. Felix reached up and pulled the chain.

'You all right, Miss Valance?' Mrs Auden called as she finally emerged.

'Fine now, thanks,' she called back. 'Dodgy sandwich on the train.'

In the bedroom she stuffed two bath towels between her legs and went to bed with a bottle of gin she'd bought from the off-licence on the way back from King's Cross.

*

Lew appeared at the end of her bed, shaking his head over the gin and telling Felix to be brave, there was a war on.

'The war's bloody ended,' she told him. 'This is the glorious sodding peace.'

'You mind your tongue, missy,' he scowled. 'Remember I'm a preacher's nephew.'

'You forgot about that when you got Phoebe pregnant. Leave me alone, you're ruining my life.'

Twenty-nine

Minna

The wind has dropped. It's so silent I can almost hear Felix breathing.

'So you lost a baby, too.'

She waves a hand in dismissal. 'Not like you did. It was early in the pregnancy. My fault, my choice.'

'Did you regret it?'

'Every day of my life. Especially when I married and it became clear I couldn't have more children.'

'Because of the termination?' I choose the word because it sounds less harsh than *abortion*.

'Because I'd performed an illegal abortion on myself, yes. Theo, my husband, was very good about it.'

'You told him the truth?'

'Yes. He said he understood and it was just a shame he hadn't met me when I was in trouble. He'd have married me and brought up the baby as his own.'

The beams above us creak as the house settles down for the night, but still I can't bear to let her go.

'Tell me how you met Theo,' I say.

'Maureen introduced us, indirectly. She was an angel, she kept me sane.'

I remember how wonderful my friends were to me and hang my head, thinking of my ingratitude.

'She just wouldn't let me wallow.'

Felix 1947

'Only me.'

Felix pulled on a dressing gown and opened the door. Maureen burst in, casting a look round the room.

194

'Bloody hell, you look seedy, what's been going on?'

She told her, without mention of Lew and Isabel, making it sound as though David had ended the relationship because Charles had threatened to expose him as a homosexual.

'Filthy little tart. He deserves a poker up the arse.' She puffed out her cheeks. 'Bet David's not really queer, it was just that school they sent him to. But he left you in trouble, did he? Bastard.'

'He doesn't know I was pregnant.'

Maureen frowned. 'Why the hell didn't you tell him?'

'It was all getting complicated.' How could she explain she didn't want him to feel sorry for her?

Maureen's green eyes, often so sharp, were soft now. 'So what're you going to do now, girl?'

'Don't know.' She stretched out her hand for that faithful companion, the gin bottle. 'I've paid the rent for this week. Want a drink?'

'Not at three in the afternoon. What happens next week?'

Felix shrugged. 'I suppose I'll just have to go home.' Home to her parents, like a little girl, instead of the confident adult she'd been until a week ago.

'You need a job, girl.' Maureen shook her head. 'But look at you, as much chance of getting through an interview as I've got of having tea at the Palace.'

'I haven't slept properly,' she muttered. 'And I can't keep anything down.'

Maureen examined her, eyes narrowed. 'I've got a plan.' She sprang up and opened the window.

Felix groaned. 'What?'

'Clever old me's got two job offers, that's what. You can have the one I don't want.'

'They'll know I'm not who they selected.'

'That's where you're wrong.' Maureen's eyes gleamed. 'The person who interviewed me was the woman I'm replacing. Leaves on Friday to get married.'

'What's the company?'

'An advertising agency. Nice people. Just doesn't pay quite as much as the other job.' She screwed up her nose.

'What's that?'

'A deadly dull bank. But full of chaps earning steady money. I want to settle down.'

Felix smiled for the first time in weeks. 'You? Settle down?'

Maureen smoothed down her skirt. 'A semi in a nice suburb, two children, and a bloke who can look after me. I'm done gallivanting.'

'I can't believe we'd get away with it.'

''Course we will.'

Felix shrugged. 'What happens if they ask for my identity card or something?'

'They won't. They were dead disorganized. Ask for cash wages, say you haven't got a bank account.'

Felix laughed. 'You'd have made a good secret agent.'

Maureen laughed too. 'Good to see you looking cheerful, Felix. You had me worried when I came in, you looked like you were about to top yourself.'

'The thought had crossed my mind.' Felix shuddered, thinking of the long night watching the bedroom spin, the endless morning listening to everyone else going off to work or school or to queue in shops. And herself, alone in a darkened room, wondering what she had to live for.

Maureen's eyes widened. 'Not for a man, Felix.'

'I feel as though I'll never be happy again.' The boulder in her chest throbbed. One of these days it would burst out and consume the world. She fought until it subsided.

Maureen's hand found hers. 'You did the right thing. My cousin had an illegitimate baby. They sent her to a home for unmarried women in the North and gave her drugs to knock her out while she gave birth. When she woke up, they'd already taken it away. She didn't even know if it was a boy or a girl. She kept reading the deaths column in the newspaper. Every time she saw a baby had died she said it was hers.'

'I couldn't have handled that.' But sometimes she wondered if she'd just imagined the whole episode, and that scared her more than anything.

'No.' Maureen squeezed her hand. 'Enough of that, let's go through your wardrobe and work out what you're going to wear.' She cast a disapproving eye around the room. 'And while you're about it you can get rid of some of these empties and clean that revolting glass. And there's clothes on the floor could do with a wash.'

The man with the parrot on his shoulder handed Felix a piece of paper with scribbles on it. 'Need this typed up in triplicate for lunchtime. Sorry about the beak marks, Rommel doesn't like that account.'

She assumed he meant the bird, vaguely remembering that the German general had taken cyanide during the war. 'Why not?'

He looked a little surprised; perhaps typists weren't supposed to make conversation. 'The client brought in some samples and Rommel didn't like the smell when they opened the tins. God knows what they put in boot polish these days.' He peered at her. 'You're not quite what we were expecting.'

Her heart missed a beat. 'Oh?'

'Carrie who interviewed you said you were plumpish and jolly.'

'Food poisoning. A dodgy can of salmon.' She thought quickly. 'I'll perk up soon.' The parrot put its head on one side and whistled and Felix grinned.

'That's better.' Rommel's owner winked at her.

'I've never seen a parrot in an office before.' Though, come to think of it, she hadn't ever seen an office before.

'She keeps the troops in order.'

'She?'

'After I'd named her someone told me I had a female parrot.'

'Couldn't you change her name?' She cursed inwardly. Too many questions, drawing attention to herself.

'She suits it. Pecks the clients if they make unreasonable changes to copy.'

'Copy?'

He smiled. 'That's what we write, sweetie, advertising copy. Didn't Carrie explain when she interviewed you?' He moved away.

Felix turned his scribbles into neat black and white type and put it on his desk. A few minutes later he returned, frowning, Rommel swaying on his shoulder. 'This is great, but why did you change the last sentence?'

'Did I?' She took it from him.

'I wrote "add a shine to your shoes". You've typed "sparkle up your shoes".'

She hadn't even noticed she'd done it. She blushed. 'I'll change it straightaway, I'm terribly sorry, Mr Curtis.'

'Don't be, Maureen. Your version is stronger than mine.' Rommel hopped onto her desk and examined Felix, head on one side.

She put out a hand and stroked the grey feathers.

'God, careful! Last person who did that had his fingers bitten.'

'I like birds.' And she'd handled enough of them in Fontwell when she'd helped David with his animal hospital to feel confident around them. She blinked. 'Mr Curtis?'

'Yes?'

'I'm usually called Felix. Rather than Maureen.'

He nodded. 'I won't ask why you prefer it, but Felix is unusual. It suits you.'

Thirty

Minna

'You married the boss.'

'Theo Curtis was nice. Even when he got dementia he was still fun. In between being bloody awful.' Felix laughs.

'I'm sorry.' I can't imagine coping with a demented spouse. 'Is he still alive?'

'He died years ago. A blessed relief for everyone. Especially him.'

'But were you in love with him? I mean, in love like you were with David?'

She considers the question. 'I liked him. I liked his parrot. Then slowly I began noticing how good he made me feel. Of course then I had to tell him my real name and how we'd tricked the agency into employing me.'

'Did he mind?'

'Said I was very enterprising. And eventually we ran the agency together very successfully. At our peak we had clients from all around Europe, drinks companies, mainly.' She grimaces. 'That was a bit of a problem for me until I stopped drinking.'

'I noticed you always ask for soft drinks.'

She doesn't blink. 'I'm an alcoholic. Alcoholics Anonymous sorted me out eventually. And Theo helped.'

'You drank because of what happened with David?'

'I suppose so. Perhaps my genes predisposed me, too. But I've learned excuses don't help.'

'You'd be justified making them.' I think of her exile from the home she loved, the drowning on the beach, the loss of David.

'Others experienced worse in the forties and didn't turn to the bottle.' She smiles. 'What drew you to Tom?' Is she being kind, realizing I can't bear to be left alone tonight?

'He made me feel strong.' The irony makes my lips curl.

Our eyes met as I got into the last carriage of a westbound Piccadilly Line train at Covent Garden tube station. I clocked him as someone who, in different circumstances, might have interested me. But I was with someone else, not the right someone, but the someone I thought was right: Hugo. Penthouse in the Barbican. Jaguar. Great taste in restaurants.

It was warm. I pulled off my jacket and opened my *Evening Standard,* burying myself in some tittle-tattle about a British film-star sleeping with his children's nanny. Long day. My hands still reeked of paint. A little burnt bit of skin stung where paint stripper had penetrated my gloves and seared me before I could wash it off. My eyes ached because the electricity wasn't switched on in the office block and the last half-hour was really too dark for painting.

I longed for a shower, a glass of wine with my feet up watching something mindless on TV. I'd call Hugo later. Hyde Park station passed in a blur of tourists and weary home-bound commuters. What was Tom doing? I seem to remember him scribbling in a Filo-fax. Or perhaps that was a memory I assembled later.

A thump. The carriage flew for a second above the rail. My news-paper fanned its sheets over the floor. Then came another crash and a smell like an iron left on too long. Screams. My eyes met those of the man in the smart linen jacket and I knew he was thinking what I was thinking. It had been a year of derailments and crashes, pic-tures of twisted metal, discarded briefcases and laptops. Bloodied faces. Stretchers. Weeping. And now it was our turn.

My side of the carriage hit the tunnel wall and I flew, closing my eyes, knowing I was dying. Then I was sitting on a lap, blushing, someone's arms around me.

'It's all right.' He grinned. 'We've stopped.'

I looked around. No blood. A woman weeping at the other end of the carriage. Crackles from the address system, the driver telling us we'd had a minor derailment. London Transport staff would arrive shortly and lead us through the tunnel back to Hyde Park. I stood, nodded a thanks to the man. Noticed how pale he was. He studied his Filofax for a few seconds, then packed it in his briefcase. I'd embarrassed him. We'd thought we were in a disaster, a tragedy, but it was only an adventure.

'I'd better get my stuff together.' I stooped to retrieve the sheets of *Evening Standard,* reclaim my rucksack. Checked my mobile was still in my jeans pocket. Sat to wait for the transport police.

The lights went off. I heard a groan opposite. 'Are you hurt?'

'Claustrophobic.' The man made an attempt at a laugh. 'I really, really do not like confined dark places. Which is going to be a problem in the tunnel.'

'Have you got a mobile?'

'Won't work down here, will it?'

'If you turn it on and off it'll act as a torch.' I turned mine on to show him. Dear God, I was turning back into the bossy little Brownie I was when I was eight. 'Doesn't last long, though.'

'Better than nothing.'

Then I remembered my jacket, lying crumpled on the floor. I picked it up and put it on. 'Just follow me out. You won't be able to miss me in this.' My silver mac. Bought in a moment of madness. Too loud, Hugo said. Too eighties. Too Abba. But useful in weather like this, and because it was old it didn't matter if the arms got covered in paint splatters. No point wearing good clothes to work.

A laugh. 'That's the best bloody coat I've seen in my life.'

And afterwards, when they helped us jump down from the carriage and reassured us that the power was off, I felt his eyes on my back the whole ten minutes we walked back to Hyde Park.

'Hunt-for-a-bus time,' I told him.

'No. Drink-in-a-pub time.' He touched my silver sleeve. 'Least I can do.'

*

I wasn't naive. I've read about the experiment conducted on a shaky rope-bridge where all the men fall for the only-moderately attractive woman questioning them halfway across. I knew we're drawn to strangers when we meet in dangerous circumstances. So I made a point of telling Tom I had to call my boyfriend.

Hugo was in a meeting when I rang. I left a message on his voicemail, feeling suddenly weepy. Tom watched me. 'There's this bar.' He took my arm. 'My brother and his partner go there. It's very camp. Do you mind camp?'

Camp would be comforting. 'Love it.' I was still only mildly intrigued by the man with the accent that was both soft and gritty, giving his words a charge I'd never felt in an Englishman's voice.

I'd just have one drink and make my excuses. A long hot bath. An early night. The bar was full of men. A young man in the most beautiful shirt I have ever seen, the colour of sunsets, danced by himself, watched by a man in his thirties who sat drinking beer. A row of pastel paper lanterns hung above the bar, bathing the drinkers' faces in pink, blue and green.

Tom nodded at the scene. 'Fairyland.' He nodded at the speakers. 'And good music.'

We danced for hours. At first I kept a foot or two away from him, feeling awkward. As the first track ended and the next one started I found myself dancing closer and closer. And I didn't feel guilty any longer. We didn't exchange a single word. I could feel the heat from his body, the question in his eyes. And I knew if I met his gaze I'd give myself away. So I kept my eyes on the parquet floor.

I managed to break the trance and go to the Ladies, where I removed a grey smudge from one cheek and found an old lipstick in my rucksack. As I walked into the bar Tom grabbed me by the arm. 'Meet my brother.' He pulled me towards the sunset-shirted boy. 'Mikey, this is . . .?'

'Minna,' I put out my hand.

'Minna?'

'Short for Wilhelmina. My grandmother.'

'How do you do, Minna-short-for-Wilhelmina.' His accent was like Tom's, but softer. 'I'm Michael and that's my partner, Gareth. I'm hiding him in here so he can't go and talk hospitals with the others. These doctors can be so dull.'

'God knows how Gareth can bear himself,' Tom said.

'We can't all have thrilling clients like you.'

'Clients?' I asked.

'I'm a public affairs consultant. Brings me into contact with all kinds of folk.'

'The specimens, Gareth and I call them.' Mikey winked at me and went back to his solitary dance.

'Mikey's the flamboyant one in the family.' Tom sounded proud.

We left at half ten. He found me a taxi, took my mobile number, sent me home alone. I wondered if I'd ever see him again. My answer phone blinked at me when I walked into my flat: my mother'd watched the evening news and was beside herself. Hugo had left a message trusting I'd got home all right, he'd heard of problems on the Piccadilly line. He'd call me tomorrow, after his breakfast meeting.

Tom left a message on my mobile at quarter to eight the next morning.

I married him almost a year to the day after the train derailment.

'We should have known,' I say.

Felix's brow furrows. 'Known what?'

'That the way a relationship begins often foreshadows the way it'll end.' *In my beginning is my end.* I studied T. S. Eliot for A levels. Tom and I thought we'd got one over on fate.

Something in the way Felix narrows her eyes makes me think she knows what I mean about foreshadowing.

I glance at my watch. Nearly one in the morning. 'A story for another time. I've been selfish, keeping you here talking.'

'I enjoyed it.' She yawns, too polite to question me further. It strikes me that our roles are getting blurred. I am supposed to be the questioner and she the one who explains. And her story seems to grow more complex every time she tells me more. Something's still missing: details don't add up, but my brain's too tired to work out where the gap is. 'I'll call you.' I wave her off, watching her car lights bend their way down the drive.

I gather up glasses and cups to take to the dishwasher. As I check the study for empties I notice Tom's left his laptop switched on. I start to log off when I see the little envelope icon showing he's got a new email. Normally I wouldn't look but I recognize Sara's address. I click on the envelope to bring up the message.

'Wonderful seeing you today. We need to meet – and soon – there's lots to sort out. Can you sneak away? I'm sure Mark hasn't guessed.'

I stare at the words on the screen and blink, half expecting to read something else when I look again. But the message remains the same. Certainly not the words of a woman diagnosed with a life-threatening disease. Ten out of ten for suspecting something's wrong, Mark. Nought out of ten for identifying the something.

One of the glasses still holds an inch of water. As I stand there rereading the email, it tips up in my hand and spills a few drops onto the wooden floor.

Thirty-one

Minna

Tom drains his coffee mug. 'Back to work.' I notice how tired he's looking. I feel sleep-deprived too. When I finally slept I dreamed I was back in the Tube tunnel again. Only this time I was alone and the tunnel walls were closing in on me. I ran towards the lights of the station, which remained unreachable as the bricks started to crush me. Just before dawn I woke, at first longing for Tom to comfort me, then glad he slept on.

Before he's even left the room he's got his mobile out to check messages.

'Tom.' I have to know.

'Yes.' He raises his head.

'Everything all right?'

He switches off the mobile and comes back in. 'Waymark's keeping me busy.'

'It's just . . .'

'What?' He sits down again. 'Are you going to talk to me?'

'Do you think we need to talk?' I'm quite pleased with this counter-question.

'Oh I think so.' He sweeps a hand towards the breakfast I've been struggling to eat. 'You could start by telling me what this means.'

'It's a grapefruit.'

'Why are you starving yourself?' His eyes could ignite the room.

'I don't mean to,' I mutter. 'I just can't seem to find an appetite.' Has he picked up on my suspicions? Is he trying to throw the ball back at me?

'You cook me these wonderful meals, but . . .' He swallows.

'What?'

'It's as though you're trying to prove something.'

I rise. 'I don't know what you're talking about.'

'Really? It feels as though you're telling me I'm heartless to keep on eating and working.'

'I don't think that.' But even to my own ears my words sound hollow. 'We have to keep going, I know that.'

'Know it, but don't believe it, perhaps.' He takes my hand. 'You need help, Minna. You've got to let me find someone to talk to you.' His eyes are still fierce and protective. If it hadn't been for that email from Sara I'd never believe he could deceive me.

'Perhaps. When we go back to London I'll think about it.' I don't mind making plans for the distant future; it may never arrive.

'Sara knows someone wonderful. She says—'

'Oh, *Sara*.' I stand. 'Since when was she the expert?'

He lets go of my wrist. 'She was so worried when . . . well, when it happened. And this anorexia—'

'I'm not anorexic,' I shout.

'What do you call it when someone stops eating?'

'Anorexics want to lose weight. I couldn't care less about my weight. I want to . . .'

'To what?'

To punish myself. To atone for my guilt by taking up less space. To control one element in a life that's out of control. 'I don't know.'

'Sara says she'll put us in touch with the clinic.'

My temper flares again. 'I wish she'd mind her own business.'

'What do you mean? She's one of your best friends.'

I start stacking plates.

'When you were in hospital after the crash she came in every day to brush your hair and moisturize your face. She even sprayed your favourite perfume on you.'

'Wonderful, wonderful Sara. Perfect wife.' I pause. 'And mother.' How could Tom resist that lush piece of pink-and-white motherhood? Two for the price of one. Sara would get custody, even though Mark's a wonderful father. Courts always favour mothers. What a sweet little family: Tom, Sara and Marina.

His face deepens to an angry purple. I take plates and cutlery to the kitchen and load the dishwasher and realize I'm shaking. I go back to the breakfast table and put a hand on Tom's rigid shoulder. 'Sorry.' By behaving like this I'm pushing him into her arms. And I still want him. 'I'll try and eat more.'

His muscles relax a little. 'Felix was here very late last night.'

'I got a bit swept up in her stories of the past.'

He fiddles with a biro. 'You seem, I don't know, more animated this morning.' He attempts a smile. 'That's good. Even if it does mean I'm getting my head bitten off.'

'Sorry,' I say again.

'It's OK. It feels like you're waking up.' He winks. 'I'd forgotten how scary you can be.' And he looks as affectionate and open as ever. If only I hadn't read that bloody email.

I go up to the bedroom to check the bed is properly smoothed down and tidy. As I put away clothes and towels I decide it's time to do some of those things I promised myself I'd attempt while we were on the coast.

The watercolour box is covered in a fine layer of dust. I haul my rucksack out of the wardrobe and pull the easel out from under the bed.

'I'm going out,' I tell Tom. 'Expect me back for lunch.'

He swivels round and beams at the painting equipment. 'Excellent. Don't worry about coming back if you get too engrossed.' His smile is encouraging, but suspicion fills my mind. Does he want me out of the house? I try to push the thought away. I've no real proof about Sara.

'See you.' I walk out of the house. The morning light glows over the cliffs. Perfect. The storm has freshened the earth and my nose is filled with the scent of the meadow.

I stop, reach for my mobile and dial Felix's number. 'Can I come round? Or is it too early?'

Felix's rented cottage is full of perfectly nice furniture. But she looks ill at ease in the sitting room, perching on the edge of the sofa as though she expects it to buck her off.

The only things that seem to belong to her are her mobile and the photograph album she's showing me. I look at the pictures on the wall (landscapes, but not local ones) and the china dogs on the windowsill. Felix and I have each chosen to unveil ourselves away from home and the presence of our own protective, yet revealing, furniture and paintings.

What would our house in Clapham tell Felix about me? I think of our drawing room, with its stripped boards and mustard walls and the paintings of the Bahamas I did when we were there on honeymoon, the sofa Tom keeps saying we should take to the tip because its springs have gone but whose bronze covers still please me, and Tom's baby grand.

'Did you ever see David again?' I admire the photograph of the tall boy with the gentle eyes and floppy fringe. After this morning's exchange with Tom, I want to hear of lovers reunited, quarrels resolved. And I want to know more about Lew's child, Louise. If there is more to know.

'He came to my father's funeral. I hadn't expected David to show but he and my father were very fond of each other back in Fontwell days. David could be loyal.' Felix pauses. 'For better or for worse.'

Thirty-two

Felix 1983

Felix didn't notice David in the church. It was only when they'd lowered the coffin into the ground outside that she became aware of his presence. The doctor had asked to be buried in Swanham parish church, the nearest consecrated ground to Fontwell. The choice had reduced the congregation, as most of his patients in Harrogate were elderly and couldn't make the journey south. Becky stood, a thin, bowed figure, clutching Felix's arm. She'd be rattling around by herself in the Harrogate house. Felix would try again to persuade her stepmother to move south to live with her.

She thought the tall silhouette by the yew seemed familiar and wished she'd remembered to put her glasses into the little patent-leather handbag she carried. The vicar finished the prayers over the grave. Mourners turned towards the cars and taxis that would take them to the reception in Swanham's one hotel. The tall man approached. She saw it was David, greying round the temples, shoulders slightly stooped, but still matching the memory she'd carried around for the last thirty-odd years. Becky spotted him too. 'David.' She held out her hands. 'You're a darling for coming.' She blinked back tears and smiled at Felix.

'Becky.' He clutched her hand, his gaze slipping to Felix. 'Hello, Felix. I'm so sorry.'

'Thank you for your letter.' The familiar neat handwriting had made her stomach lurch.

'Your father was one of a kind.'

'It's wonderful to see you.' Becky beamed at David through unshed tears. 'Did you drive down?'

'I did. Can I take anyone to the reception?'

'You could drive Felix.' Becky propelled her towards him.

'I thought I was going with you,' Felix said.

'I want five minutes alone at the grave.' She smiled. 'You do understand, don't you?'

'This way.' David nodded towards a Mercedes.

'You've done very well.'

'The last few years have been good ones.' He paused. 'Work-wise.'

'I married too, you know.' What a fool; she sounded over-keen to assure him that another man had found her worth keeping, even if David hadn't.

'Becky told me.' He gave her a sad little smile. 'I was sorry to hear about your husband. Dementia's cruel.'

'We had some good years before he went into the home.' Now wasn't the time to dwell on those last months, Theo growing more and more confused and unhappy, instead of the cheerful companion he'd been.

David was saying something.

'Sorry, I missed that.'

'I was saying you deserved a happy marriage.' He blushed. 'Sorry. Not for me to say. Forgive me.'

'I had one. And you?'

'I married. Her name's Barbara.' His face retained its redness. 'I met her a year or so after I got my first consultant's post. She'd have come today if our son hadn't been home from university with glandular fever.'

The illness obviously ran in the family. 'I'm sorry. How many children do you have?'

'Two. One of each.'

'I'm glad.' Glad her heart had turned to stone years ago and couldn't feel pain like it used to. 'And Charles, do you still keep in touch with him?' Impossible to keep a tone out of her voice. Too bad.

'Charles died in San Francisco years ago, some exotic virus. His lifestyle became increasingly outrageous. God knows how he coped with National Service.'

'They made him do it?'

David laughed. 'He wanted the education corps but got some bog-standard infantry posting. Two years cleaning latrines.' He glanced at her. 'You're probably wondering about me. I came to terms with my sexuality. By the time I'd finished at medical school I knew I wasn't gay.' He frowns. 'I could never forgive him for what he did to us.'

A silence fell between them. 'And medicine was all you hoped it would be?' she said at last.

He shrugged. 'Sometimes I think I can't stand seeing any more suffering.'

She couldn't believe she was hearing this. 'But you were always so good with hurt animals.'

'It was different when I was young. Now watching people in pain tears me apart.' His face was set as he turned the ignition. They were driving through the small town, past shops and buildings Felix had known since her earliest childhood. Funny how small they all looked now.

'How's Isabel?'

He glanced at her. 'You know what happened to her?'

'What?'

'She left Barrington after the war.' He grinned. 'Took the baby and upped sticks and went to live in a cottage in Sussex.'

'But she was always desperate to live in London.'

'I know. Who'd have thought it. Turns out she really did have a flair for horticulture. She ran a nursery for a while, until the Squire died and left us each some money.' They'd reached the hotel and David slowed the Mercedes. 'I'll let you out here while I park.'

In the lounge she made straight for the drinks table, reaching for a glass of sherry before she realized what she'd done. She pushed the glass back and picked up a glass of tomato juice instead, marching away before she could weaken. Would it always be like this every time she saw booze? A tide of pensioners claimed her, pinning her down with memories of her father. She saw David in deep conversation with Becky while silver-haired men and women reminisced about the chickenpox epidemic of '34 and the false alarm over diphtheria in '37.

He came over to take his leave, a process that involved fresh group-reminiscences about flower-and-veg show winners and whether or not there'd been a village fête the first summer of the war. Finally Felix had him to herself. 'I wish we'd had more time to talk,' he said. 'But I've got evening appointments.'

'It's a shame.'

'You're the only person who understands.'

'Yes.'

'If you're ever in Dorking, do pop in.' He blinked and gave her his gentlest smile.

'I'll take you up on that.' They both knew she'd never go to Dorking to meet Barbara and the family.

She watched him walk to the door and clutched the glass of tomato juice to herself.

Thirty-three

Minna

'And that was the last time you saw David?' I ask. Felix doesn't need to nod. We sit for a few minutes and the only sound is a blackbird in the garden outside.

'Minna?' She gives me a direct look. 'Tell me.'

I could pretend I don't know what she's talking about.

But I do know what she means. I start talking and I can't stop. Words tumble out. I tell her what happened on the way home from the party.

It was pouring by the time I'd extracted Tom from the conversation he was having with the American in the expensive-looking cashmere jumper. 'Come and have a last dance with me.' He put his arms round my waist.

'It's too late.' In his car seat on the hall floor Benjamin was turning his head from side to side and stuffing his hand into his mouth. 'He's starving. Shame I started him on bottles, or I could have fed him myself.' I pulled on my coat. Tom spotted another friend from university days and swayed over to say a prolonged hello. Benjamin opened his eyes and gave me a look that warned of trouble if he wasn't soon reunited with his bottle. 'Come on, Tom.' I tugged at his sleeve. 'He's going to start bawling.' I covered the baby with his blanket.

'Mustn't keep a man from his bottle.' Tom gave the friend a slap on the back and started burrowing under the rack-full of coats for his jacket. Then there was another five minutes of thanks to our hosts. By now Benjamin was properly awake, grizzling slightly, kicking his feet, warning of the bellowing to come. I dragged Tom out onto the street, where the rain beat down in rods. He took the keys out of his pocket and unlocked the door.

'I hope you don't think you're driving.' I took the keys from his hand.

'Oh come on, Mins, I had two glasses.'

'Three.'

He groaned and surrendered the keys. 'Give me Benjamin, he's getting soaked.' He took the baby seat from me and opened the passenger door. I saw him pull the belt over the seat. Did he check the tension as you're supposed to each and every time? Did he check I'd pulled the straps tightly enough round Benjy's chest? I can't be sure. I was diving into the driver's seat, relieved to be out of the pouring rain, anxious to get home before the baby started screaming.

Tom jumped in beside me and I pulled out. By now the rain was lashing the windscreen. The car swayed in the wind. 'Quite a storm.' Tom was quietening down. 'Wasn't it just grand to see them all?' He yawned. 'We should go out more often. And it was useful to meet Jeremy socially.'

'Was that him, in the cashmere jumper?'

'Likes his smart clothes, does Jeremy. But we had a good talk and I think there'll be some more work for me from Waymark.'

Benjamin started to roar. Through the rear-view mirror I caught a glimpse of his tiny wrists waving in the air. My foot pushed down on the accelerator. 'Careful,' Tom warned.

'You're a fine one to speak, getting plastered on my first night out.'

He grinned. 'Sorry.'

Was I as angry with him as I seem to remember? I'm not sure. I was probably just exasperated. And tired. The baby seldom slept through the night. Now it would be difficult to get him to take a bottle. He'd want me. It would be an hour at least before we'd get him down and sleep was possible. Taking him with us and disrupting his schedule had been a mistake. Next time we'd get a babysitter.

These thoughts were still buzzing round my mind when the van pulled out. I didn't stand a chance, that's what Tom and the police told me. Nobody could have avoided the collision. I shouldn't blame myself.

I had flicked the windscreen wiper to its fastest setting but still the rain poured down the glass, blinding me.

The white van turned out of a side street in front of me. I slammed down my foot. The ABS braking system juddered a few times and we slowed. But not enough. The car was still skating across the road.

Tom muttered something under his breath. Now the van filled the windscreen. I could read the writing on the side – G JONES WINDOW-CLEANING.

The crash wasn't as loud as I'd expected. I had just enough time to note this as my head shot towards the window and the world fragmented into silvery-grey slivers. Before I lost consciousness I heard Tom cry out.

The van was packed with building materials: stone slabs, metal girders, bags of cement and bricks the driver had stolen from a building site. Its weight meant it couldn't skid out of harm's way when we crashed into it, so our lighter car absorbed the force of the collision. The van driver jumped out unharmed, I'm told. Apparently he called the emergency services on his mobile and tried to resuscitate Benjamin while we waited for the ambulance. He wasn't to know Benjamin's neck was already broken.

The driver got two months in prison. If I hadn't hit him he'd have got away with his robbery. If he hadn't stopped to try and help he might still have escaped the police. His wife had just had a miscarriage, he'd lost his job, and he was desperate for money so he could take her away on holiday. Tom tried to reassure me they'd let him out early for good behaviour.

When I woke up after the crash I was in a side-room which spun and refused to come into focus. I squinted and made out Tom beside me, a white object round his left arm. He saw me looking at him and smiled. 'Hey, you're back with us.' A nurse appeared.

'Mrs Byrne.' She took my wrist and checked my pulse and shone a torch into my pupils. 'Good. You're doing well. I'm just going to fetch the doctor.'

The room still spun but now it was slowing. My eyes started to make out objects: roses in a vase beside me, cards, my sponge bag – who'd brought that here? The white object round Tom's arm was a plaster cast. 'Are you hurt?'

'Small break. Nothing to worry about.' He smiled again and I noticed how grey his skin was. Something had happened. I knew that I knew what it was but I couldn't remember. I closed my eyes again, replayed the last seconds of the drive home. *The van pulls out in front of me. I brake, the airbags spring out, the car keeps sliding across the road and the van doesn't move out of the way and there's a crunch.* Then what? I remembered blue lights, the young man in the hoody standing in the car doorway – the thief whose van I'd hit. And he was saying something about a baby. Our baby. Benjamin. I opened my eyes again and sat up.

'Where is he?' I pulled off the white sheets and blankets. 'I want to see him. Or is he with Mum? I'm well enough to look after him now.'

'Minna . . .' Tom tried to stop me. 'You can't—'

'Where is he?' And something terrible was coming for me like a grey monster, trying to flatten me. And I knew where Benjy was, or rather, where he wasn't. I screamed and the noise filled the room, filled the whole world.

They let me see Benjamin in his little casket at the chapel of rest. There wasn't a mark on his body that I could see. He looked like a wax mannequin, pristine in a way he never looked when he was alive.

Tom stood beside me. 'I gave them the red and white outfit to put on him because I thought it was your favourite.' Mikey and Gareth had bought it from a designer baby shop in Milan: three-quarter length trousers and a long-sleeved top with a train pattern.

It had come with a matching cap, which had usually ended up lop-sided over one of Benjamin's ears, giving him a piratical air.

'It's a bit tight in the body since he had the last growth spurt.'

'I'll drive back and get something else.'

'No, it's fine.'

'I didn't know whether or not to bring the cap.'

'Do people wear caps in coffins?'

'Don't know.' Tom looked like a small, uncertain boy. 'But I'll go home and get it if you want.' I sensed how unbearable he was finding it to stand here beside me.

'We never had him christened.' I'd only just started thinking about organizing the ceremony. 'He'll be floating around in limbo for eternity.' *Limbo*? Where did that come from? I didn't consider myself a religious person. I wasn't even Catholic, although we'd married in a Catholic church to keep Tom's family happy.

'Forget all that bollocks. Even my mother doesn't believe it.' Tom's mother is a regular at her local church in Belfast, hasn't missed Sunday mass in fifty years.

Tom found me a priest with a Liverpool accent, a school friend of Gareth's, who kept trying to reassure me about limbo, saying even the Vatican no longer believed in it, and reminding me how Jesus suffered the little children to come to Him. And I smiled and nodded.

So convinced was I that I'd committed my son to some never-ending waiting room, I didn't even want to bother with a funeral – what was the point? But Tom insisted and the Liverpudlian priest conducted the service at the same church where we'd been married. I couldn't get the thought of unconsecrated burial grounds out of my mind, even though they assured me this wouldn't be the case for Benjamin. So I made Tom agree to a cremation.

I brought the ashes down to the coast with me and put the urn on the shelf above the television. I keep wondering what to do with them. I'm not sure I want to part from them.

*

Unlike most people, Felix doesn't twitch or look uncomfortable, or rush to tell me how sorry she is. Her eyes don't move from mine, she hardly blinks. 'And how are things between you and Tom now?' she says finally.

'Bad.' Just saying it makes me realize how bad.

She's silent again, I can almost hear her thinking. 'You must try and talk to him.'

'I think he's involved with someone else, one of our friends.' Despair floods me and experiencing emotion is such a novelty I clutch the edge of the seat to steady myself. 'Oh God, supposing he leaves me?' Tom, my lover, my companion. My friend. Whom I've ignored, neglected, and pushed away for so long.

'All the more reason to talk.'

'I can't.' I sound almost panicked. 'And he's so busy with work.'

Her mobile rings. Her face falls as she listens. 'No, you're right to ring me,' she tells the caller. 'I'll have to phone the roofing company and tell them to get started immediately.'

'Bad news?' I ask as she puts the phone down.

'My roof. I've been losing tiles for a while but the neighbour who's watering the plants tells me there's a leak.' Suddenly she looks her age.

'Will it be a big job?'

She nods. 'I should have sold the house years ago, to be honest. But like a sentimental fool I clung onto it. I'd already lost Rosebank, and my marital home – had to sell it when Theo moved into residential care.' Her hands fall open in resignation. 'I suppose the house is only bricks and mortar.'

'Bricks and mortar mean a lot to most people.'

The silence between us feels companionable and deep. I think of how many people Felix has lost – friends, lover, husband, parents. 'You never found out what happened to Phoebe?'

'She was impossible to find. I kept thinking about her and the child. At least now we know Louise grew up. But we know nothing else. I wish I could see her.'

'Why?'

'I want to confess, Minna. Tell her what really happened to her father.'

'Why now? After all these years?'

Her shoulders sag. 'You finding his body like that, it's as though he was telling me it was time to draw a line under the whole thing. But I can only do that if I tell the truth.'

'To the police?'

'Why do you mention them?' Her eyes widen.

'No reason.'

'They never found his skull, did they?'

'I don't think so. We certainly didn't see it when we found the rest of his body.' Why is she asking about Lew's skull? Is Felix growing confused? I pull my cardigan tighter round me as I remember my grandmother's last months, a foggy muddle of past, present and imagined events that nobody, least of all her, could interpret.

Felix's gaze darts round the room as though she seeks distraction. 'Did I tell you about the time I saw Isabel again? I found a telephone directory for the Midhurst area. There were only two *I. Barrington*s listed.'

Is she trying to divert me or is this just one more indication of her confusion? But my curiosity about Isabel makes it impossible for me to resist. 'Go on,' I say.

Thirty-four

The first was a semi-detached thirties house with net curtains and garden gnomes fishing round a pond. Felix didn't even bother ringing the doorbell. The second address lay up a rutted, muddy lane. If this was Isabel's new home Felix hoped she'd abandoned her youthful love of white clothes.

She stopped the car and switched off the engine. Smoke curled out of a chimney and a clothes line of washing jigged in the April breeze. Red tulips blazed in a flowerbed and late narcissi poured over the lawn beneath a magnolia. Felix caught the papery scent of hyacinths. A cold frame housed neatly labelled terracotta pots of seedlings.

She walked up the path and found the front door open. 'Hello?'

'Who's that?' a woman called from upstairs. 'If you've come for the jam jars for the WI, I left them in a box on the kitchen table. Help yourself.'

'It's Felicity Valance.' Isabel wouldn't recognize her married name.

Silence.

'Felix?' Isabel sounded uncertain. 'Hang on, I'm coming down.'

The first Felix saw were her legs, her ankles and calves still elegantly slim, in sheer stockings. Or had Isabel switched to tights like most of womankind? Her tweed skirt stopped just below the knee. Her face came into view. Isabel must be in her late fifties by now but her smooth skin and slim figure could have fooled Felix into thinking her at least a decade younger. 'Well, well, haven't seen you since Fontwell days.' Her still-languorous eyes examined Felix.

'The night on the beach.' Felix had no wish to make this easy for her, even after all these years. And she didn't want to admit to having gatecrashed Isabel's wedding. Not yet. Or having taken shelter in her

London house during an air raid. Or having read her diary. So many secrets.

'Poor Lew.' Isabel sighed. 'They never found his body, did they? Used to keep me awake at nights worrying about that.' She looked Felix up and down, just as she'd done when they lived in Fontwell. 'Are you coming in, darling? Or do we have to do our reminiscing standing up?'

Felix followed her into the front room. Two small sofas faced one another, faded but still expensive-looking. Photographs crowded the fireplace. Felix peered at them and saw they were all of the same blond boy, growing up to become a tennis-playing adolescent and a handsome young man on a chestnut hunter.

'That's Justin. He's forty now. Hard to believe.' The pride in Isabel's voice was unmistakable.

'What does Justin do?'

'He's a farmer, in the north. Barrington bought him a place up there. Good of him, really.'

'Why good?' Of course Felix knew.

'Well, Justin's not his son is he?' Isabel gave that old teasing smile of hers and pulled a cigarette out of a silver box. 'Want one of these, darling? No? You always were a straight little thing.'

'So whose son is he?' Felix smiled back. Two could play the cool game. 'Sorry, terribly rude of me to ask.' Not that she had any doubts, but she wanted to hear Isabel say the name.

'Johnson's.' Isabel took a puff and smiled again. 'Not who you'd choose to father your child. At first I thought I should get rid of the baby. But I didn't.'

Felix shifted slightly in her chair.

'I always wanted the society wedding, life among the best kind of people. Johnson couldn't exactly have given me that. Even if I'd loved him enough to marry him. So I let Barrington take advantage of me almost as soon as we met. He thought Justin was his. For a time, anyway.' She stubbed out her cigarette. 'Bit of a shock when I realized I'd been wrong about what I wanted.'

'What sparked that?'

'We were on the way to some big do in the City – colleagues of Barrington's. Must have been about five or six years after the war. He was moaning away about his shares going down and taxes going up and the bloody socialists. He kept droning on that he hadn't fought the war – as if he'd ever lifted a weapon – to have a bunch of communists steal his property from him. I just sat there in the car and looked at his piggy face and had – what's the word they use about the Three Wise Men?'

Felix's puzzlement must have shown on her face.

'Epi-something?'

'Epiphany.'

'You always did better at lessons than I did. Anyway, darling, I looked at Barrington in his dinner jacket with the cummerbund straining over his stomach and I had an epiphany. Told him I wanted to leave. "You always said you wanted money, and money you've got," he said. "Well it hasn't made me happy," I told him.' Isabel sighed.

Her gaze returned to Felix and she studied her, taking in her clothes and shoes. Felix had taken trouble with her appearance for this trip. 'Do you keep in touch with that half-brother of mine?' Isabel put a hand over her mouth in mock concern. 'I'm assuming you know the dirt about the Squire? Could never get used to calling him Daddy.'

'I know you're David's sister, if that's what you mean.'

'Bit of a shock, I expect.'

Felix shrugged.

'So have you seen David?'

'He came to my father's funeral.'

Isabel's expression softened. 'I was sorry to hear the doctor'd died. He was very kind to me. God knows what would have happened to me if he hadn't been around in Fontwell. I really think they'd have put me in some ghastly asylum. Your father understood depressive illnesses, and not many did back then.'

Felix couldn't trust herself to talk to her about her father. 'Apart from then, no, David and I don't meet.'

'True love doesn't always mean love that lasts.' Isabel sounded as though she was reading the blurb on the back of a romantic novel. But her expression was thoughtful.

'You knew?' Felix leant forward. 'About David and me?'

'About your affair?' Isabel nods. 'He came to me one evening, would have been '47 or '48. Said he was in turmoil. That obnoxious little queer Charles was clinging to him but he wanted you. He went on and on about how wonderful you were, how awful we'd been, blaming you when . . . well you know, that night on the beach.'

Felix felt the lump in her throat grow larger.

'I never knew why it didn't work out between you two.' Isabel peered at her as though hoping Felix would explain. When she said nothing, Isabel laughed. 'Discreet as ever. Talking of old lovers, Johnson came to see me, you know.'

Felix nearly shot out of her chair. 'When?' She couldn't help glancing out of the window, as though he might be prowling around outside.

'Don't panic, it was decades ago. God knows what would have happened if Barrington'd found him there.'

'Where?'

'In our Grosvenor Square house, darling. There was an air raid, not V1s, proper bombers. I thought I ought to get down to a shelter with Justin, it sounded nasty. We'd just reached the front door when the bell rang.'

1944

Isabel opened the door, the baby in one arm, and stared at the man in the shabby coat on the doorstep. 'Johnson?' She stepped back, remembering there was nobody else in the house with her. Justin gave a faint cry and she rocked him in her arms.

'Miss Isabel, Lady Barrington, I mean, sorry to come and see you unannounced.' The house began to shake as the first of the Dorniers approached.

'You'd better come in.' She took him downstairs to the kitchen,

223

supposedly the safest part of the house. 'What can I do for you?' She tried hard to disguise the shaking of her hands and sat down on a kitchen chair, jigging the baby on her knee. A parachute mine crashed down a few blocks to the south. God, this didn't sound good, and here she was stuck with Johnson.

'Shouldn't you go to the shelter?'

'No, it's fine.' She couldn't bear the prospect of him taking her there, people seeing them together, listening in to their conversation. 'Why did you come to see me?'

The full intensity of his stare hit her like flames. 'I've joined up.'

'I thought your lungs—'

He waved a hand in dismissal. 'There's always ways into the Forces. Surprised you're not doing something useful yourself, Isabel.'

She wasn't going to let him talk to her like that. 'How do you know I'm not?'

His smile took in her jewellery and the hair she'd had set that morning.

'I could call the police in here and tell them you're harassing me.' The fierceness in her voice surprised her.

'But you won't.' He pointed upstairs. 'Wouldn't want to lose all this, would you? Wouldn't want your husband to know what you were like before you married him.' He leant towards her. 'Wouldn't want everything to come out, would you? It's been, what, a year now? You've kept very quiet about that nigger.'

The engines rumbled overhead now. On the shelf an earthenware teapot danced to the vibrations. Isabel felt the pressure drop in the kitchen. As the air swooshed out of the basement, smashing through the window, she dived under the kitchen table with Johnson's son. Too late, they should have gone to the shelter.

Felix 1985

'A direct hit?' Felix asked.

'Not quite. Else I wouldn't be here now. It landed next door. The blast travelled through the dividing wall. Justin and I were all right, but the glass shattered and a piece of the window-frame hit Johnson on the head. The housekeeper had been saying the window needed re-taping but she hadn't got round to it. I suppose she never imagined there'd be anyone else down there apart from her and Cook.' Isabel puffed on a second cigarette. 'I thought the whole house must have come down on top of us, but when I got to the ground floor you'd hardly have known. Just a few bits of plaster on the floor.'

'And Johnson?'

'He wasn't moving.' Isabel rolled her eyes. 'Bit awkward really, didn't know how to explain him, so I stuffed his identity papers in the stove and went outside to call in the auxiliaries. I said I'd no idea who he was, that I'd taken him in when the alert started. But when we got down to the kitchen, he'd gone.'

'Gone?'

'Must have passed out and come to while I was away. God knows what happened to him. It was a hell of a night. Perhaps he got caught up in another bomb. Perhaps he joined up and pegged it somewhere in Europe.' Isabel glanced at the window. 'Perhaps he survived and he's still out there somewhere. I can never quite be sure he won't come and track me down.' She caught sight of Felix's face. 'Don't worry, darling. He'd be far too decrepit to do anything to us now.'

'Were you ever in love with him?'

Isabel smirked. 'I fancied him a bit. He wasn't bad-looking in an intense, working-class, kind of way. And I was terribly mucked up inside, you know. The shrinks say I needed to show myself how little I valued myself by having sex with men I despised.' She shook her head. 'He was so intense, though. And one day in the boathouse I let him go all the way, just to see what it was like, a day or so before Lew turned up. Unfortunately I rather enjoyed it. Tried hard not to let him see, though. Kept saying he'd forced me.' She rolled her eyes. 'I couldn't stop seeing him, even though I hated myself. Then when Lew appeared I realized how stupid I'd been. He was so much better-looking than Johnson, but he wouldn't even kiss me, kept saying he'd treated Phoebe wrong but he was going to stick by her and her child.'

'A gentleman.'

'He was that, all right.' She sighed. 'Funny, really. It took a poor black from Georgia to show me how people should behave.' Her eyes were fierce. 'He was better than all of us. Think what he could have become if he'd lived.'

'He'd have gone back to the South. Things wouldn't have been good for him there.'

'Perhaps. But he had talent, don't forget that. And character.'

'And a child.' Felix often found herself thinking about Lew's unknown offspring.

'You worked that out, too, did you?' She blew out smoke. 'I sometimes wonder what happened to Phoebe's little half-caste baby. Must have been born just a few months before my Justin.'

The clock on the fireplace struck the hour. Nearly time for her to go. 'It was a nice house you had in Belgravia.'

'You saw it?'

'I took shelter in it during a raid when I happened to be in that part of London.'

Isabel raised an eyebrow but said nothing.

'Someone left your basement door open.' Should she tell Isabel she'd read her diary? No. Better not.

Isabel didn't seem perturbed. 'Damn servants. They'd run out to the shelters and forget to lock up. Sometimes we'd come back and find people had looted our stuff. Barrington got quite unpleasant with the staff.'

'Was he really that bad?'

Isabel nodded, stretched out one of her wool-clad legs. 'Ghastly man, a real parvenu. Made his money canning vegetables, would you believe? Nice about alimony, though. Paid for all this.'

'Was he unkind to you because of Justin? Did he find out about his real father?'

'Yes, but not who it was. Hadn't got a clue about Johnson. Barrington just didn't know how to handle me. I was so much younger, of course. And I suffered dreadfully with my depression. Funnily enough, that cleared up a bit when the bomb landed next door. Must have shaken the wires in my brain or something.' She grinned. 'Doesn't sound very scientific, does it? But that's how it felt. And the doctors tried out some new drugs on me as well.' Felix had to admit that the face in front of her showed no signs of melancholy.

There seemed no more to be said. Felix rose. 'I should go now.'

'Listen darling, what I said all those years ago about your father,' Isabel stubbed out the cigarette. 'I didn't mean it, you know. I was just jealous.'

'Jealous?'

'You got on so well with David, you were always together. And I felt left out. When Lew arrived I was so worried he'd prefer you two to me. So I said . . . those things about your clothes and your father to hurt you. Shouldn't have. Sorry.' For a second or two it was possible to see Isabel as David's sister, for a moment her face wore the same expression as David's had when he'd found a wounded blackbird or a mouse the cat hadn't finished killing.

Felix bowed her head. 'It's fine. Thanks for saying it, though.'

'Should have said it years ago.' Isabel looked almost wistful. 'Come again, won't you? Gets dull down here.'

'You wouldn't think of moving back to London?'

Someone opened a door at the back of the house. 'Isabel, you in?' A deep male voice with a rural burr.

Isabel lifted an eyebrow. 'There are some attractions to country life.'

Minna

'You sound as though you liked her in the end,' I say.

'Annoyingly enough, I did. She was less brittle. And she had her plants to occupy her. And her rustic admirers.' A smile, wry but admiring, twists Felix's face.

'Is Isabel still alive?'

'She died a few years ago after a bad fall. Apparently she went out at night to protect a particularly precious shrub from the frost and slipped. She caught pneumonia while she was still in hospital.'

'Did you tell David you'd seen her?'

'I never spoke to him again after my father's funeral.'

'Is he . . .?'

'Still alive? Yes. He's retired now but I sometimes see him mentioned in the press as sitting on various prestigious boards and committees.' Felix looks wistful. 'Perhaps I should have told him about finding the cormorant sketch. Perhaps he read the newspaper accounts about you finding Lew's body. The nationals gave it a bit of coverage.'

Something else occurs to me. 'What happened when you rang the local paper? Did they give you Louise's details?'

'No. They rattled on about confidentiality. I made them promise to give her my mobile number if she ever calls them. I bet they forget, though.'

'What about the Electoral Register?' I suggest.

Her face brightens. 'That's an idea. I'll find the woman if I have to knock on every door in Bournemouth.' Her chin juts forward. I can imagine her doing it.

Thirty-five

Minna

Tom and I sit watching the ten o'clock news. I say watching but really I'm lost in a world that died sixty years ago and he's frowning at the stack of bank statements and cash-point receipts beside him. My abandoned task – I never told him the final balance, the amount we needed to borrow. He sighs. 'This'll have to wait until tomorrow – I've got to finish a report for Jeremy.'

'I'll do it. I'd forgotten.'

'Would you?' His face lightens. 'I don't really know what I'm doing. Never had your eye for figures.'

'I'll finish it tomorrow. First thing, so we can ring the bank.'

'There's something I need to tell you.' He can't meet my eye and gets up to stand at the conservatory windows.

'Oh?' I shiver in the warm air.

'I should have told you a long time ago.'

So it's not money. 'Is it Sara?' The words burst out of my lips.

'Sara? No, I meant Benjy.'

'What about Benjy?'

'The coroner said in his report that the car seat was in good working order and the straps fastened properly.'

'Yes.' Is he worried I think he was careless?

'What he didn't know, what I hadn't told anyone, was that the car'd been in a slight accident the week before.'

My puzzlement must be written clearly on my face.

'I'd taken Benjy out with me to go shopping. We hit a bollard in Sainsbury's car park, just nudged it really. I checked the baby and the car seat and it all seemed fine. Benjy hadn't even woken up. The car was hardly dented.' His voice grows very quiet. 'To be honest, I didn't give it a second thought.' He turns from the window and sits down again.

I remember noticing a hairline crack on the car's number plate.

He leans forward. 'Don't you see? Suppose the crash damaged it? They say if a seat is involved in an accident you should buy another one.'

'But this was hardly an accident. You just bumped the front of the car.'

'It might have caused some hidden damage.'

I take his hands between mine, surprised to find myself feeling protective towards him. 'They'd have found it when they were investigating. The seat was fine. We lost Benjy because of what I did.'

'The van pulled out too suddenly. Nobody could have missed it. That's what the police told me.' He pulls his hands from mine and buries his head in them. 'If I hadn't drunk all that wine I'd have been the one who hit it, not you.'

'You only drank three glasses.'

'I was supposed to be driving home, not you. It's my fault you've had all this unnecessary guilt to deal with. I wish it had been me.' He raises his face, ashen, eyes shadowed. 'I've seen you looking at me in the last few weeks, I've seen your expression, how you blame me. I've seen how you serve up these meals just for me as though you're telling me I'm callous.'

'I don't.' I think of the events of the last months and shiver.

'I've seen your face, Minna. And you've been so cold the last couple of days, as though you hate me. I don't blame you, Lord knows.'

'I thought you were having an affair with Sara.'

He stares at me

'Mark told me she was acting strangely.' I pause. 'And I thought she was seeing you.'

'Me?' His face shows such surprise I can't believe he's bluffing. 'What on earth gave you that idea?'

'She sent you house details. She rings you on your mobile at odd times. And emails you. I thought you were planning to leave me for her.' I give a hollow laugh. 'Perhaps you are.'

I wait for him to tell me I've guessed right after all.

'You've got this all wrong.' His fierce stare compels me to meet his eye. 'The house details were for you.'

'For me?'

'Friends of hers have bought that house. They live abroad and they're moving back. They want someone to sort out the decor, help them choose paints and curtains so they can move straight in. Sara told them about you. We were waiting for the right time to tell you about it.'

I'm aware my mouth is hanging open.

He smiles at me. 'You need to start thinking about your work again, Minna. We thought this house would be a start.'

'I couldn't, it's much too soon,' I gabble. My brain can't make sense of this.

He nods. 'It's your decision. But you will think about it, won't you?'

I'm about to dismiss the idea again when I remember how excited a new project used to make me: trips to fabric warehouses for curtain material, scrutinizing paint charts, expeditions to second-hand furniture shops and auction rooms. The thrill of seeing people's faces when they see the new world you've created in their homes. 'I'll mull it over.' And I don't just make the promise to get him off my back. But there's something else I need to clarify. 'So Sara's not having an affair?' The idea's been so firmly welded into my head it's hard to believe it was just a phantom.

'Of course she's not. She's very happy with Mark. In fact, as well as trying to sort out this house for her friends and looking after the baby she's arranging a big do for his fortieth, something extravagant. She's been on at me to pull some strings to get her a room at the House of Commons.' He rolled his eyes. 'She's no idea how impossible that is right now with security sky-high.'

'So how come you bought her the laptop?'

He sighs. 'It's for you. I thought it would be a spur to getting your career recharged. It's not new but I've bought all kinds of weird and wonderful design software. They wouldn't deliver down here.'

So many reasons for Sara to ring Tom's mobile all the time. I laugh. Tom looks anxious. 'It's all right,' I say. 'I'm just realizing how easy it is to read into things whatever you want.'

'So you'll come and see the house?'

'Of course. When?'

'Hang on, I'll ring Sara now.' He goes off, leaving my mind bubbling over.

When he comes back he looks determined. 'Tomorrow afternoon. Sara'll be there with the keys – and your new laptop. We can be back here in time for supper. Or we could spend the night at home.' He catches a glimpse of my face. 'Or not.'

The thought of entering our home still terrifies me. I try and switch into work mode to distract myself. 'I'd better dig out a pad and pencils.'

'Just a moment.' He puts down the mobile, rifles behind a sofa cushion and pulls out a paper bag from Swanham's art shop. 'Thought you might like some new stuff.' He smiles like Father Christmas as he pulls out the contents. He's got it all right: the exact brand and softness of pencil, the exact size of pad. I smile back. Can it be, finally, things are getting better? His mobile rings and he snatches it up, mouthing a sorry to me. 'Jeremy. I've got a time for the meeting. I think we're making headway . . .'

We lie in bed together. Tom reaches over my shoulder and pulls Benjy's sleep-suit from under my pillow. 'You still need this?'

I nod. 'Sorry.'

'I can't exactly complain it takes up too much of the bed.' He takes the suit from me and examines it. 'I just don't know how much it's helping you now. The psychiatrist said—'

'What does he know?' I snatch back the garment.

'Sorry.'

'It's all right. Just give me a bit of time. I'm getting there.'

Tom's hand touches my shoulder. 'You certainly are.'

'Felix has helped me.'

'Ah.'

'Not that you haven't.' God, I've put my foot in it again. I move closer to him and his arm encircles me.

'You must know all there is to know about her friendship with Lew.'

'Not quite. Sometimes I think she's holding back on me.'

'It's as though you're on some kind of personal mission.'

'I suppose I am. But we'd both like to find Louise, Lew's daughter. It would complete the puzzle. And I'd like to find out—'

'What?'

'Whatever's still hidden.' I sigh. 'You must think I'm obsessed, but it's helped me, in a funny way.'

'It seems strange that other people's sad stories could do that.' He strokes my hair.

'Perhaps I feel less alone, knowing others have had sad stories.'

Silence. Then, 'Do you really feel so alone?' And he sounds so despondent I turn to him.

'No. I know you're here for me. And I will pull through, I will.'

'Perhaps one day we can think about another child.'

I can't believe he's said it.

'Minna?'

I pull myself out of his embrace. How can he even dream I'd be able to be a mother again. 'You know what happened!'

'It doesn't mean you can't have a second baby.'

'It means I'd be mad to try.' My voice is shrill.

'Goodnight, then.' Now he's the one who sounds alone. And distant, as though he's a long way from me.

Thirty-six

Minna

We both make a supreme effort over breakfast. I even manage to nibble half a piece of toast.

We're getting into Tom's car when Felix's Vauxhall shoots down the drive, throwing up dust and gravel. She springs out like a woman thirty years her junior. 'Thank God I caught you.'

'What's happened?'

'I've spoken to Louise.'

'You got hold of the Electoral Register this quickly?'

'Didn't have to. Mrs Ogle rang to tell me she's organized a plumber to mend that kitchen tap. It struck me she might have older telephone directories in her office – people don't always throw them away when they get new ones. She found the number for me and I rang Louise.' Felix's eyes sparkle. 'The remarkable thing is we're only just in time. She leaves for a long holiday in Canada tomorrow.'

We so nearly missed her. 'I'm just off to London,' I tell her.

'We're back late tonight,' Tom says, opening the passenger door for me. 'We need to be on our way now.'

'If we don't go to see her now we've lost the chance for months. And you'll be back in London and I'll be back in Yorkshire.'

I look from one of them to the other, feeling as though I'm standing on the edge of an abyss. I know I should go with Tom but the prospect of meeting Louise is irresistible.

I close the passenger door. 'I'm sorry.' And I am. But I can't meet Tom's eyes. 'I've got to do this, I've got to finish this now.' He still says nothing. 'Tell Sara I'm sorry.'

'I'll ring her.' He sounds resigned. Sad, but resigned.

I pick up my rucksack.

Felix looks from Tom to me. 'I should have rung before I turned up.'

'No, it's fine.' It's not, I can see hurt on Tom's face.

'We can take my car,' Felix says. 'But we've got to hurry, she's frantically packing.'

'We could go to London another day,' I tell Tom, even while I know that's not the point. I squeeze his arm. 'I'll be back this evening. We can talk then. I'll cook.'

He walks over to Felix's car and opens the passenger door for me. 'I'll see you later,' he says. I kiss his cheek and he forces a smile.

'Poor Tom,' I say, as much to myself as to Felix. I sit clutching the rucksack, full of the art materials he bought for me.

'We shouldn't be leaving him like this.' She sounds guilty, too, but her eyes have a zealot's gleam.

'He's had a lot to put up with.'

'Losing the baby must have hit him hard.' She turns the car, giving me a glimpse of Tom's taut face as he stands at the front door.

'It wasn't just that.' I pause. 'I was acting strangely before we came here.'

I've done it, I've finally found the courage to extract this part of my past and look at it.

She nods to show me she's paying me attention but says nothing as we reach the road.

'When Benjy died, after the initial shock, I couldn't accept he was gone. I took his sleep-suit into our bed. It's still there; it helps me.'

'Sounds natural enough to me.'

'But that's not all. Until recently I kept looking for him.'

'Where did you look?' She sounds so neutral she could be asking me for directions.

'I'd go out into our back garden and imagine I'd find him having a nap in the pram. Or out to the car, thinking I'd left him in his car seat. Of course he was never there.'

'So you started looking in other places?'

'I became convinced he must be at his nursery. I'd only recently started leaving him there a couple of mornings a week. It gave me the chance to do some painting or go shopping by myself. Or do a Pilates class.'

After Benjy died I slept a lot, couldn't bear to be awake, so I'd suspend myself in nothingness. But there are only so many hours a fit young human can opt out of wakefulness, even with sleeping tablets. I'd wake at lunchtime, heart racing, and hunt for my car keys. I'd drive to Benjy's nursery, three miles away. One of the reasons I'd chosen the nursery was its good parking facilities: I could always get a place on the paved-over front garden, especially as I collected Benjy hours earlier than most of the mothers returning from jobs in the City.

The first couple of times I went to The Willows Nursery for Children Aged Six Weeks to Five Years Old after his death I just sat outside in the car with the engine running, telling myself I knew he was dead and I was just doing this to feel better for a few minutes. I imagined myself unobserved; certainly nobody ever twitched curtains or came out to me. I'd drive home feeling simultaneously relieved and guilty, like a recovering smoker sniffing empty cigarette packets.

On the third occasion I parked the car and switched off the engine. The front door opened. A woman came out carrying an infant in a car seat. I knew I could ring the bell, they'd let me in and they'd bring Benjy out to me. Maggie and Colleen would tell me what he'd eaten for his lunch and reassure me he was getting used to his formula. All these weeks had been a nightmare, nothing more. I reached for my mobile to ring Tom and tell him there'd been a terrible mistake but I'd sorted it out, but decided it would be better to do it when I'd taken Benjy safely home.

I got out of the car and walked up the steps. Did I pause for a second before I rang the bell? Did my reason try to tell me this was all wrong? I can't remember. Maggie came to the door, very pale I thought. They'd been working her too hard, asking her for too many extra shifts. 'Did he have a good lunch?' I asked.

'Mrs Byrne.' She'd used to call me Minna. We'd been on good

terms, enjoyed a gossip and a laugh. But now I had passed through some kind of door marked untouchable. 'Come in.'

Usually parents can't breach the outer defences of The Willows. Social Services or OFSTED or someone lay down strict rules about security. And quite right too. As I passed the rows of baby seats and pegs bearing hats and fleeces, I began to feel worried. Had Benjy had a bad reaction to his milk? Was he, God forbid, one of those children who turn out to be allergic to every foodstuff known to modern mothers? Had he had a fall; banged his head? They'd be worried I was going to make a fuss, but I understood about accidents. Hadn't I met Benjy's father as a result of a train derailment?

She bundled me into an office. 'Take a seat. I won't be a second.' Her footsteps clattered down the corridor. I heard murmurs.

I sat at the computer surrounded by time sheets and invoices. Perhaps they were just going to ask me if I wanted Benjy to do baby music classes. Tom had laughed when I'd mentioned them, said he was far too young for that kind of stuff.

The door bell rang.

I don't remember standing up and walking out of the office to the front door but obviously I did. I opened the many mortise locks and found a woman about my age standing on the steps with a baby in a car seat. 'Hello,' I said.

'Hi.' Northern accent. 'Here we are. A bit jittery as it's our first session. Silly really, when it's only for two hours.'

'A taster session?' I remember doing something similar with Benjy when he stared nursery.

'That's right.' A nervous smile. 'Just time for a Yoga class. And a raid on Sainsbury's. I'll reassure myself he'll be happy here when I go back to work next month.' She handed me the car seat. 'Be a good boy, Rory.'

'He'll be fine.' I smiled at the little boy, who was pulling off a sock to examine his toes. 'My Benjy's the same age.'

'And you've got my mobile number? And my husband's direct line at work?'

'Don't worry,' I reassured her. 'Nothing will go wrong.' Of course it wouldn't.

I watched Rory's mother get into her car, looking relaxed. I'd put her mind at rest and she'd go off to enjoy herself at her exercise class. I waited until she'd backed out of the drive and closed the door, half expecting Maggie to emerge and take Rory from me.

Nobody came. I looked down at the baby, now engaged in putting his feet into his mouth. Benjy used to do the same thing; I was forever hunting down discarded socks. I walked down the steps carrying the baby seat. Opened the rear door of my car. I was pleased to see this was a high-quality seat, safety's so important. I strapped the seat into the back of the car, testing the tension of the straps to make sure it couldn't budge an inch. 'There we are, sweetie. We'll be home in ten minutes.'

The baby's chubby hand waved at me. Chubby. Benjy's hands were slender, even for an infant's. This little boy wasn't Benjy. A chill ran down me. What the hell was I doing? I undid the straps and pulled the seat out of the car, flinging myself up the steps to ring the door bell. I deposited the baby on the top step and sprinted back to my car. I turned on the ignition and backed out, without looking. A lorry honked at me. I turned right into another side street. I hadn't a clue where I was going. People stared at me from the pavement.

I closed my eyes and switched off the engine.

'How long did you stay there?' Felix asks in the same casual tone.

'Until a motorcyclist started pounding on the window.'

By then my head was resting on the steering wheel. He must have thought I'd fainted. I remember him shouting at me to hang on, he'd fetch help. I remember a policeman. He was very kind, kept telling me he understood as he helped me out of my car and into his. I told him what I'd done, that I was so sorry. And Tom, pale and shaking, coming to sit in the back with me, clutching my hand so hard it hurt. 'But you didn't do anything,' he kept telling me. 'You didn't take the baby.'

'But I could have done.' What had stopped me?

238

Then I was back in the hospital – the same one I'd been in after the accident, but in a different ward. They gave me something to sleep – as if I hadn't spent most of the last weeks asleep. When I woke up they made me take some tablets. A psychiatrist talked to me. I screamed at him that I had to have Benjy's sleep-suit. He looked grave. 'Was that what he was wearing in the accident?' he asked.

'No. It was what he wore at night in his cot.' He'd been wearing smart trousers and jumper to the party, I'd wanted to show him off to our friends. I hadn't seen these clothes since Benjy died. I think they gave them to Tom to take home. The psychiatrist nodded and called Tom, told him to bring in the sleep-suit when he visited.

The policeman came back and told me of course nobody would bring charges against me – I'd done nothing wrong.

'I have,' I told him. 'I killed my child.'

The policeman blushed and turned to Tom. I saw my husband shake his head.

'I have to leave London.' If I stayed, I'd do something even more terrible.

'I was going to take you to France next month,' Tom said.

'I need to leave now. Please.'

The psychiatrist insisted on another meeting and talked to Tom in a low voice. Tom nodded, said he'd find a cottage on the coast. A friend might be able to help.

'So Tom drove you straight down here?' Felix asks.

'After the shrink had assured everyone it was extremely unlikely I'd actually steal a child. I could see he still thought I was completely mad.' Especially as I was still clutching the sleep-suit.

'I doubt it. Or else he wouldn't have let you go.' Felix continues to use the same dry tone, thank God.

'I knew what they were thinking. I could see the pity in their eyes.'

We're leaving behind the countryside now, picking up the tell-tale signs of the conurbation that is Poole and Bournemouth: roundabouts, DIY stores, schools. I feel almost bereft – me, the town mouse. 'People never used to pity me,' I continue. 'They thought I had it all, husband, baby, nice house, interesting job.'

'And you can still have all those things. Even the baby.'

'I don't know if I'd dare.' I remembered the little boy on the beach trying to hold water in his hands. 'Or if I deserve to.'

'You're very brave.'

'Me?'

'You face up to the truth.'

'Hasn't done me much good.' I shudder, remembering the grey days.

'But eventually you'll move forward. Not this year, perhaps. But next year. The pain will still be there, but you'll be living again. Things will seem meaningful.'

'I'll always feel guilty.'

Felix says nothing but her eyes flicker towards me for a second. 'We're nearly there,' she tells me at last. My hand goes to the cormorant sketch in my pocket. I almost open my mouth to ask what the thumping noise is and realize it's my heart.

Thirty-seven

Minna

Louise lives in a quiet cul-de-sac on the outskirts of Bournemouth. Sedate is the word I'd use to describe the neat gardens and semis, most of them sporting petunias in flowerbeds, crazy paving where the lawn should be, white lace curtains and hanging baskets.

'Does she live alone?' I ask.

'Apparently. She said a niece is coming to house-sit while she's in Canada.' Felix pulls into the drive, behind a grey Ford Focus. Louise has kept her lawn and her flowerbeds are full of red campion and hollyhocks. No hanging baskets. No net curtains. Felix switches off the ignition and for a second we just sit there. I sense that if I told her I want to go home she'd agree.

'Right.'

She opens her door, her expression reminding me of Tom when Mikey dared him to dive off the high board when we were all on holiday two years ago: do or die.

The front door opens the second the bell chimes. 'Hello.' Louise's skin is caramel-coloured. Her curling hair, greying now, looks as though it was once a mid-brown. She smiles: a broad, open smile that makes me think of Felix's description of Lew's grin. She stands upright like a queen, her skin smooth and soft, belying her age, which I calculate must be just over sixty. Beside me Felix sighs.

'You're like your father.' She takes Louise's hand. 'I'm so very pleased to meet you.'

'Come through.' She ushers us over wooden floors into the back room. Rugs hang from walls. A dresser displays pottery bowls and a guitar sits in an open case. The walls are rich cinnamon and gold. Photographs of young women stand on shelves: waterskiing, collecting degrees, dressed up in evening gowns. Other photos show them clasping babies and toddlers. Lew's granddaughters and great-grandchildren?

'What a beautiful house.' I allow myself to feast on the colours and textures.

'You only just caught me.' She laughs, a rich, low sound. 'I'm going to be in Toronto for six months staying with my daughter, Danielle. She's having another baby.'

'Do you have just the one child?' I ask.

'Three. All girls. Jill's a barrister in the Middle Temple.' A note of pride. 'Danielle's a doctor. And Sally's a headmistress.'

'A talented family.' Felix nods towards a chair. 'May I?'

'Please.' Her smile is warm. 'Why did you want to see me?'

I've rehearsed this moment a hundred times but all I can think to do is to pull the cormorant from my pocket. 'This is for you.'

She frowns. 'What's this?'

'Your father drew that bird on the beach at Fontwell in October 1943,' Felix says. 'He gave it to me. Then Minna found it. We think you should have it, something to take with you to show Danielle.'

Louise runs a finger over the bird. 'He wasn't a bad artist, was he?' I see her eyes are brimming. 'Sorry. It's hard – finding all this out. You see, Mum and I always thought he'd just abandoned her, gone off to Normandy and never come back. Or survived and returned to the States without telling her.'

'Lew would never have done that.' Felix's voice was fierce. 'I was there when he died. The last thing he said was your mother's name.'

Louise shakes her head and blinks away the moisture in her eyes. 'When Mum didn't hear from him . . . She was desperate. She was only nineteen, a girl.'

'What did she do?' Felix leans forward.

'By the time she was expecting me she was living in Portsmouth. She'd moved there to get better-paid work. She'd been bombed out, second time it'd happened. They put her in a home for single mothers and wanted to take the baby – me – from her to adopt.'

I look at Felix and see her eyelids fall over her eyes for a second or two as she registers the parallel with her own story.

'Mum agreed – anything to get them off her back. But then she got up early in the morning, wrapped me in a blanket, crept downstairs and managed to force one of the windows on the ground floor. They locked them in at nights as though they were dangerous: a bunch of women and their babies.' Louise laughs. 'Perhaps they were. She had enough cash for the bus fare so she went to Southampton and found herself lodgings. The landlady agreed to mind me for extra and Mum got a job in the Pirelli cable factory. When I was four months she was allowed to leave me in a state nursery.' Louise sniffs. 'They were keen enough to have unmarried mothers in the workforce when it suited them, even mothers of half-castes like me.'

I flinch at that term. Louise notices.

'That wasn't the worst thing they called me, I assure you. Little brown bastard, nig-nog, coon, I heard them all.' Louise lets out a sigh, long and deep. 'But then the war ended and they wanted all the women back in their homes playing housewife. Mum lost her job, found it hard to get another one. We kept moving. Sometimes she'd get odd bits of work, as a barmaid, or seasonal jobs picking fruit. When I started school it was easier. I was bright. Despite my unfortunate circumstances, they said. They pressed Mum to have me adopted but she refused. Even though we were so poor we didn't see meat for months. They even wanted to send me to Cincinnati; they'd found American families who'd adopt coloured children.' Louise takes a deep breath. 'Eventually I passed my eleven plus and went to grammar school. Nearly killed Mum saving the money to buy me the uniform. But she did it. And I was always the best turned out in my class. Even though my gym tunic was second-hand.'

'Were you good at art?' Felix asks. 'Like your father?'

Louise smiles, points to a cardboard portfolio leaning against the dresser. 'Look in there.'

Felix opens it, revealing paintings and sketches: fruit, flowers, trees, animals, children.

'I was a teacher. My pupils loved my art lessons.' Her eyes half close. 'Only stopped teaching a year or so back when Al, my

243

husband, died.' She studies me. 'What's the connection between you two?'

'We met on a bench in the old village.'

Her gaze is intent. 'Tell me what you came all this way to say. You didn't come all this way just to give me this, did you?' She touches the cormorant. 'You could have posted it.'

Felix reties the strings on the portfolio. 'I came to tell you the truth.' She finishes the bow. 'Your father was murdered.'

I look at her as though she's out of her mind, but her expression is serious and calm.

Thirty-eight

Felix 2006

Louise sits up. 'The police said he drowned, slipped off the rocks or something.'

Felix closes her eyes to block out the scene that's unfolding in front of her. 'I didn't tell you everything, Minna. Lew was hit on the head with a shotgun until he went under. They never found his skull or they'd have seen the evidence.' She puts a hand to her face. 'It was all my fault.'

1943

A pheasant coughed in the bushes as Felix reached the woods on her way to the beach. No time to take the longer, less eerie route along the lane. Every second counted. The moon, no longer the fat globe it had been a few nights earlier, vanished behind clouds. She switched on her torch. Branches creaked as the wind caught them. She hesitated. Something rattled in the dark. Felix knew what it was: Johnson's traps. She forced herself forward, step by step. She could see him now, stooped over something metallic on the ground. An animal screamed. Felix trembled. Then there was silence. Johnson rose, picked up his gun. She switched off the torch. He'd heard her. Her mouth opened and closed. He moved towards the path. From behind came the sound of the motorbike. Felix forced herself to creep behind an oak.

The engine stopped. 'Say, you're the gamekeeper, aren't you?' Hardy said.

'That's right.'

'We've heard our fugitive's on the beach. You seen anyone down there.'

'No.'

'We've had sightings.' Laurel got out of the sidecar.

'There's nobody down there except those kids.'

Laurel shrugged. 'OK. You may be right, but keep your eyes open.'

He turned to stare towards his traps. 'I'm a little busy right now . . .' His hand tightened on the gun.

'Mr Johnson? Something you want to tell us?'

'Seems like it's my duty to help you search.' The words came through clenched lips. 'I'll take a look in the cove.'

'Thank you. We're going back to leave the bike in the lane, can't get it along the cliff path. See you on the beach.'

He watched them head back towards the village then nodded to himself and set off.

This wasn't supposed to happen. Felix's mouth opened in mute protest. He knew the paths better than the police, he'd reach Lew before them. Her stomach somersaulted as she crept after him, then she broke into a run to keep up.

The path bent. Felix was breathless, didn't see he'd stopped and turned. 'Who's there?' She crouched behind a fallen tree, praying. His footsteps came nearer. 'Is that one of you kids? I know your games. You've sheltered that coon down on the beach, haven't you?' He must hear her heart pounding, her breath coming in short, painful bursts. He'd pull her out of her hiding place and beat her. She closed her eyes in anticipation. Nothing happened. She opened them again. He'd gone. She'd have to be careful, though. He'd still be looking out for her. And he'd hear the slightest sound.

It was so dark she knew she couldn't go further without switching on her blackout torch. Her hand went to her pocket. Gone. Must have dropped out while she was behind the dead tree. She paused. Looking for it would take valuable time. But she couldn't carry on without some light, even a feeble glow. Her fingers swept the ground. No torch.

The low moan she heard was her own. The shadows formed themselves into a shape. Johnson stood before her.

'Hey you, what's going on?' The beam of his torch ran over her face. A scream rose in her throat and dissolved.

'It's Felicity Valance.'

'What you doing here?'

'Going to find David.'

He scowled. 'At this time of night?'

'I need to tell him something.'

'What?' He stepped closer.

'Nothing.'

'Then you just push off home, Felicity Valance. I bet your father doesn't know you're out here, does he?'

She said nothing. Something crunched beside them. An animal screamed. Felix shook.

He was watching her. 'Just a rabbit in a trap.'

'Can't you . . .?'

'Put it out of its misery?' He moved into the bushes. She heard a thump. Then she spotted her torch beneath an exposed root and grabbed it, and she was running, tripping over branches, scratching her legs on brambles, heart thumping. His shouts followed her, coming closer. She came to the bank, closed her eyes and jumped down, landing legs together like a parachutist and springing forward into the lane to continue her dash. Her heart was coming out of her chest. She reached the cliff path and threw herself up it, hearing her breath jagged and hoarse. She was lighter than him, faster on the incline. The distance between them opened up, his curses seemed further away. Then shingle was flying up under her shoes and pain cutting her chest.

She reached the rocks, almost unable to speak. 'He's coming. Hide, Lew!'

'Who?' David emerged from the shadows.

'Johnson. The police told him they were going to search the cave.'

'How did the police know about the cave?'

'I told them.'

Now the faces of Lew and Isabel appeared in Felix's torchlight and they were throwing questions and accusations at her. Isabel was telling Lew the Squire would help get him to Ireland.

'There's no time for this now,' Felix hissed. 'Lew's got to hide before Johnson finds him.'

David called for Lew, who appeared from the cave, eyes wide with fear. 'Get over the rocks before he gets here,' David urged the GI.

Felix bent over to ease the stabbing in her chest. Heavy footsteps came towards her and Johnson stood there, his light in her face. 'Got you. What's going on down here?'

'Nothing.' A pebble dropped from a rock behind her.

'Where's Miss Isabel?'

'Don't know.' Something splashed and she heard a cry.

Johnson's beam moved to the sea. 'Someone's there. Show yourself.'

She took the opportunity to move behind him and creep towards the rocks. 'Felix!' David's shout was almost a scream. 'Help us. He's in the water.'

Isabel's white face appeared in the shadows. 'Is it Lew?' She grabbed Felix's coat. 'Has he fallen in?'

'That you, Isabel?' Johnson's torch beam caught her face. 'You've been out here for hours. And last night, too.'

'Spying on me, are you?'

'What if I am? There's dangerous types on the loose.'

'Dangerous, my foot.'

He moved towards her. 'You've been down here with that nigger.'

'What if I have?'

David shouted again, words that the wind swallowed.

'He can't swim. Oh God.' Isabel put a hand over her mouth.

'Who can't swim?'

Felix jumped across the rocks, hands scrabbling on wet surfaces, saltwater flooding her eyes and mouth. She reached David and stooped down to grab Lew's sodden jacket. He was heavy, as though the sea were trying to pull him back. Her heart pounded as they laboured.

'Don't give up,' David cried. Lew's fingers clutched at the rocks, his arms began to take his weight.

His chest was clear of the water, his mouth opening in a grin of triumph when Johnson's boot smashed into it. One of his hands slid from the rock in surprise. He spat out a mouthful of blood.

'Get off!' David struggled with Johnson on the rocks. 'He can't swim.' Johnson pushed the boy off as though he were a feather.

Lew still clung to the rock with one hand, the other grabbing at thin air. 'I'm slipping!' His hand scrabbled and found purchase. Groaning, he started to pull himself out of the water again, eyes glassy with shock.

Johnson stamped on his fingers. Lew screamed and let go of the rock, vanishing beneath the surface for a few seconds. Felix ripped the tissue paper off her torch, clinging to the rocks and shining the full power of the beam over the water, willing him to surface. Then he was in front of her again, arms flailing, gulping mouthfuls of air.

'Missy,' he panted. 'You get clear, now.' His head went under and bobbed up again. 'Run away.' The last words came out as pants.

'Lew!' she screamed.

Johnson picked up the shotgun he'd dragged over the rocks and swung it high. Felix's beam caught it mid-arc before it crashed down on Lew's head. Lew gave a small gasp.

'Phoebe . . .'

He sank again.

Felix screamed.

'Cut it out.' Someone shook her. Johnson had moved so silently she hadn't heard him come up behind her. 'Deserting bastard.' He spat. 'You children go back to bed and keep your mouths shut.'

Felix looked up at him. 'I hate you,' she shouted over the roaring wind. 'I hope you die and go to hell.'

He scrabbled towards her. 'Hold your tongue.'

'I'll tell the police.' Felix heard the quiver in her voice. 'They're on the way down here. We'll show them what you did.'

'I was only defending Isabel. We had a scuffle, he fell in. Nobody'll believe anything else.'

'You, defending me? That's rich.' Isabel laughed, a thin, harsh sound against the roaring of the waves.

'That's what they'll say,' Johnson turned for the beach, 'when I tell them I saw you and him together.'

Felix followed him. 'What do you mean, saw them together?'

Johnson gave a tight smile.

'You're lying!' Isabel's eyes blazed.

'I'll tell them how you're like a bitch on heat, couldn't get enough of me.'

David jumped down beside them. 'Shut up, both of you.'

Johnson folded his arms. 'Go ahead and tell the police. Then I'll say my bit and all your hopes for a big society marriage will just melt away. Who'll want a nigger's leftovers?' He turned to Felix and bared his teeth in a grin. 'Thanks, you led me straight to him.'

David's eyes bored into her. The sea seemed to cease its roar for a second. They stood motionless, David, Isabel and Felix.

'My life will be ruined if you tell the police, Felix,' Isabel said, in a voice so soft she could hardly hear her.

'Perhaps you should have thought of that when you wouldn't let Lew leave,' Felix told her. 'Let us tell the MPs.'

Isabel shook her head.

'The Squire'll believe you, not Johnson.' David touched Isabel's hand. 'You know he will.'

'I can't take the risk.' She pulled her hand away. 'My reputation . . .'

Johnson swivelled sharply. 'I'll be off.' He turned back to them threateningly. 'And if I hear you've said a word about what happened here I'll come and find you. You hear? I'll track you down.'

He stared at Isabel, as though trying to commit her face to memory, before darkness swallowed him. Felix thought she caught his outline against the cliffs for a second before he vanished.

David turned to Felix. 'This is all your fault. He'd never have found Lew if it hadn't been for you.'

And then Laurel and Hardy were scrunching across the sand towards them and they were telling her to keep quiet, pulling her down behind the boulders.

Thirty-nine

Minna

Felix looks at me. 'The rest of what I told you was true, about what happened when the MPs reached us, how they searched the cave and didn't find anything and how they thought Lew had tried to run away. And about how we pulled him out and I took the money from his pocket.'

'God.' There seems no other word capable of expressing my reaction. 'So that's what you felt so guilty about – it wasn't the police at all, it was Johnson Lew was running from.'

'And Johnson would never have found him if it hadn't been for me.'

'I'm lost.' Louise looks from one of us to the other.

'A storm was brewing and I thought Lew'd be safer in custody. The military police said they'd treat him well so I broke my word and told them where to find him. I went down to the beach to tell Lew what I'd done, so he wouldn't be frightened. But Johnson followed me.'

Louise lets out a sigh. 'You were how old?'

'Nearly fourteen.'

Louise shakes her head. 'A child.'

'Sometimes I almost thought I'd dreamed it. It was so dark down there, so noisy with the waves crashing down on us. Sometimes I persuaded myself Lew had just slipped back into the water.'

'I still don't understand why you didn't tell the MPs what Johnson did to him?' Louise's eyes burn with emotion.

'We were scared.' Felix reaches for her handbag. 'And there was Isabel to consider.'

'Isabel?' Louise's lip curls.

'Later on David found out she was his sister.'

Felix tells her about the Squire's confession. 'He was very con-

252

cerned about ruining her prospects. Even so, we were wrong to say nothing.'

Louise sits quietly. Her eyes drop to Lew's sketch. She sighs. 'So far as the military was concerned, he was just a deserting nigger. They wouldn't have bothered looking for his killer.'

'There's something else.' Felix removes a brown envelope from her handbag. 'Your father saved this money for your mother. I've kept it for you all these years.'

Louise takes it, opens it, pulls out the large, old-fashioned notes. 'How much would this be worth in modern money?'

'Probably not much,' Felix says. 'I wish I could have tracked your mother down and given it to her. I tried once.' She tells Louise how she travelled to Isabel's wedding in the hope of seeing David and enlisting his help finding Phoebe. 'I didn't even know Phoebe's surname.'

'She moved all the time, you'd have had no chance of finding us.' Louise's fingers flick through the notes, but she doesn't look at them. Her eyes are focused on scenes that took place more than sixty years ago. 'She always said he wasn't the type to leave her in the lurch. She said he was a gentleman.'

'He loved her.' Felix's words are firm.

'And Isabel?' Louise almost whispers.

'She was just a distraction. I don't think they had a relationship.'

'She cost him his life.' Louise sighs but her eyes are softer now. 'She cost me my father.'

'Lew would have married your mother.' I picture Phoebe on a boat heading across the Atlantic, baby in arms. 'Perhaps you'd have grown up in America.'

'Maybe it's as well he didn't take us there.' Louise's eyes narrow. 'A white woman married to a coloured man, in Georgia? They'd probably have jailed Lew and deported my mother for breaking race laws.'

'I wonder what happened to Tom, Leenie and Marcus?' Felix says.

'Who?' Louise doesn't know she has, or had, aunts and uncles.

'Lew's brothers and sisters.'

'We tried to trace members of the Campbell family before we buried Lew. Couldn't find anyone in the state who was related to him,' Louise's shoulders slump, remembering. 'Perhaps they moved to New York or the Midwest after the war. Plenty of black people headed north for better lives.' She falls silent.

I wonder if she's remembering the petty and undignified economies of her childhood: shabby clothes, school trips untaken, cruel jibes in the playground.

'Thank you.' She folds up the notes again. 'Taking this with me to Canada will make me feel I've wound things up here.' She touches the cormorant sketch again. 'I kept wondering how he'd come to die on that beach. And I promised myself I'd find out. But there was no time to do anything before Toronto.'

'What about the police?' I ask. 'Shouldn't we tell them now?'

'Why?' Louise shrugs. 'My father's long dead.'

'So's Johnson, in all likelihood. He was already middle-aged when he went off to fight in the war,' Felix says.

'I just wanted to know what had happened to him.' Louise nods to herself. 'That's all.' She picks up the cormorant drawing. 'Funny, this would have taken him, what, five minutes to do?'

I know what she means: this sketch Lew dashed off has reached across sixty years to touch us.

Forty

Minna

Miles pass, on the way home, without either of us saying a word. My mobile gives the brief two-tone ring that announces a text message. Kris is planning her move north for her new job and needs somewhere to live in Yorkshire that will accept a cat. 'On streets soon. Any ideas . . .?'

I'll ring her. And this time I really mean it. 'I've thought of something,' I tell Felix. 'Don't know why I didn't click before.'

'Hmmn?' She looks tired. Telling us about Johnson's part in Lew's death must have taken it out of her.

'My friend Kris. She's just got a job in Leeds, she's a museum curator. But she doesn't want to live in the city, she wants somewhere calmer. She'd suit Harrogate.'

Felix raises an eyebrow. 'I hadn't thought of taking in lodgers.'

'She doesn't smoke, doesn't have loud parties. She's a bookworm. She just needs somewhere for a few months while she gets herself sorted out.' I deliver the clincher. 'Oh, and she's got the most adorable Persian.'

'What colour?'

'Grey.'

Felix is silent for a few minutes. 'When can she move in?' she says at last.

We turn off the main road and the traffic dies away. Dust blows onto Felix's windscreen and she shoots the windscreen washer at the rusty specks. The drops of water rolling down the window remind me of that night, months back, when my life stopped. I blink. 'Why didn't you tell me about Johnson?'

It takes her so long to answer that I'm not sure she's heard. 'Didn't think I was going to tell anyone,' she says at last.

'Not even Louise?'

'Not until I saw her.' She pauses. 'I didn't know what I'd say to her. I've lived with this thing for so long. It was almost as though . . .'

'As though what?'

'It sounds daft but I was almost scared that I'd just be a shell without my big secret. Empty. Dead. I thought people would see me as a silly old woman who should have told the truth and got over the fact she hadn't kept a promise.'

'Nobody would think of you like that.' But I know how guilt can be a kind of glue, holding things together. And it's frightening when you know it's time to let go of the guilt. Supposing you just melt into nothingness? My heart goes back to Tom, to the way I jumped into Felix's car and abandoned him this morning. I eye my mobile but know this is something we can only discuss face-to-face. My heart drums out an uneasy message: I don't deserve him.

As we approach the town I know what I've got to do. I just don't know if there's enough time. Swanham's little market comes into view, stallholders packing up their fresh fish and fruit and vegetables. 'Stop!' I scream. Felix spins the steering wheel and indicates retrospectively, causing a Volvo behind us to honk its horn. 'Sorry,' I say as she halts outside Woolworths, her face full of alarm, probably worried I'm having a seizure. 'I'd like to cook something special for Tom. I'll jump out here and grab a taxi home.'

'You'll do no such thing, I'll park and wait.' She folds her arms. I spin round the stalls, begging the stallholders not to close their tills until they've sold me an organic chicken, asparagus and strawberries. I root around in boxes of Jerseys until I find the most delectable, tiniest potatoes and scoop the juiciest-looking French beans off the display. Nothing but the best tonight. With my last ten pound note in my hand I dash across the high street to the off-licence and grab a bottle of white Burgundy.

Felix opens the boot for my shopping, eyeing the carrier bags but saying nothing. We drive through the green lanes with their dog roses and rosebay willow. I know I'm seeing these things for almost the last time now. I've decided, soon I'll be back in London.

'I hope your meal goes well.' Felix's smile goes right to my heart.

'Thanks for driving me there. I needed to see this through to the end.'

'And what an end.' She stops outside the house and we get out. She sweeps me into her arms. 'What a woman Louise is.'

'Yes.'

She lets me go. 'Do you think you can be happy now, Minna?'

'Yes.' The realization hits me. 'God, I hope so. But only if I haven't ruined everything with Tom.'

'Make it work.' There's a quiet urgency to her tone. I know she's thinking of all the things that didn't work for her. We stand together for a few seconds in silence before Felix gets back into the car. I watch her until the car reaches the end of the drive and turns out of sight.

Forty-one

Minna

I dump the bags in the hall, tear upstairs into our bedroom and pull Benjy's sleep-suit from under the bedclothes. For the last time I hold it to my face and breathe in the scent. By now it probably smells more of me than Benjy. I go downstairs to the utility room and stuff it into the washing machine with the soap capsule, slamming the door and pushing the on button before I can change my mind. Time to let go.

I unload the carrier bags in the kitchen and start work. As I rub olive oil over the chicken I notice my senses coming alive again, the golden oil soft under my fingers, the aroma of the thyme, the blast of heat on my face as I open the oven door. I've been cooking delicacies for Tom for months, but I haven't really noticed what I've been doing. Today there's a sensation inside me I can barely remember: appetite.

The pile of bank statements reproaches me from the table. I sit down, find my place among the sheets and finish ticking off receipts. I'm left with a figure, a very red figure. But it's OK – I know I can work again now, I can whittle down that debt until we're solvent again. I divide the number by twelve, by twenty-four. Two years. We'll be back in the black again by then.

I tear back into the utility room and find the washing machine's finished the cycle. I tug out the sleep-suit and hang it over the clotheshorse. Once it's dried, I'll fold it carefully in tissue paper and pack it away in a drawer with the blue plastic tag they put on Benjy when he was born and all the cards people sent to congratulate us.

Tom's car grinds up the drive. No time for me to change. My heart thuds. I feel like I did when we were first courting. I pull a brush through my hair and pull out an old lipstick from my handbag to smarten myself up and go out to meet him.

His face is set and for once he ignores the loose frond of sweet pea waving in the breeze. Normally he'd stop to tie it back (he says he's not a gardener, but he can't resist this kind of outdoor task). Not tonight. He's a man ready for confrontation. Or worse.

'Hello.'

'Hello.' He carries a smart charcoal-grey case: my laptop, I guess. 'I'm not staying, just come to pack up a few things before I go back to town.'

'Tom.' He looks bemused by my detaining hand on his arm.

'I think you need some space.'

'No.'

'I'm not helping you.'

'That's not true.'

'I wish I could believe it. But I just seem to put my foot in it. What I said last night about having another baby, I've been kicking myself. I'm not surprised you wanted to get away from me today.'

My hand tightens its grip. 'We need to talk. Come and eat.'

He gives a short laugh. 'You mean, you load a plate for me and nibble on a piece of carrot yourself?'

'No. I mean eat together. Really.' I point towards the dining-room table, the two placemats. 'Look.' He ducks his head round the door.

'Lovely.' His voice is tired.

'Roast chicken. With asparagus. And strawberries and cream, your favourites. And this time I'm eating with you.'

'It's too late, Minna.'

'Don't say that. It's never too late.'

He swallows. 'I'm sorry, I don't think we're doing each other any good.' He looks a decade older this evening, as though all the grief of the last months has suddenly hit him. He turns towards the staircase. 'I'll clear my stuff out. I imagine you'll want to stay down here for a bit longer. Let me know when you come back to London and I'll move out of the house.'

'No.' I stand in front of him. 'This isn't what I want. Really.'

'When you drove off with Felix this morning I realized how far we'd grown apart.'

259

'I shouldn't have done that. I'm so sorry.'

'I'm sorry, too.'

'It's all over now. I'm ready to move on.' As I say this I almost feel something shift inside me, as though a layer of molten lava has started to burst out.

He sighs. 'I've got no energy left. My business is collapsing around me.'

I think of the clients who can never get enough of him, who call at all hours. 'What do you mean?'

'It's almost impossible to run the business remotely. I've got to get back to London to sort things out. Some of my clients are threatening to go elsewhere.' He gives a dry laugh. 'Some of them already have. If it weren't for Waymark I wouldn't have a business left.'

'I'm sorry.' I force him to make eye contact with me. 'You don't deserve this.'

'I need to salvage what I can.' His shoulders seem to slump. 'If I can just bring Waymark through successfully there's a chance I can turn things round for us.'

The 'us' gives me a little hope our marriage is salvageable, too.

'I'm going to stay with Michael tonight,' he adds, and my hope diminishes. But not completely.

'I want to show you something.' I point at the utility room door. 'Look.'

He follows me in there and blinks at the sleep-suit hanging over the clotheshorse.

'I can't promise to get rid of it, but I'm going to store it with Benjy's other bits and pieces. I'm moving on, Tom.' The skin on my arms prickles. What have I started? For a second I want to hide in my old, frozen self. But I can't.

He puts out a hand to touch the suit. 'I was trying to tell you last night there'd come a time when you could pack it away. I'm glad for you, sweetie.' He bites his bottom lip. 'I just don't know about us, though.'

'Whatever you decide, you won't get to London until late

tonight, you'll need to eat before then, won't you? And dinner's ready, I just need to carve the chicken.' I grab his sleeve. 'Come on.' I all but drag him into the dining room. He puts down the laptop and sits down, as though he's in the dentist's chair awaiting root-canal work.

The white Burgundy sits chilled on a coaster. I pour him a glass. 'I don't know if I should.'

'You should.' He takes a sip. I pick up one of the asparagus spears on my plate and dip it into the hollandaise. How long is it since I've eaten something this rich? My taste buds give little jumps of recognition. I swallow the first mouthful and dip the next spear into the sauce. Tom's watching me all the time, as though he suspects I'm going to make a dash for the loo to rid myself of what I've eaten. I chew slowly and resist the panic signals my brain sends me. Then I pick up another spear and repeat the procedure. I eat four of them and excuse myself to bring in the carved chicken and vegetables from the kitchen.

While he finishes his asparagus I serve the main course. He takes another sip of his wine and my heart lurches – he wouldn't drink if he was expecting to drive.

I've given myself a small slice of breast, half a dozen beans and two new potatoes. No point in pushing myself too far, it's months since I've eaten so much at one time. But I finish everything on the plate in front of me. By the time I've finished the last bean I feel almost drunk on food. 'There are strawberries,' I mutter. 'And cream.'

'I'll fetch them.' He clears the plates and goes out into the kitchen.

He's hardly spoken a word to me. His wineglass is still half full. He's going to leave. When he returns with the strawberries I strain my face into a smile. He stares back at me.

'You haven't eaten like that since Benjy died.'

'I know I have to change. And eat, I want to eat.' As I say it I realize how true this is. I pick up a small strawberry and I eat it.

261

Tom watches. 'I felt I'd lost you.' His face still shows hurt. 'Lost Benjy. Then you.'

'I know. I think the not eating and throwing myself into Felix's story was a distraction away from what mattered most.'

'Don't know about distraction. I think she's helped you.'

'I'm surprised, I thought he was barely tolerating my interest in Felix.'

'She's obviously had her troubles. Survived.'

'Yes.'

'Perhaps you needed to see it was possible to move on, too.' He looks down at his crumpled napkin. 'And now?'

'I've seen Lew's daughter. I've given her the cormorant. It feels ... finished.' I blink. 'I can be ready to go back to London in a few hours,' I say. 'Just let me clear up the kitchen and pack.'

He sits back in his chair and examines me. 'Sara was really pissed off when I rang and told her you weren't coming. She'd had to move heaven and earth to get the afternoon off. She only works three days a week and her boss wasn't thrilled with her.'

'I'll ring her.' I force myself to meet his gaze. 'I know I haven't behaved well to her, to anyone. And I'd like to see her friends' house, really. I've already had some ideas.'

He's still staring at me. 'He was my child, too, you know.' He pushes back his plate. 'I miss him.'

'I know.'

'Do you?'

'Of course I do.'

'I thought I had to be strong for you. I felt selfish when I let myself give in to my feelings.'

Now I'm the one who's staring.

'Oh Jesus.' He puts out a hand towards me. 'What am I saying? Don't pay any attention, it's late and I'm tired. I've been on the phone with MOD officials all afternoon.'

'I thought ...' I don't know what I thought. That he was coping better than I was? That he had his work to distract him? That a mother would always suffer more than a father? The full extent of my assumptions strikes me for the first time.

'I'm so sorry.' My hand covers his. He'll pull away. But he doesn't, he shakes his head.

'Don't worry, ignore me.'

Like I have for the last four months. What kind of human being have I become? Something is happening, pressure is building behind my eyes. I start to shake. I can't resist this force pummelling me. I look up at Tom, try to speak, can't. My hand falls out of his. 'Oh Tom' I say. 'What have I done?' Then my voice fails me. And it begins. Months of pent-up grief and guilt flood me, pushing down dams, deluging parts of me I thought were arid. And it hurts, it hurts so much. Sounds I've never heard myself make before, sounds that barely sound human, break out of my throat. Tom's getting up, coming round to me, holding me.

'Let it all out.' His voice sounds choked. 'This is what we've been waiting for.'

I shake my head, finding it hard to believe that this emotion won't suffocate me. Just at the moment I think grief is going to throttle the life out of me; tears start falling. My sobs are harsh, rasping. I can't believe it's me making this noise. My head rests on the table. A single strawberry observes me from my abandoned bowl. A small puddle forms on the mat where my tears land. And still they come. I cry for Benjy in his red and white suit lying still in the hospital chapel. I cry for the child he'll never grow up to be: a uniformed boy arriving for his first day at school, a muddy-kneed lad playing football. A child I'll never take to the seaside.

Wave after wave crashes over me, battering me without mercy until I can't sit up any more. I slip to the floor. Would these tears have been easier if they'd come out after the death? Perhaps they wouldn't have felt so acid. I curl up on the carpet, helpless.

But Tom's with me, whispering words I can't make out, stroking my hair just as he was the night Benjy was born. I see tears on his face. It's not the first time he's wept for his son but it's the first time he's wept with me. Our eyes lock and I feel a connection that's even stronger than the one I used to feel when we had sex.

When it finishes he brings me a blanket from the bedroom and wraps me up like a newborn. 'You know what we need, don't you?'

'Not a cup of your bloody tea.' I try to smile.

'Yup. Just as my granny used to make.'

'It'll kill me.'

'It'll build you up.'

'I should be looking after you,' I tell him. 'I've neglected you for so long.'

He shakes his head. 'You'd only make some of that poncey Earl Grey. I'll do it. All I ever wanted was for you to let me look after you.'

And the brew is strong and sugared, which I'd normally hate, and very slowly it revives me so I can sit up. 'I feel like a husk,' I say. 'Dried out, barren.'

He takes my hand. 'You've just flushed out all the bad stuff. Now you can start to let the good things in again.'

'I don't know if there ever will be any good things for me.'

He smoothes my hair. 'I promise there will be.'

And I believe him.

'I'm so sorry for thinking you were having an affair with Sara,' I tell him.

He puts a finger to my lips. 'I'm just going to ring Michael and Gareth and tell them my plans have changed. I'm staying here.'

Forty-two

Minna

'Danny Boy' flutes into my sleep, Tom's mobile – I used to tease him about his ringtone. I reach over him to switch if off but he's already grabbing it.

'Sorry, it's Waymark.' He puts a finger to his lips.

I stick my tongue out at the Nokia.

'Hello, Jeremy.' Tom sits up. I run my fingers up his naked chest and he smiles at me. But then his face grows hard. 'Really? That doesn't surprise me. Well, I'll have to think again.' He grimaces. 'I'm sorry too, but I can't . . .' Now he's getting out of bed, pacing up and down. 'No, we won't give up. We've seen politicians and ministers, we've briefed the press, but there must be something else we can do.' More static. 'Yes, I'm aware how much money you've spent already. But what we need to do now won't involve more cash, it's hearts we have to win over.' He ends the call.

'Is he being a bastard?' I tug at his hands to bring him back to the bed.

'Jeremy? No, he's always civil. But he's like a bull terrier with this project. And I need him to pull it off too because part of my fee's contingent on getting planning permission.' I notice how tired Tom looks. I've put this down to worry about me. Now I remember that huge pile of emails in his inbox.

'Tell me?' I run my hand along his chest.

'You don't want to be bothered with it, honest.' He looks away.

'Oh, I see.' I sit up, let my hand drop away. 'You don't think I'm up to dealing with it.'

He replaces the hand. 'It's like this. Waymark found me this cottage.'

I frown. 'I thought Sara did?'

'Sara suggested the location. But Jeremy gave me the trust's telephone number.'

'Why?' It seems odd for Jeremy to show such concern for one of his consultants' wives.

'Why indeed?' Tom lets out a slow groan. 'He wants to get his hand on the next parcel of MOD land to be released.'

I sit up. 'Which bit of land?'

'Upper Farm and the surrounding fields.'

'He can't. Surely it'll go to the Barrows Trust like this house?'

'That's what everyone thinks. The original landowners were compensated decades ago, so they've got no claim. But the local authorities have a big say. They might find Jeremy's proposition too attractive to turn down. And the MOD has a responsibility to tax-payers to get a good price for the land.'

'What's Jeremy offering?'

'A big donation to the new swimming pool in Swanham.'

Of course – what better way to ingratiate himself with the council? 'In return for?'

'A sort of holiday village.'

I picture tennis courts and hacienda-style villas spreading over the valley.

'It'll all be perfectly tasteful, he'll use local materials and building styles,' Tom adds, as though reading my mind.

'But the whole point of this place is that it hasn't been developed at all in the last sixty years.' I fold my arms, feel anger claiming me. 'No fertilizers, no intensive farming. In return for driving people out and mortaring their houses, the army's protected the environment. It's like a war dividend.'

'Exactly.'

'So you're not going to help him with this, are you?'

Tom's head drops.

'Tell me you're not?'

'I'm in a hole, Minna. I can't afford to lose his work.'

A sick feeling washes over me as I remember the debit card that wouldn't work in the supermarket, the bangers on the barbecue instead of the fish, the cheap wine, Tom's concern about the overdraft.

'You've seen the bank statements. You know we can't pay this month's mortgage. That makes two months in a row. I need the Waymark account, at least for a few more months until I can find some new clients.'

'You really need to be back in London, don't you?'

He looks down at his mug of tea to avoid my eyes.

'We're going back.' I throw back the duvet. 'Tomorrow, as soon as we can.'

'No, we can't. We've got to stay until . . .'

'Until I'm better. But I am now.' As I say it I realize how true the words are.

'I've got to stay a bit longer, anyway, Jeremy's coming down today. I'm meeting him at the Cygnet in Swanham.'

'Good. I can tell him what I think of his plans.'

'Minna . . .'

'I know, I know, we need his money. But not at any price, Tom, not at any price.' I think of something. 'I need to speak to Felix about this.'

His eyes narrow. 'You realize, don't you, that if you help scupper this project we lose money we badly need?'

I stare out of the window at the fields and trees. My sigh seems to fill the view. 'OK.'

He starts pacing up and down, something he does when he's had an idea that excites him. 'On the other hand . . .'

'What?'

'It's a high-risk strategy but sometimes those are the best.'

'What are? Stop talking in riddles.'

He sits down next to me. 'Suppose we could get someone like Felix to approve the project? Wouldn't that prove it was worthwhile?'

I stare at him, speechless, as if he's crazy.

He pulls me up. 'Come on. You need to see the plans. You need to talk to Jeremy. So does Felix.' He hands over his mobile. 'Ring her now. Tell her we'll pick her up in an hour.'

*

Felix's eyes blaze when Tom opens the car door for her. 'This should never be allowed. I can't believe the council are even giving it consideration.'

'Think about the swimming pool,' I say. 'You were only saying the other day that Swanham didn't have much going for it.' Funny, given all I've just said against the project, how I spring to the defence of Waymark. Well, of Tom, really; of my husband.

'True. But even those things wouldn't compensate for the loss of the valley.' Her hands clasp one another in her lap.

'There's hardly anyone left round here who lived in Fontwell before 1943.' Tom's voice is neutral. 'And Waymark aren't planning to touch the village itself, just the old farm. Locals might be glad of the employment opportunities.'

'Tell me more about this Jeremy.'

'Jeremy Wilson. He's the MD. He's built similar schemes in other parts of the country, and America.'

'Tom says we can talk to him for five minutes before their meeting starts.'

'Good.' Felix's jaw is set like a bulldog's. This Jeremy won't know what's hit him.

Her mobile trills. 'That'll be the roofers telling me when they can start work on my house.'

'You've got problems with your roof?' Tom asks.

'Age and neglect.' She turns off the phone. 'I can't deal with it now.'

Forty-three

Minna

'Jeremy Wilson.' I watch Felix shake the man's hand and grip the coffee table to steady herself. She busies herself fiddling in her handbag for a handkerchief. He's in his late thirties, strong-featured rather than handsome. I was expecting him to be slick-suited but he's wearing an open-necked shirt and chinos. A fleece jacket hangs on the back of his chair and his feet are clad in expensive looking lightweight walking boots.

'Excuse my appearance, I've been walking around the proposed site.' His accent is American. He turns to me. 'We've never met, but we were both at a party in London back in April.'

That party.

'And I think I saw you in the village a few days ago,' he adds.

'Of course.' I remember the man in the graveyard.

'I saw you there, too,' says Felix. 'On the cliff path.'

We sit. 'So Jeremy, tell us what you're planning in the valley.' I'm surprised at the firmness in my tone. This is how I used to be. No, it's not. I never used to sound this sure of myself.

'The first thing to say is I've absolutely no intention of wrecking the place.' His gaze doesn't falter. 'It's beautiful down here and I won't do anything to spoil that.'

'So why don't you let the trust buy the land? They're best placed to preserve it.'

'They've got very little cash left after the purchase of Rosebank. I'd like to do some work on the river, the weeds need clearing and the banks need shoring up.'

'You can't argue with that,' Tom says.

'Or with our plans to restock the meadows with approved indigenous wildflower seeds.'

'No,' I concede. 'But I can argue with some chi-chi development that completely changes the character of the place.'

'What chi-chi development? I'm going to knock down some old corrugated-iron barns that are covered in rust and build farmhouse-style houses using local materials and local labour. And "village" is a misnomer. I'm talking half a dozen houses and a pool room. We won't spill out of the old farm area. And the people who stay will be mainly families who want to go walking and cycling.' He leans forward. 'In fact, that's how we'd market the place, as a holiday base for people who care about conservation. We'd even put aside a certain percentage of profits each year to feed into local environmental projects. Like the Barrows Trust.'

Felix is studying him carefully, every word, every movement, the way his chin juts forward. 'Do you know this area well?'

He turns to her. 'I'm from the States, as you'll have noticed.'

'You don't have family here?'

He frowns. 'Not immediate family.'

'But you do have some links?'

'Going back years. My maternal grandfather lived in the village.' She nods.

'I don't mention it because it's such a tenuous connection.' He shifts under her gaze. 'I don't want people to think I'm trying to use it to influence them.'

'But you're quite prepared to work on them through a rigorous public affairs campaign,' I say.

He smiles at Tom. 'I've certainly had some good advice from your husband.' I scowl at Tom. Or try to. 'So what more can I tell you to put your mind at rest?'

'Can we see the plans?'

'What was your grandfather's name?' Felix says.

'I'm sorry?'

'Only I think he was Philip Fuller.'

He looks at her as though he thinks she might be a witch. 'How on earth do you know that?'

'Philip's brother Sam was a friend of mine.'

'Great-uncle Sam.'

'Of course you won't have known him.'

He grins, looking more like a mischievous boy than a business-man. 'But I do.'

'Do?'

'Sam lives in Florida. On the coast.' Amusement flickers across his face. 'Still goes out on his boat most days. He and Grandpa are tough old boys. They always say growing up in cold, damp cottages prepared them for anything.'

'But Sam drowned in the North Atlantic when the liner was hit.'

He stares at Felix. 'You didn't hear? Sam was concussed. Some-one dragged him into a lifeboat but he was in a bad way. Took them months to work out who he was. By then he'd been fostered by a family in Florida. He stayed with them through the war and then decided to make America his home. But he always kept in touch with my grandpa.'

'It's hard to believe Sam's alive.' Felix looks stunned. Another of her ghosts can be buried.

I sit back and study Jeremy. 'Did you choose this valley because of the family link?'

'I suppose I did. Grandpa and Sam told me how they rode on top of the hay wagons at harvest. And the cave on the beach. And the Squire in the big house. It sounded very romantic.' He pauses. 'Perhaps it coloured my view more than I'd like to admit.'

'Did they talk about the war years?' I stare at a mark on the oak table.

'They said they were very quiet in Fontwell. Until they were evacuated.'

Felix's mouth forms a small smile. I can see her opposition to the scheme wilting. 'Your scheme still doesn't seem to do much for the local community,' I say. 'I know you're donating money to the swimming pool, but even so.'

'I'm being as generous as I can afford to be.'

'What about building a few low-cost houses to sell or rent to a local family?' Felix suggests. 'Most people can't afford to buy round here, the prices are ruinous.'

He lets out a breath. 'You don't ask for much, do you? I'll have to think about it.' He turns to Tom. 'Remind me to be careful next time I employ a public affairs adviser.' But his frown's cancelled out by the sparkle in his eyes.

I rise. 'Thank you.' We shake hands. 'You're not what I was expecting.'

He rolls his eyes. 'I won't ask what that was. I've a feeling it won't be flattering.' He takes my hand. 'Perhaps you'd like to get involved with the interior design when we're at that stage? I've seen that office block you worked on in Holborn. And Tom's shown me pictures of some of your domestic projects.'

'I'd love to, thanks.' Can this be me, talking about work?

'Come to think of it, there are some other projects we might need help with. We've bought some offices in Limehouse. They're looking very tired.'

'Not trying to bribe me, are you, Jeremy?' I hope he can tell I'm joking.

He grins. 'Not now I've met you – I'd be much too scared.' He makes a note on his Blackberry. 'I'll ring you, Minna. Come and take a look at Limehouse, see if you're interested.'

'I'd love to.' I hope I don't sound as stunned as I feel.

Planners Give Fontwell Project Green Light
District Councillors and MOD officials have announced
the planned sale of part of the decommissioned army
ranges to Waymark Holdings, a developer.

'Waymark's delighted that our offer has been
accepted,' said Tom Byrne on behalf of the company. 'We
recognize that this part of the coast is suitable only for
the most sensitive development. For this reason we're
limiting our plans to rebuilding an old farmhouse and
buildings a mile outside Fontwell village. One of the new
units will provide housing for local families. And we'll be
taking advice from the Barrows Trust, which owns the
first tranche of land released by the MOD, on how best to
protect the land we buy.'

Councillor Colleen Narrow said: 'We're happy that
Waymark is the best developer for this project. They've
shown a clear commitment to the area and it's
heartening to find a developer with such enlightened
environmental policies. Their donation to the swimming
pool fund means work can be completed by October this
year, instead of next spring.'

Councillor Narrow went on to say that the council's
change of heart had partly resulted from support for the
scheme shown by former residents of the village of
Fontwell.

Forty-four

Minna

The cars are packed, Rosebank locked up. Tom and I walk through the garden and out into the field. The wildflowers have passed their best now, I have to look hard to make out ox-eyed daisies and cornflowers. Blades of grass swish against our legs as we make for the path down to the beach. I feel as though a giant press has been lifted from me, allowing me to savour colours and scents again. On the beach I lift my head to the breeze so I can feel it touch my cheek.

We stand on the sand at the spot where we found Lew all those weeks ago. The police have moved the tape now and the high tide last night has smoothed the sand so the beach is sheet-smooth. In one of my hands is the urn containing Benjamin's ashes. In the other I hold Tom's hand so tight his circulation must be at risk. And I feel I've reached the end of a journey.

I never met Lew. All I know of him is what Felix told me and she only knew him for a few days. But I gave his sketch to his daughter and feel I can claim some knowledge of him. When I rang Felix and told her what I wanted to do she approved of the idea. She also told me that Lew hasn't appeared at her bedside since we visited Louise. She doesn't think she'll ever see him again. 'Was he a ghost?' I asked.

'No such thing. He was a figment of my imagination,' she replied in that dry tone of hers. 'Generated by my guilt.'

'You had nothing to feel guilty about.'

A laugh. 'You and I both know that makes not a jot of difference.'

'No.'

A pause while we both consider the things we wish we'd done differently. Or left undone. 'Now, what's Kris's telephone number?' Felix says briskly. 'Work starts on my roof next week, she can move in after that.'

*

I take the lid off the urn, wait to feel the breeze on my back, and throw the ashes into the air. The wind picks them up and unfurls them like a grey banner across the sky. They float in the air for a few seconds before falling into the waves. Too light to sink, they start to float away almost immediately. I close my eyes for a second or two and picture Benjy as he would have grown up to be.

When I open my eyes again I see the ashes have almost vanished into the immensity of the sea.

'Time to go.' Tom, my husband, lover, friend, confidant, tugs me gently back to the here and now.

Felix 2006

Felix watches the cars pull out of the drive. Rosebank is left, temporarily, to itself. Minna will make a fresh start back in London, with her husband, friends and work to sustain her, still grieving, still hurt, but whole again. She'll lose her papery insubstantiality as she eats more and more. Life will grab her back.

Next week a fresh party will claim Rosebank for their own, admiring the smart decor, the proximity to the beach, and the well-stocked garden. None of them will know about Lew.

She finds herself walking past the house, peering up at the windows just as she did the first afternoon she came back. For the first time she feels a kinship with the place; it's not just some yuppie retreat with its past firmly covered in smart paints and fabric. She remembers picking raspberries in the garden with her mother the summer they moved in, how butterflies fluttered over the buddleia and her father's mower whirred on the lawn, scenes unshadowed by the years to come. If she empties her mind of all dis-traction she can make out the smile on her mother's face as she hands her the very last raspberry. 'You spoil that child.' Her father's voice is indulgent as he moves behind them.

'Of course I do!' Her mother laughs. 'Who knows what life will throw at her?'

And then the garden with its scents of wisteria and honeysuckle are behind her and she's crossing the meadow to the cliffs. As a child she seldom came this way; David's house lay in another direction and they always used the path from the village to get down to the beach. Below her the shingle bends a lazy curve against the whispering sea. She walks down for a last look. She'll imprint this scene on her memory. Perhaps she'll come back to Fontwell some day, perhaps not. But now she's ready to return to Harrogate. She's got a roof to fix. And Minna has written down the name and number of this friend of hers, Kris, with the Persian cat. If Kris does rent the top floor of the house Felix will need to organize some hasty decorating and the construction of a cat flap in the back door.

She takes the pebble from her pocket and weighs it in her palm. It's been decades since she last tried this. She throws it, flicking her wrist so the pebble skims the waves. One. Two. Three. Four. Five.